Rosie Arche born in Gosport, Hampshire, where she still lives. She has had a variety of jobs including waitress, fruit picker, barmaid, shop assistant and market trader selling second-hand books. Rosie is the author of several Second World War sagas set on the South coast of England, as well as a series of gangster sagas under the name June Hampson.

Also by Rosie Archer

The Girls from the Local
The Ferry Girls
The Narrowboat Girls

THE MUNITIONS GIRLS SERIES

The Munitions Girls
The Canary Girls
The Factory Girls
The Gunpowder and Glory Girls

THE BLUEBIRD GIRLS SERIES

The Bluebird Girls
We'll Meet Again
The Forces' Sweethearts

ROSIE ARCHER

Victory *for the* Bluebird Girls

Quercus

First published in Great Britain in 2020 by Quercus
This paperback edition published in 2020 by

Quercus Editions Ltd
Carmelite House
50 Victoria Embankment
London EC4Y 0DZ

An Hachette UK company

A CIP catalogue record for this book is available
from the British Library

PB ISBN 978 1 52940 533 0
EB ISBN 978 1 52940 534 7

10 9 8 7 6 5 4 3

Typeset by CC Book Production
Printed and bound in Great Britain by Clays Ltd, Elcograf S.p.A.

MIX
Paper from
responsible sources
FSC® C104740

Papers used by Quercus are from well-managed forests and other responsible sources.

For Maureen Swire, extraordinary singing tutor, thank you

Chapter One

1944

'When you're old you'll regret not doing the things that scared you.'

Bea Herron stole a look at Rainey Bird's tired, earnest face and considered her words. If anyone knew about taking chances, it was Rainey, Bea thought. During the past year hadn't her friend gambled on having what she'd wanted? Only to find it snatched cruelly away because of this damned war?

'I regret nothing, except . . .' Rainey faltered.

Bea felt for Rainey's hand and squeezed it comfortingly. How Rainey had come through everything was a mystery to Bea. But, like the trouper she was, Rainey was back on stage once more.

In silver sequin-studded evening dresses that clung to their bodies the two young women were standing in the wings at Dartmouth Town Hall, in Devon.

'There's no need to say more,' Bea said. Now was not the time to dwell on misfortune. Now was the time to celebrate that the the Bluebirds were together again and performing for the United States 5th Army Corps to raise their spirits before they crossed the English Channel.

'You've got to do what I did, Bea, and take a chance.' Rainey's voice was insistent, but her heavy make-up didn't quite conceal the shadows beneath her eyes. 'Not all men are untrustworthy.'

The curtains had already closed on the first half of the show and the Bluebirds, top of the bill, now waited to go on.

Clouds of lily of the valley perfume announced Ivy's sudden appearance. Out of breath because she was late, as usual, she moved quickly into her place next to Bea. She took a deep breath. 'You all right, Rainey?' She didn't wait for a reply but instead addressed Bea: 'That bloke's here again!'

'You're only telling her what she already knows,' Rainey said.

'I don't want to talk about him,' Bea broke in. Then she

said, 'Ivy Sparrow, you're cutting it fine – we're about to be introduced.'

With both hands Ivy smoothed her dark chin-length bob. 'We don't need no introduction! Just listen to those men already whooping and whistling for us.' Ivy carefully pulled aside the edge of one of the red velvet curtains so she could peep at the audience.

Bea craned her neck. 'Let me look, then.'

Men were clustered around little tables, their smart uniforms of olive-coloured jackets and light trousers enhancing well-nourished bodies and tanned faces. They all looked so young and innocent, Bea thought. Unlike the world-weary British servicemen the girls had entertained abroad and at home.

Frothy pints cluttered tabletops. The men were evidently intent on enjoying themselves. Snatches of dialogue reminded Bea of how American film stars spoke. Her eyes searched the busy bar below the stage until they found the one man she was looking for. 'Is it so wrong for me to want to care for somebody? To have what you two have already had?' Bea paused. 'I want to understand how it feels to have that special someone.' Her voice grew stronger as she tried to add substance to her words. 'I mean, even if the person who loves you isn't in the same room with you, they're still there, aren't they?' She looked at Ivy for reassurance.

'So, the Ice Queen's melting, is she?' came Ivy's sceptical reply.

'Ice Queen?' Rainey's voice was sharp. She shook her head, her shoulder-length Titian hair gleaming under the lights. 'I wish you wouldn't call Bea that. When a woman's endured an assault she'll often keep away from men.'

There was an awkward silence.

Ivy's face had reddened. 'I'm sorry, Bea,' she said. 'I let my mouth run away with me, I didn't mean anything.'

At the time Bea hadn't thought of that sailor's unpleasant groping as an assault but, of course, it was. Afterwards her relationships with men had changed. She had never been interested in a serious romance with any man, until she'd spotted the tall broad-shouldered fellow a couple of nights ago with a paperback copy of *The Brothers Karamazov* tucked into his back pocket. She admired men who read intelligent books. She'd spotted him leaning casually against the bar, his weight thrust heavily on one hip. He'd looked content, at ease with himself. She'd wondered if he'd always been that way, the end-product of loving parents and a secure homelife. Or perhaps it was an outer skin, a sort of shield he'd fashioned to keep away unwelcome individuals.

This man's skin was a rich brown and his close-cropped

hair a mass of tiny tight curls. His eyes were dark, like the chocolate freely available before the war but now as precious as gold dust. When she looked at him now, Bea felt an effervescent tingle deep inside her and she couldn't turn away.

He was slender, but beneath his short jacket she could sense the strength of his muscles. Obviously, he was no stranger to hard work, either in the services or before he'd joined them. She wondered what it might be like to touch him, first with her fingertips and then perhaps with her lips.

She'd known he would return the following evening, just as she'd been certain he'd be here tonight for this was the Bluebirds' last performance on the Devon coast. Tomorrow morning they'd be travelling back to Gosport in Hampshire. Which meant that this beautiful man and she were destined never to meet. Unless she or Fate made it happen.

So, what had happened to her?

She'd been standing on stage singing when she'd been struck by awareness of his presence. Cupid's dart? Not possible: Bea didn't believe in love at first sight. That only happened in books and films. Nevertheless, what she was experiencing must mean she was healing from the effects of that long-buried assault. Perhaps it even suggested that something wonderful might be about to happen.

Her thoughts whirled away as the curtains drew back and Sammy, their pianist, stood up and introduced them.

Amid fresh cheers and wolf whistles the girls sashayed in their high heels towards the microphones at the front of the stage.

Bea, as usual, calmed the audience with a short speech and then, with a nod towards the piano, allowed Sammy to take them into their first song, 'Boogie-Woogie Bugle Boy'. The three girls shimmied seductively to the music and the men went wild.

Ivy's solo came next. Bea marvelled that her husky tones could so easily dictate the sad mood of the song. A pin might have dropped during 'Stormy Weather' and everyone would have heard it, so intently were the men listening. 'As Time Goes By' came next followed by 'You'll Never Know', both sung sensually by the three. Then Rainey moved towards the central microphone to sing her solo, 'I'm Nobody's Baby', the Judy Garland favourite.

As Bea listened she admired the way Rainey kept her true feelings hidden and even flirted with the audience as she gave herself over to the lyrics. She inhabited a different persona on stage. Her friend caught her eye and gave her a hint of a smile, which turned into a laugh when, assuring the audience that she had no one to love,

6

a tall American soldier stood and called, 'You can have me, babe!'

The air inside the hall was charged with electricity amid the good-natured laughter. And then Sammy began to play the second to last song of the evening's performance and it was Bea's turn to stand alone in front of the microphone.

For the first time that evening Bea allowed herself to study the man at the bar. The look in his eyes gave her the courage to fasten her gaze to his face. "'You'd be so wonderful to come home to,'" she sang. He chuckled, showing square white teeth, and she returned his smile, confident he was laughing with and not at her. He was now looking carefully at her and Bea, in that split second, was nervous, unsure what was happening between them.

"'So easy to love . . .'" came Bea's next words.

Suddenly he looked away, and, leaving his drink on the bar, pushed through the crowd of men, ignoring their grumbled jibes at being disturbed while the show was on. Then the exit door closed behind him.

Bea's heart plunged.

Professionalism took over and, despite the tears welling in her eyes, she immediately turned her face to the next table of men and allowed them to believe she was singing straight from her heart to each and every one.

As she finished, the audience cheered, and Sammy began the introduction to the Bluebirds' final song of the evening, 'Coming In On a Wing and a Prayer', a rousing tune that encouraged the audience to sing along with them. Bea smiled brightly even as her heart was crushed to a million pieces. What had she done to make him leave?

Blowing kisses to the men, Ivy led the way down the tiny flight of steps that took them into the very heart of the overcrowded hall. At the end of each night's performance the girls, along with the previous acts, mingled with the audience. Shaking hands and offering a few kind words made such a difference to men separated from their families and loved ones. Photographs of wives, children and sweethearts were produced from pockets or wallets and proudly displayed while their owners congratulated the Bluebirds on their singing.

The girls scribbled their names on napkins, menu cards and the fan photographs pushed in front of them. They signed autograph books, too, smiled and listened to the men eagerly greeting them.

Bea felt as if she was sleepwalking, playing her role by rote. Her mouth asked questions, her eyes smiled, yet over and over again she was asking herself why the one man she wanted had walked away without a backward glance.

And then, a tattered photograph was pressed into her hands. It was so familiar to her that she couldn't help exclaiming, 'Oh, this is one of our very first publicity shots.' She remembered when it was taken, long before the girls had made a name for themselves.

'So you'll know how long I've treasured it,' he said, in his American drawl. It was a soft Southern accent. A lemon-scented cologne emanated from him. For a moment all Bea could do was stare into his smiling brown eyes. He hadn't abandoned her but had disappeared to bring her the photograph. Bea's eyes were glued to his face, and her knees were almost buckling. She wondered if she'd fall at his feet for joy. With more confidence than she felt, she touched the picture, running her fingers across the familiar faces of herself, Ivy and Rainey, reliving the memories it conjured for her.

He grasped her hand and held it to his lips. 'Before my courage kinda disappears, Bea, let's get outta here.'

Chapter Two

Rainey pressed the off button on the cord of her bedside lamp. Despite her tiredness, she knew she'd be unable to sleep. This wasn't due to the over-excitement that followed from singing her heart out on stage in Devon but because she had realized she must face up to the pain she'd caused the person who loved her most.

'Mum, I need you,' she whispered, into the pillow. 'I'm so sorry.'

Her own pig-headedness was continuing the rift between them. But how could she apologise? How could things possibly return to normal between them after all that had happened? She squeezed her eyes tightly shut to stop the tears spilling out.

'I'd give everything I own to feel like a little girl again,' Rainey whispered into the darkness. 'To have you pull back the covers and climb into my bed, as you've done so many times in the past, to comfort me . . .' She remembered how Jo would hold her close until, safe in her mother's arms, Rainey would fall asleep. The last time Jo had held her like that had been after Charlie died.

It seemed to Rainey that her mother, maybe all mothers, possessed a special skill to take away their children's pain. After all, the words 'Let me kiss it better' magically made a grazed knee or elbow feel better, didn't they?

But Rainey was no longer a child. Now, she was a young woman whose madness had passed but she needed her mother more than ever. What if Jo had had enough and had taken seriously Rainey's refusal to see her? Surely not.

Her eyes lingered on the washstand where the blue and white jug and bowl sat. Treasured items bought from a jumble sale with money they could barely afford to spend when Jo and Rainey had first moved to Albert Street. This terraced house had been their refuge from Alfie Bird, Rainey's father, who had used his wife as a punchbag until Jo had eventually realized nothing would change for the better unless she escaped him. Together, mother and daughter had left Portsmouth and survived in the hovel that gradually they'd made into a welcoming, comfortable home. Jo had worked while Rainey finished school. Later Jo had helped

Rainey achieve her ambition to be a singer as one of the three Bluebirds, travelling abroad with ENSA, cheering the troops while the war raged about them.

Rainey loved Bea and Ivy – they were more than friends, practically sisters. But when Charlie, the man Rainey had worshipped, had been killed in that bomb blast, it had been Jo's love that had saved her – that, and the approaching birth of Charlie's child.

Back on stage in Dartmouth, she'd had to hide her grief. Troops leaving to fight on foreign shores deserved to be sent away with the memory of three smiling Bluebird girls encouraging them to defeat the enemy. With Bea and Ivy's help, she had turned the corner on the long journey back to sanity by doing the one thing that made her happy: singing.

If only Rainey had the courage to begin to heal the rift she had created between herself and her beloved mother . . .

She lay wide awake remembering the day when Bea and Ivy had brought her back from the nursing home in the taxi.

'You sure you'll be all right if I pop up the road to Peacocks to buy fresh bread? Ivy's here should you need anything.' Bea was anxious.

From the armchair in the kitchen, with her feet on the stool, Rainey took her eyes from the dancing flames in the grate, and said, her mind in turmoil, 'Please don't be gone a long time.'

'I won't.' The front door closed behind Bea, but without the usual tinkle of metal swinging on string and hitting the wood. Rainey had removed the key. She couldn't face well-meaning visitors letting themselves in. Not now, possibly not ever again, after all she'd been through.

She'd been dozing when the banging on the door started.

'Rainey, I must talk to you.'

Indignation filled her at the sound of Jo's voice from outside the house. How dared her mother think she could come visiting when, at the time Rainey had needed her most, Jo hadn't been there for her? 'Don't let her in, Ivy!'

Ivy looked at her despairingly. She'd been on her way from the scullery to answer the knocking.

Resentment built within Rainey. 'I don't want to see her,' she snapped.

'But it's your mum . . .' Ivy was edging her way towards the passage leading to the front door.

'Don't you dare!' Rainey shouted. 'This is my house and I say who comes in!'

Ivy stared at her, then backed away. 'You can't leave your mother out there in the street . . .'

But Rainey allowed her anger to take hold of her. Through

the black fog that had descended in her brain she could see Ivy's wisdom but chose to ignore it. 'Tell her through the door that I don't want her near me.'

Ivy said, 'I can't do that! You don't really mean it.'

Furious, Rainey had risen from the armchair.

'Stay there. You've just come from the nursing home and you need to rest. I'll go.' Her face was hard, her normally warm eyes steely dark.

Rainey settled back in the chair. She kept her eyes on Ivy as she left the kitchen to walk down the passageway. She heard muffled voices, knowing Ivy wouldn't upset her more by opening the door despite what she'd said.

Rainey's head was spinning. The anger, the madness made her believe she was paying her mother back for ignoring her pain when she'd most needed help. In her scrambled mind it was retribution. She was aware of her mother's love for her but she deserved to suffer as Rainey had suffered.

'She's gone, for now,' said Ivy, coming back into the kitchen. After a short silence she added, 'You've hurt her.'

Rainey had expected to feel jubilant that she was getting her own back. All she felt was a deadness inside her.

When Rainey didn't answer her, Ivy took a deep breath and said, 'I've heard of normally happy women who've given birth, then become depressed, even when their babies are strong and well. You've been to hell and haven't come back yet. I understand all that. Just don't try shutting the door like that on me or Bea because we've all been through too much together. What I've just done for you is because I care about you. But I owe your mother a lot so don't expect me to share any of your misguided feelings.'

Ivy came over to her, bent down towards the armchair and pulled her into her arms. 'I understand and I feel for you,' she said. 'So does Bea.' She let Rainey go before she added, 'So does your mother . . . I'm gonna put the kettle on, I think we could do with a cuppa.'

After that, Rainey ignored Jo's visits, ignored her phone calls, and allowed her own unreasonable behaviour to continue.

Now she was ashamed she'd allowed that madness to take hold of her.

Rainey had to face up to the anguish she'd caused her mother, but how?

'You know how much I love this child, don't you?' Ivy looked down at Gracie lying star-shaped in her cot. Tendrils of white-blonde hair stuck damply to the little girl's forehead and to the neck of her white cotton nightdress.

'You won't be saying that if you wake her and she refuses

to go back to sleep,' Eddie said. 'You know what a tartar she can be.' Eddie was making sure the thick blackout curtains were pulled tight so the light at the top of the stairs didn't escape through the bedroom window.

Ivy smiled, first at Eddie, then down again at the little girl. After tenderly replacing the patchwork cover over the precious child, Ivy nudged Eddie from the room, leaving the door slightly ajar so they could hear her if she woke. Eddie switched off the light.

Their bedroom was at the back of the house and over-looked the long thin garden with the brick lavatory and the lilac bush at the end. Before flooding the room with light, Ivy crossed in front of the iron bedstead and drew the blackout curtains, shutting out the late white frost that illuminated the darkness outside. A laugh bubbled from her throat. 'Mr Edwards at number eight, so I heard, put up a new blackout curtain in his window facing the street. Then he went outside to check it was all right just as the ARP warden was passing on his bicycle and caught him with his front door open, letting all the light out! Talk about bad luck. He got a court fine!'

'Bloody little Adolf Hitlers, some of those wardens,' said Eddie. He pulled off his shirt and threw it onto the chair, then poured cold water into the china bowl from the jug on the nightstand for his usual quick wash before bed.

Ivy was still brushing her hair when Eddie threw back the bedcovers and, climbing in, said, 'Come on, love, don't keep me waiting for a cuddle.'

'Didn't you get enough of them in the pictures tonight?' She smiled, remembering Eddie's arms around her all through *Jane Eyre*.

'Cuddling in the Criterion isn't the same as being alone in bed together,' he said. 'And, before you ask, the picture didn't quite follow the story as written in the book.'

'I'm surprised you always remember the exact plots of all the novels you read,' Ivy said. She remembered how put out he was on seeing *Gone With the Wind* after reading the book. She'd spoken lovingly. Many men, after being hard at work all day, preferred to go to the local pub and sink a few pints. Not Eddie – he rarely visited the Alma at the end of the street. He escaped his worries about his building firm and a truck that had seen better days by delving into the written word. Ivy loved him all the more for it. She stared at her reflection in the dressing-table mirror, put down the hairbrush and ran her hands over her straight dark hair until her fingers met beneath her chin. She hated it when stray hairs stuck up, spoiling its symmetry. Her glossy locks shone in the glow from the bedside lamp. 'Bea's fellow reads books,' she said.

'I should hope he reads everything, newspapers as well,' said Eddie. 'Though I wonder sometimes how much they print of the truth about the war.'

Eddie had met Brian Baxter, who was always called Bing, and the two men had instantly liked each other.

'He had a copy of *The Brothers Karamazov* on him the night he asked her out,' said Ivy. 'Did I tell you that?'

'Only about a hundred times,' said Eddie, with exaggerated patience. She watched as he smoothed his blond hair. 'Anyone who reads Dostoevsky has to be pretty smart,' he added. Then, changing the subject, he asked, 'When you've finished titivating yourself in front of that looking-glass I'd like you to come to bed.'

'Any special reason why?' Ivy's eyes glinted mischievously and held his in the mirror's reflection. It was a look that meant she wanted him as much as he wanted her. She liked it that they knew each other so well and that there were no secrets between them. They talked about everything and anything.

He smiled. 'I thought we could get some more practice in, trying for a little brother for Gracie.' He sat up in the clean but now rumpled sheets with his arms outstretched, willing her to go to him.

She slid off the chair and climbed onto the bed, moving

towards the man she'd loved all her life. His lips touched hers, then travelled down towards her neck with a passion that set heat flooding through her body. His tongue caused shivers to race along her spine, making her moan with desire.

'Ivy?' Eddie stopped. One word. It held a question that meant so much. Ivy's eyes filled with tears. Sadness flooded her.

She locked her eyes with his. Why did the months go by with no sign of a child for her and Eddie?

'Just because it hasn't already happened doesn't mean it never will,' she murmured. She tried to push his unspoken thoughts from her mind. They enjoyed making love, enjoyed each other's bodies. Eddie loved her and never tired of her, or she of him.

Gracie had been conceived after one hurried attempt at lovemaking between Eddie and Sunshine, Gracie's biological mother. It didn't seem fair that Ivy's body let her down, month after month. 'It'll happen when it happens,' she said, making herself believe her own words. 'All that matters right now is that I want you to make love to me.' She stared into his eyes and saw the relief there. His arousal was fully apparent, the strong muscular contours of his body pressed against her.

'Ivy, you're so beautiful,' he said. The words were gentle,

soft, yet heart-breaking. Instinctively she arched into his body. Eddie pulled at her nightdress and she lifted her arms so it could slide up her body and above her head. She heard it slither to the lino and gasped as Eddie once more pressed his warmth against her. Slowly he began to explore her body. He took his time to arouse her, to give her pleasure that was charged with passion. Ivy moved against him and responded with all the intensity her love could give.

Afterwards they lay face to face on the bed, the soft light of the bedside lamp making shadows in the cosy room.

'I have something to ask you,' she said. She didn't wait for him to question her. He'd never once lied to her and she believed he never would. 'If I can't give you a child, will you still love me?'

The sigh he gave was long and laboured. Then, his arms still wrapped around her, he began to kiss her face, her lips, pulling her head back so he could kiss her neck. Suddenly he let her go.

'You are the only mother Gracie has ever known and you are the only woman I've ever loved or will ever love.' He paused, his two big hands now tenderly holding her dark head. He didn't wait for her to reply. 'I don't care that you won't marry me. I admire you for carving out a career for yourself with my sister and Rainey. And you're content to stay here in my childhood home and have my mother live with us . . .' With the corner of the sheet he gently wiped her damp eyes.

Ivy spoke haltingly, 'But I couldn't do any of those things, be with you, travel around the country and sing, if it wasn't for Maud,' she said, sniffing and putting a finger across Eddie's mouth to stem his further words. 'She's my rock.'

Eddie pretended to bite her hand. She smiled and allowed her fingers to fall away. What she didn't say was that all she'd ever wanted since she'd first met him was to carry his child and be his wife.

'And you're mine,' he whispered. 'We're a tightly knit family and nothing, I repeat nothing, will ever change that.'

Chapter Three

'Mum, the key's on the end of the string. Why are you knocking on the door?' Rainey's words came as naturally as she could utter them.

She stared at the well-dressed pretty blonde woman standing in her doorway and waited for her to speak. Instinctively she wanted to fly into her mother's arms, but pride held her back. As if to prove a point, Rainey fumbled behind the door at 14 Albert Street and triumphantly pulled forward the means of entry. She didn't say she had only recently returned the key to its usual place.

'I can't just walk in and out of here as I like,' Jo said. Her green eyes flashed and a hesitant smile offset any other words Rainey might have spoken. 'This is your home now. I don't live here any more.'

Rainey stifled a sigh and dropped the key so it swung

back to its original resting place with a soft clink. She pulled her pink candlewick dressing gown closer against the cold February air and took a deep breath. 'We're standing here letting all the heat go out of the house. Come on in, then.'

She turned and walked down the passage. Once she heard the front door click shut, she was satisfied that her mother was following. She waved an arm at the comfortable kitchen and the fire burning steadily in the grate to show her mother that she hadn't, as perhaps Jo might have thought, only just got out of bed.

'I'll put the kettle on,' Rainey said. Bing Crosby crooned softly from the wireless.

At least, Rainey thought, her mother wouldn't ask if she was eating properly. On the table a plate was covered with toast crumbs and the smell hung in the air mingling with the scent of lavender polish.

In the scullery Rainey topped up the still warm kettle and lit the gas. From the white-painted cupboard on the wall she took out china cups and saucers and set them on a tray. She noted a movement out of the corner of her eye. Jo had taken off her green gabardine belted coat and had thrown it over the back of a kitchen chair, which proved that she didn't intend to leave soon.

Jo now stood in the doorway between the kitchen and

the scullery. There was a look of deep concern on her face. 'Are you all right, Rainey?'

Rainey took a deep breath before answering. 'Course I am. I'm back on the stage, aren't I? Best place for me. How's married life treating you, Mrs Blackie Wilson?' There was little warmth in her voice.

Jo stared at her. 'I didn't come to talk about me. I'm worried about you.'

'Not worried enough to cut short your honeymoon, though, eh?'

Jo put up a hand as though the door frame was about to collapse and her touch could magically hold it in place. She sighed. 'I got no message. When I did find out I came straight back.' Jo's voice tailed off, then grew stronger again. 'I wish you'd let me come to you sooner. Who would have thought such a thing could happen? Everything was fine when Blackie and I left after the wedding party.'

Rainey watched the steam shooting from the kettle. She took it from the gas jets and used a little of the boiling water to heat the brown earthenware teapot. She replaced the kettle on the flames and emptied the hot water out of the pot. In went three spoonfuls of tea from the caddy, then the boiling water. She turned off the gas. Her hands were shaking. She was glad she'd managed the task without mishap.

Rainey felt as if the scene unfolding in her home was unreal. Part of a film, perhaps, in which her mother and she were the actors. She jammed on the teapot lid, then glanced about the work surfaces.

Jo, anticipating her daughter's needs, handed Rainey the knitted tea cosy.

'Thank you,' Rainey said. Her voice was very small and suddenly she couldn't control the tears.

Jo pulled her into her arms. 'I'm so sorry I wasn't there for you, my love.'

'Oh, Mum,' Rainey cried, unable any longer to keep up the pretence of coldness, her hostility now completely swept away. 'It was awful! It's still awful.'

She fell against her mother's softness and clung to her.

With her mother's arms around her, Rainey felt safe, wanted. After a few minutes Jo said, 'Come and sit by the fire and tell me everything.'

Rainey allowed Jo to lead her into the cosy kitchen and to the armchair near the fire. She then pulled the small wooden stool from beneath the table and perched next to her daughter, getting as close as she could.

Rainey could smell her mother's shampoo. Its familiarity brought back childhood memories. 'Friday night is Amami night,' the advertisement had claimed, and Jo was still using number five, for blonde hair. Its scent comforted Rainey, made her feel safe.

'Talk to me, Rainey.' Jo pressed a white handkerchief into Rainey's hand.

'What can I say? My baby's dead.'

There, she'd said it. For weeks she hadn't wanted to believe it but she'd finally said the words. She felt her mother's arms tighten about her. 'I think the excitement of the day and your grand party at Thorngate Hall were a bit too much for me . . .'

As soon as the words left Rainey's lips she realized her mother might think she was blaming her for her own natural excitement at the wedding. She said quickly, 'Not that I felt the least bit unwell then or afterwards on the way home.'

'Did you feel any signs during the evening? Any backache?' Jo asked. She kept her arm around Rainey's shoulders, her face close to her daughter's cheek.

Rainey said, 'Nothing. You'd have thought I'd know if I was about to give birth, wouldn't you?'

Jo sighed. 'Not necessarily. Every woman's labour is different, love.'

Rainey pulled away and looked into her mother's anguished face. 'I was so excited for you, Mum. I couldn't think of anything except how pretty you were and how proud and handsome Blackie looked.'

The marriage of the Bluebirds' manager to Jo had been a longed-for event. The morning's nuptials had been held at Fareham Register Office, the afternoon and evening spent dancing and celebrating at one of Gosport's most prestigious venues in a blur of happiness. Even the sun had put in an appearance for the day. Practically everyone who had touched Blackie Wilson and Jo Bird's lives had accepted an invitation. Rainey was so happy for them that her feet hadn't touched the ground all day.

'I didn't think my baby was due for at least another three or four weeks,' said Rainey. 'I'd been feeling fine.' She breathed out slowly. 'I thought you'd be home and with me . . .'

'As we all thought,' agreed Jo. Rainey felt the dampness of her mother's tears mingle with her own on her cheek.

'I was very bad-tempered at Thorngate before we left for home,' Rainey said. 'I put it down to tiredness, and all the excitement. I was snappy with Bea and Ivy. Bea insisted on stopping the night with me . . .'

'Thank God for friends who know us inside out and love us all the same,' said Jo. 'That girl is worth her weight in gold. And Ivy.'

27

'You think I don't know that, Mum? I woke Bea up when I discovered my bed was all wet. Everything started happening so quickly then.'

'First babies usually take a long time.'

'Not this one,' Rainey said. 'He was in a hurry. Bea phoned for a taxi and got me to Blake's.'

'You'd been going to the maternity home for check-ups, hadn't you? It's a wonder they didn't find anything amiss beforehand.' Jo had put Rainey's own thoughts into words.

Rainey shrugged. 'If they did, they kept it quiet.'

Jo said, 'Oh, love. Bea telephoned the bed-and-breakfast on Dartmoor where Blackie and I were supposed to be spending our wedding night. But we'd not reached it. We were broken down in the car in the back of beyond in Dorset.'

Rainey was only half listening: she'd begun reliving her nightmare. 'Mum,' she said, 'he was so little . . .' Her mind went back to the white-walled room, to the pain and herself straining to rid the agony from her body.

'Push! Use the rope!' urged a woman's voice.

Rainey saw again the thickly woven cord attached to the bedhead. She remembered the terrible cries that hurt her ears and that she wished would stop. Then she'd realized the sounds were coming from herself. She'd called for Charlie, forgetting he was dead. Gone in the blast that had ripped through the flat on the night before their wedding . . . She'd felt a sliding sensation over which she had no control.

Then Rainey heard another, different sound start up, softer, like the mewing of a kitten. Followed by silence. It was a quiet that Rainey had never experienced before. Next came the frantic bustle of people moving, whispers, heightened antiseptic smells. The murmur of heated voices. A mask stinking of rubber was put over her nose and mouth. She'd pushed it away.

'I heard the word "syringe",' Rainey told her mother. 'Then everything became muffled, unreal. I was fighting to stay awake, Mum. I desperately wanted to sleep but I knew something wasn't right and I had to stay awake. The blackness was pulling me down into it. I called for Charlie again and said I wanted my baby. The darkness was stealing up on me, like it wanted to drown me . . .

'"Hold him," someone said, and laid a wrapped bundle on my breast. A very still and silent bundle. I defied the tiredness and unwrapped my child. When I looked at his beautiful little face, which they'd wiped, but not properly – his cheek still had a covering of white stuff and blood streaks on it – I saw he wasn't breathing. That first cry I'd heard from him was his last.

'I saw his perfect feet with tiny toenails and miniature fingers that were like Charlie's. He was so still, so small, Mum, so . . . so not alive. I was willing him to open his eyes, to take a breath. I tried to love him into life . . . Mum, it wasn't any use . . .'

Jo released Rainey, rose from the stool. 'I should have been with you,' she said. 'I'm so sorry.' Her voice was cracked with tears.

'I was too weak, too tired to hold on to him. They took him away from me. The next time I woke I was in a little room. Bea was watching me from a chair, Ivy standing beside her. Before I had a chance to ask them anything a nurse came in, all blue, white and starchy. "'Now don't go talking about the birth,'" she said to them. "It'll only upset her. Leave everything to us." She was speaking to Bea and Ivy, as if I wasn't there. When the door closed, I said to Bea, "They've taken him, haven't they?"

'She didn't answer, she didn't need to. Her eyes were all red from crying. "Take me home," I said. "Please take me home."'

Rainey stared at her mother, into the green eyes that mirrored her own. She used her hands to wipe her face then patted the front of her dressing gown for the handkerchief. 'I'm so sorry I wouldn't see you, Mum. You didn't deserve to be treated like that. I was hurting so much and wanted to lash out at you because I blamed you for not being there.'

Rainey pulled the handkerchief out of her dressing-gown pocket and frantically scrubbed at her eyes. After a while she said softly, 'I really am so very sorry. None of it was your fault. I've missed you so much. I've been out of my mind . . .'

'Don't you worry about that, my love.' Jo was looking at her intently. 'It's doing you good to talk now.' Then she added, 'We always lash out at our nearest and dearest when things go wrong. I understand and I love you.' She sighed. 'I'll get us that cup of tea now, Rainey.'

'I'll bring it in, Mum.' Rainey wanted to show her mother that she intended to make amends. A start would be making tea.

'No, I will,' Jo insisted, and pushed herself upright.

Rainey realized her mother was glad to do something, anything, rather than continue listening to her apologising for her behaviour. Perhaps, too, she wanted to show Rainey everything between them was back on a more normal footing. Rainey settled in the chair, listening to the rattle of crockery.

'Both girls have been good friends to you,' her mother called from the scullery.

'Bea and Ivy fetched me home in a taxi. They stayed with me,' Rainey shouted back. 'Wouldn't even let me carry in the box of supplies Blake's sent me home with.' She got up and walked towards the scullery door. She thought how like old times it was to see her mother pottering about in there, as she used to do before she married and moved in with Blackie.

'Mum, I heard him cry, I know I did. It wasn't a dream or something I made up. I heard him cry.'

Jo stopped pouring the milk into the cups and said, 'I believe you. But, Rainey, you said he was so little . . .' Her voice petered out. Rainey knew the silence that followed held more meaning than if her mother had continued talking. When Jo finally spoke, she said, 'You wouldn't have wanted him to suffer through life, would you?' She replaced the milk bottle on the draining board. 'I came home to Gosport on the train immediately I heard,' she added. 'Blackie followed as soon as he could get the car on the road again.'

Jo removed the cosy and began to pour the tea. 'I didn't expect you'd refuse to see me.'

Rainey felt more tears rise. She'd been wrong to take out her unhappiness on her mother. She tried to explain how it had been. She spoke quickly, her words running into each other.

'It wasn't only you I didn't want to see, it was anyone – everyone. I hid in this house, didn't get up, didn't wash myself or comb my hair, didn't answer when anyone phoned or called and took away the key from the back of the door. Bea made me give her the key so she could let herself in and out. She and Ivy took it in turns to shop and cook for me, not that I ate much. When I started to feel a bit more like myself, Bea and Ivy took me out for walks. Places where it was quiet, where I wasn't going to meet anyone I knew.' The corners of her lips rose in a small smile. 'They made me sing, as well! We'd walk along arm in arm singing stage songs. There was nothing wrong with my voice, and my body soon adjusted itself. The midwife had given me Epsom salts and some other medicine to help dry up my milk, and Bea brought me Savoy cabbages so I could put the leaves in my bra to cool my breasts . . .'

Jo handed Rainey the cup and saucer. 'I should have been with you,' she said again.

'Mum! I was out of my mind.' Rainey put her tea on the draining board and pulled her mother into her arms. Once more she breathed in the scent of Amami shampoo.

Jo kissed the side of her face. 'I'm here now,' she said.

Jo then asked a question that seemed utterly out of context. 'How did you feel going back on the stage singing for the Americans in Dartmouth?'

Rainey collected her thoughts and answered as honestly as she could. 'Apprehensive, scared. It was so soon after . . . but I knew if I didn't force myself to snap out of it, I'd let my nerves get the better of me and probably never sing in public again. Besides, I had Bea and Ivy to hold me up and two Savoy cabbage leaves stuck inside my dress.' Rainey gave another small smile.

'When you were a little girl you sang your way out of problems,' said Jo. 'Singing was like medicine to you, a cure for all ills. You sang when you were happy as well,' she added. 'The night we left Portsmouth and I drove to Gosport to start a new life I remember you sang all the way . . . Fifteen you were then.'

'Bea persuaded me . . .'

'Yes, if it hadn't been for Bea and Ivy,' added her mother, mysteriously. 'We all knew if anything could bring you back to life again it would be singing up there on the stage.'

A sudden silence filled the scullery. Rainey watched her mother drink from her cup. Then Jo smiled at her, as though she was hiding a secret.

'You all knew?' Rainey said. 'All . . . of . . . you?' There was another silence as she digested her thoughts. 'Of course! I should have realized. It was all down to you, wasn't it? It was you who suggested to Bea that she persuade me to sing at Dartmouth!'

Jo smiled at her.

Rainey hadn't finished. 'You sorted it all out with Blackie. I thought Bea had arranged it, with help from Ivy, but it was you . . .'

Jo put her hands on Rainey's shoulders and looked into her eyes. 'And we were right, weren't we? You should have known I'd do anything to help you on the road to recovery. And now do as your mother tells you and drink up your tea!'

That didn't happen because those words had hardly left Jo's mouth when the long wail of Moaning Minnie rent the air. Rainey grabbed at her mother's arm. 'I thought it was too good to be true. We've all been saying how quiet it's been along the south of England without the daily whine of bombers and now here they come again! Damn Hitler!' She pointed to the Morrison shelter erected in the living room. 'Get in there, Mum. There's no telling how long this air raid will last. You're not setting foot outdoors now.'

Jo was checking inside the small shelter that could accommodate two or possibly three people. 'There's a quilt to keep us warm. A pack of cards, a couple of books, two pillows, a big torch . . .'

'And I'm just about to put the kettle on again,' said Rainey.

'Got any sandwiches?' Jo asked.

Rainey decided she was making sure her daughter ate properly. 'There's a loaf and a tin of corned beef,' said Rainey, grabbing the flask, which had been washed out and allowed to drain. Jo grinned back at her.

Rainey pulled her dressing gown tighter about herself and blessed the timing of the air raid. Suddenly it felt as if everything was going to be all right, somehow. Maybe not today but sometime in the future, and she and her mum would face it together.

'I'll do the sandwiches,' Jo said. 'I heard Blackie talking to Jack Warner's agent yesterday on the telephone . . . You know Jack Warner, the star of *The Dummy Talks*? It's a new film . . .'

'I do know who Jack Warner is,' said Rainey, with just a hint of sarcasm.

'Of course you do,' answered Jo, taking the bread knife from the drawer. 'I was only going to tell you that they were talking about a Baby Blitz. Apparently, Hitler is going to chuck everything he can at us now in an all-out bid to win the war.'

'There's nothing about that in the newspapers or on the wireless,' said Rainey, spooning more precious tea into the pot.

'I'm only telling you what I heard.'

'Mum, you, of all people, know you shouldn't repeat things. You don't know who could be listening!'

Jo made a noise that sounded like 'Huh!' Then, 'No, and a mother never knows when her own daughter is going to tell her off.' Rainey looked at her and returned her smile.

The days were still short and barely bright. Now the dull sky was criss-crossed by searchlights looking for the enemy. Then came the noise of throbbing bombers. She couldn't see them but they were there, all right. Rainey heard the whistle of falling bombs and the blasts that shook the ground. Anyone with any sense would be in their shelters, she thought, as she let the corner of the curtain drop. Jo was struggling with the key that opened the tin of corned beef. It was the same with sardines – her mother always made a mess of them too.

'Let me finish making the sandwiches,' she said, passing Jo the newly filled flask. 'Take this into the Morrison with you. I nearly lost you once through my own pig-headedness. I don't want to risk it again.'

Chapter Four

'Tell me what you think of him, then.' Bea leaned across the ring-marked Formica tabletop and touched Eddie's sleeve to gain his attention. It was difficult to hear above the band's loud music in the Connaught drill hall. The many dancers of all nationalities on the floor, shrieking with laughter at the mistakes they were making during the Paul Jones, didn't make it too easy to talk, either.

Bea could see Bing trying not to fall over his feet while cavorting with an extremely large middle-aged lady, who had just become his new partner. He'd started off by accompanying Rainey, but the Paul Jones being a participation dance meant that, after a series of complicated steps, everyone swapped partners.

Bea's brother stopped mid-laugh at Ivy's contortions with a sailor who didn't seem able to grasp the difference

38

between his left and his right feet. Instead of answering Bea, he asked, 'Are you going to marry him?'

Bea sat back on her chair in amazement. 'It's early days yet but we have talked about me travelling to America after the war . . . if we win.' She saw sudden shock on Eddie's face and added, 'When we win.'

Eddie, who was still bitterly disappointed that he hadn't been able to enlist on medical grounds, was a firm believer that Hitler would never win the war. 'Of course we'll win. You could be a GI bride.'

Bea knew that 'GI' had originally stood for 'Galvanised Iron', which was stamped on tins and buckets, and that it also meant 'General Issue'. But American servicemen billeted in England had been dubbed GIs, which in this case meant mass-produced or 'Government Issue'. 'I thought you liked him!'

Eddie punched his sister's arm playfully, dislodging an empty glass on the table but catching it before it rolled off. 'You know I do but you can't get away from the fact that many people think the American servicemen are more privileged than our boys and resent them joining the war to help us win. Overpaid, over-sexed and over here – isn't that what they say?'

The air was thick with cigarette smoke, which had begun

to sting Bea's eyes. Eddie waved to Ivy as she danced by with a partner.

Bea blinked. 'That's what stupid people think. Do you resent Bing?' She tucked a strand of golden hair behind her ear. It had come loose from one of the tortoiseshell combs she wore. She'd put it up in a chignon but it was so silky the combs couldn't contain it.

Eddie shook his head. 'God, no, I don't. After the Japanese bombed Pearl Harbor, I believe that if the Americans hadn't joined forces with us, we would now be batting against a very sticky wicket indeed. Instead we're going to win the war against those damned Germans.'

Bea smoothed a crease out of her brown woollen dress. She particularly liked it because it made the most of her small waist. She gazed across the table at her brother. It wasn't often that Rainey, Ivy, Eddie, Bing and she were able to go out and enjoy themselves all together. Maud had volunteered to stay in and look after Gracie so Eddie and Ivy could join them, and Rainey had been persuaded to come along, instead of moping around at home in Albert Street.

Bea glanced across the crowded floor at Rainey, now paired again with Bing and laughing up at him. It was early days yet, she thought, but Rainey was taking each one as it came. This evening was a success for everyone.

Eddie interrupted her thoughts. 'Look, I think Bing's a great man and he's good for you. I happen to believe he really does love you. There's not many blokes fall in love with a photograph of a girl, then move heaven and earth to find her.'

'Oh, I don't know.' Bea chuckled. 'If it hadn't been for Rainey's father, before he got blown up, pressing her photo into Blackie's hands in France and extolling her virtues as a singer, the Bluebirds wouldn't have happened, would they?'

'Bea Herron, you've got an answer for everything, you have,' Eddie said.

'Actually, Bing saw us on Pathé News in a cinema in Mobile – that's where he comes from ... Alabama,' she added. 'There was a bit on ENSA in the desert and the Bluebirds were filmed during a show. He, like many men, wrote to us for a picture that we all signed. And he's kept that photograph ever since. He says that was when he first fell in love with me, watching me sing to all the troops on a makeshift stage among the sand dunes!' Bea grinned at her brother. 'I knew the moment I set eyes on him in Dartmouth that he would be special to me.' Bea saw the concerned look on Eddie's face and knew what he was going to ask her almost before he opened his mouth.

'You have explained what happened to you when you were a kid?'

Bea took a deep breath. 'Yes, I have. It took a lot of effort to tell him why I'd never had a man in my life . . . He's so understanding.'

'Well, it wasn't your fault.' Eddie ran his fingers through his blond hair. Bea knew he hated remembering the sailor and how he'd tried to take advantage of her in the back-yard of the town pub. 'You were a kid,' he went on. 'It's not something you can forget, and it's caused you damage. Thank God it wasn't made public – it might have blighted your chances of becoming a Bluebird . . .'

'In a way I've been lucky, Eddie. But I don't want secrets between me and the first man I've ever cared about,' she said. 'Bing began telling me how some of the white people in America treat black people . . . the segregation, the cruelty, the hate.' She shook her head contemptuously. 'When he worked in the shipyards for the war effort the race riots were terrible. It all started when a dozen or so black men were given jobs that normally only white men did in the factories. He joined the army in the hope he'd experience a better life and get away from all that.' She frowned. 'It hasn't always worked out that way for him.' For a moment she was silent. Then she said, 'I knew I had to explain why I needed to take things slowly with him.'

She used her thumb to wipe away a tear that had formed in the corner of her eye. 'Did you know Hattie McDaniel won an Oscar award for playing Mammy in *Gone With the Wind*? Well, when it came to the presentations in Atlanta, she was advised not to attend because she's black and the theatre on Peachtree Street is a whites-only establishment. I think that's just inhuman.' Bea paused. 'Because Bing's had terrible things happen to him and has witnessed stuff we can only imagine, he understands how cruel people can be. I believe that's why he, like you, escapes into his beloved books.'

'Possibly,' Eddie said. 'Reading a book is like watching a film going on in my head and it helps me stop worrying about this blessed war . . . So you might travel to America when it's all over?'

'I wouldn't like to lose Bing now we've found each other,' she said. 'But I'm not sure it would be right for him or me in his country, a black man and a white woman. It would take a lot of guts from both of us. Maybe I could persuade him to stay here.'

'Maybe. But there'll be animosity towards coloured people here as well. And what about your career?'

Bea made a face at him. 'Racial problems aren't as bad in England as they are in America. You only have to look at him enjoying himself here—' Bea broke off to wave at Bing dancing. He waved back at her.

She turned to Eddie. 'Black and white Americans are over here helping us to win the damn war. As for my career, you know how much it means to me. Perhaps Blackie will be able to get me some work across the ocean. Who knows? Anyway, that's enough about me. When are you going to tell me you and Ivy expect the patter of little feet?'

Bea saw a frown cross his forehead. 'It doesn't seem to be on the horizon yet.'

'Well,' consoled Bea, 'you have Gracie and she's a gorgeous child . . .'

Bea was suddenly aware of a whiff of fresh sweat, lemon and bergamot, as a man appeared next to her. His large hand caught up her own, which was resting on the table. 'Bea, your turn to dance with me.' He gave her a look and a smile that made her heartstrings jangle with happiness. At his side, Rainey was in a red dress that should have clashed with her hair but didn't. Instead the vibrant colour added warmth to her pale features.

Rainey tugged at a grumbling Eddie's arm . 'Git up, Eddie, an' take a turn around the floor with me! I don't think I've ever danced with so many different servicemen, ever, and now I want to dance with you!'

Eddie tutted, but entered into the spirit of things and bowed deeply to Rainey. 'Will you do me the honour, Miss Bird?'

'Of course,' she giggled, 'but I'm thanking my lucky stars this dance is a quickstep because I'm not snuggling up close to you for a waltz!'

'Certainly not!' Eddie said. 'Then it'll be time for me to parade around the floor with my Ivy.'

Bea watched her handsome brother take her friend's hand and move onto the crowded dance floor as she settled into Bing's arms. The air about them smelled of stale perfume mixed with tobacco smoke and sweaty bodies as they melted among the other dancers on the floor.

Bea said, 'Thank you for dancing with Rainey. It's lovely to see her smiling again, despite everything that's happened.'

'Happy to be of service, ma'am,' Bing said, and stopped dancing to salute her before once more pulling her into his arms and continuing the dance. All evening Bea had wanted to share with Bing something that was on her mind. The moment to do so hadn't as yet materialised and even now, in his arms, she realized, because of the noise, she would have to shout to make herself heard. Not at all what she wanted. Oh well, it would have to wait until later.

After the last waltz had been played and everyone stood for the National Anthem, the people spilled noisily onto the town's pavements to catch buses or walk home. Bea clasped Bing's hand as the cold enveloped them. Eddie, with his arm around Ivy, had already shepherded his flock back to his temperamental truck, which he'd parked on the road nearby. After shouting goodbyes to the others, Bea and Bing walked towards North Cross Street.

The moon exposed the town, showing the effects of war. Any remaining windows were blacked out and looked like the dead eyes of corpses, thought Bea. The town hall, now in ruins, was positively ghostly. At any moment Bea expected vampires to sweep through its damaged brick arches screaming like banshees. She stepped even closer to Bing and looked up at him. 'You're sure you don't mind staying in a room over the café tonight?'

'I'd like it better if I could stay with you.'

Bea felt herself colour. 'I think I'd like that, too,' she said shyly, 'but it's not possible. Della and Bert would never let us sleep together.'

'A separate room, that's what I'll give him,' Della had said sharply. 'And no sneaking into each other's beds. This is a respectable place, this is, not a knockin' shop!'

Bea had blushed. She hadn't wanted to tell Della that she and Bing hadn't actually got beyond the kissing stage. She was apprehensive about going the whole way with him because it would be her first time. She wanted everything to be perfect when they made love, which wouldn't be easy while she lodged at the Central Café and Bert looked upon her as a daughter.

'You can trust me,' she'd said to Della.

'Aha, but can I trust him?' Della had tartly replied. 'He's a man, ain't he?'

Bea hadn't told Bing about that, but she had explained why she was living at the café instead of at her family home in Alma Street.

'With Ivy and Eddie a couple, and Mum and baby Gracie in the house, there wasn't much room for me so I moved down to Bert's café. Bert and Della are like family, you see. Della is Ivy's mum, so it was a bit like them swapping daughters.' He'd nodded to show he understood.

Now Bea began talking again. 'Rainey said you and I could share a room at her house in Albert Street but I didn't want that. Gosport people gossip. It wouldn't do her reputation or mine any good.'

Bing stopped her flow of words with a kiss. 'I understand, Bea, I sure do.'

When he released her, he said, 'Folks can be just as narrow-minded where I come from.' He shrugged. 'And often what they don't know about any situation, they make up. My mom says a good girl could stay home every night of the week and the neighbours would wonder who she was indoors with!'

Bea laughed and looked up at the sky, which was covered with glittering stars. No enemy aircraft tonight. She felt the magnificent canopy was an omen that she and Bing were meant for each other. 'Your mother is a very wise woman. That sounds like something my mum, Maud, might say. We're not so different, then, you and I?'

'No, we're not.' He stopped walking and pulled her close. His lips strayed to her nose and he left a small kiss imprinted on it. 'I thought about a hotel room for the night. Or there's plenty of bars here with rooms,' he said. 'Then I thought about how well-known the Bluebirds are in this town and if gossip got about that you'd stayed with me . . .' He smiled down at her. 'It wouldn't be good. I don't want that for you, honey.'

Bea thanked him silently from the bottom of her heart. She stared into his eyes and knew she loved him with every fibre of her being.

As they reached North Cross Street she looked along the pavement at the tall darkened building on the corner and wondered if the Central Café had closed for the night. But, approaching, she could hear music tinkling from Bert's wireless. She smiled to herself. Momentarily she'd forgotten he kept strange opening hours. Possibly he might even be waiting up for her – he worried about her. The blackout curtains were doing a wonderful job, she thought.

Before she unlocked the side door, her usual method of entry, she took a deep breath. Perhaps now wasn't the right time to tell Bing her thoughts. But tomorrow morning he would be catching the eight o'clock ferry to arrive at Portsmouth Harbour station for his train to Dartmouth. Time was of the essence. Bea decided to take a chance.

'Wait a second before we go in. I've been wanting to ask you something all evening but I couldn't summon the courage. How far is Brixham from where you're based in Devon?' Her words came out in a rush.

'I've heard the name. Maybe five or ten miles.' He looked at her questioningly.

Bea took another deep breath. 'George Formby is supposed to be appearing there at the Alhambra Theatre soon, for three nights. His wife Beryl, she's also his manager, has double booked him . . .' It occurred to her that he might not know who she was talking about. 'You do know who George Formby is?'

Bing nodded. 'I've watched him in shows at the cinema. A funny man.' His brow furrowed.

'Yes – and as he can't appear at the Alhambra, Blackie's booked us in instead!'

For a moment Bing stared at her, then the meaning of her words dawned on him. 'So that means you'll be singing on a stage near me in Devon?'

Bea nodded.

His smile widened. 'So, you'll be staying in a hotel with Rainey and Ivy for several nights?'

Bea was thinking it was one of the hardest things she had ever needed to do. She was hinting – no, telling him – that in Devon they could be away from the prying eyes and gossipy tongues of neighbours. Why, oh why didn't he grasp what she meant?

'Ivy and Rainey would understand. You and me . . . We could stay together in a different hotel.' Bea's mouth seemed to be full of cotton wool. She tried again. 'If you wanted to be with me, and if you can get the time off . . .'

For a moment he was silent. Then he grinned at her, his eyes twinkling. Bea realized that the penny had already dropped but he couldn't resist teasing her.

'Yes, yes, yes,' he chanted. Then he picked her up and whirled her round and round on the pavement until Bea squealed to be put down.

The door opened and Bert stood there. He'd folded his arms and was staring at them. Bing almost stumbled as he set Bea on her feet.

'Get inside, you daft buggers,' Bert said, pulling the blackout curtain closed after them so the light wouldn't shine out into the street. A welcome blast of warm air tinged with bacon fat surrounded Bea. 'Della told you no funny business, Bea.' Bert scratched his chin, glaring at the man Bea loved. 'Bing, you know where to go, where you left your belongings, on the top floor. Don't you dare try creeping down – I've got the sharpest ears in Gosport!'

Chapter Five

The fresh sheets were icy cold to Bing's upper body. The small room was spotlessly clean, with an iron bedstead, a chair with his army duffel bag lying across it, and a wardrobe with his clothes draped over the door ready for his departure in the morning. There was a fireplace, but instead of flaming coals to warm the room, a newspaper fan filled the cleaned grate. Coal was precious in England. On the bamboo bedside table a tumbler of water was covered with a saucer. He couldn't drink it because it was tepid. Had the British never heard of ice cubes? Next to that was his copy of Homer's *Iliad* where he'd left it earlier that day, but he couldn't be bothered to read: so many things were running through his mind.

His foot searched for the stoneware hot-water bottle that either Bert or Della had thoughtfully placed in the bed.

Della most probably, he decided. Della, who reminded him of Hedy Lamarr and who clucked around her Bert and Bea like a mother hen. What Bing liked most about Della was her ability to speak her mind. You knew where you were with her.

The hospitality of Bert and Della was legendary and had been from the moment Bing was introduced to them. He'd made a few flying day visits to Gosport but this was the first time he'd spent a night under their roof. He'd quickly realized that without Bert's tenuous ties to the black market and the half-closed eyes of the local police, in exchange for free meals, he would have found it difficult to provide good food for his café customers.

Thinking about food, or the lack of it, reminded Bing of what it was like to go hungry and without decent clothing. Back home in the summer months he'd gone barefoot to school, as had many of his friends in Mobile, Alabama. Going without had never stopped him getting what he wanted, though. He remembered being a skinny, ragged kid of nine, wearing glasses bound up with tape, waiting outside the majestic library building day after day until Mrs Henshaw had finally allowed him to have his own library ticket. He knew he'd got under her skin when, on one insufferably hot day, she'd brought him a soda and told him to come inside the building when he'd finished it. She didn't allow eating and drinking in the library.

Thirty degrees, and more, in the summer without shoes wasn't such a problem, but in the winter when it rained constantly, he hated the warm mud squelching between his toes. He'd have hung about outside the free library forever just for the possibility to escape inside a book.

His mother, Dawn, had brought up three children by taking in white folks' washing and ironing, cleaning and maiding for them. He didn't remember his dad, who had disappeared just after Bing was born. His family ate well when the sea gave up Mobile's delicacies of shrimp, crab and oysters. Bing and his brother George had spent most of their time with nets and lines near the sea wall of the dock-yard. His mouth watered, thinking about fat king prawns and his mother's fragrant freshly baked cornbread.

Bert was always pressing food on him. It didn't seem to matter to him that Bing protested he was well fed in the US Army. Saying he was already full-up became Bing's mantra. He had seen the empty Gosport shops and the queues of weary women with ration books in their hands.

After leaving the stores at Brookley airfield, he had joined the army to gain skills, ending up as an engineer, first class. Now he was on *LST 507*, one of the tank landing ships belonging to United States 5th Army Corps, based in Dartmouth, Devon. His mom was proud of his achievements.

Even in the army there were racial taunts but now he was no longer a skinny kid. At six foot four he could look after himself. And he didn't invite trouble.

His mother had laughed and teased him because he'd told her he was in love with a white girl he'd never met. He'd shown her the Bluebirds glossy photograph and she'd said, 'You got as much chance of meeting her as you have of finding the gold at the end of a rainbow!'

He'd reminded her of yet another of her sayings, 'If the Lord wills it.'

Well, not only had he met Bea, the girl of his dreams, but she loved him. Maybe the Lord was looking out for him after all.

He thought about Bea's shyness in telling him that the Bluebirds would be appearing at Brixham. It had taken her great courage to say what was on her mind. If she wanted to back out of going to a hotel with him, well, that would be fine, too. He'd already waited a long time to meet her and he would wait forever to make love to her if she changed her mind.

He smiled in the darkness. Bea was in her room on the

floor below and he knew she wanted him, possibly as much as he wanted her. He could slip out of bed and creep down to her. Perhaps Bea half expected it. Bert and Della certainly did! But he wouldn't betray their trust. He always kept his promises. Even though he loved that blonde downstairs more than life itself.

'Come on, wakey, wakey!'

Bert's gruff voice woke him and Bing scrambled to sit up. He took the mug Bert was handing him. 'I'll bet you don't get tea in bed in the army!' Bert gave a belly laugh. He'd brought frying smells into the room with him. Bing's stomach grumbled. 'Della's cooking breakfast and Bea's waiting downstairs. She's already dolled herself up to look good for when you says goodbye to her.'

Bing swallowed a mouthful of hot dark liquid and tried not to shudder. 'Thanks for the tea, Bert. I meant to ask you for an alarm clock last night but it slipped my mind . . .'

'Don't matter. I wouldn't have let you sleep in, mate. I knows how important it is for you to get back to barracks on time.' Bert turned and made for the open door. He gave a small cough and looked back at Bing. 'Would you mind if I asked you a question?'

'No,' said Bing. He didn't really want to finish the tea. He much preferred coffee and didn't understand the English with their constant tea-making. But he didn't like to refuse Bert's hospitality.

'You Americans ain't 'alf got some funny names but the only other Bing I've heard of is Bing Crosby, the American film star and crooner. How come you're named Bing?'

Bing treated him to a wide white-toothed grin. 'My real name is Brian Baxter, my initials, BB. The boss at one of Mobile's clubs I used to work in when I was seventeen first called me Bing. I got a low voice and I used to ape Crosby's tones. The girls loved it. So, BB became Bing.'

'Sing a bit, do you?' He reached across and received the half-empty mug Bing handed him.

'And I play the piano.'

'Well, I'm blessed!' Bert stood staring at him, twisting the mug in his hand. 'You read music then, like Blackie Wilson, our Bea's manager?'

Bing laughed loudly. 'Nah! My mom had no money for nonsense like that. I play by ear. Jazz mostly.'

'Well I never,' said Bert. 'Bea never let on to me you 'ad a voice.' His forehead creased a bit. 'We got an old joanna – that's rhymin' slang for piano – in one of the rooms. Next time you're in Gosport, I'll get it set up in the café. I like a bit of music, I do.'

'Is that a promise?' Bing had never played to white folks in the club. Sometimes, though, he played in the canteen back at barracks. That seemed to go down okay, unless a white soldier said something derogatory. Then Bing would simply get up and move away. No sense in asking for a fight.

Bert gave him a gap-toothed smile. 'Yes! And I'll 'old you to that, son,' he said. He made to leave but again turned. 'Next time you come down I'll show you my collection of walking sticks. Been collecting them for years, I 'ave.'

Bing had heard all about Bert's passion from Bea. He felt a tug at his heartstrings. The gnarled café owner really had taken a shine to him if he wanted to show him his most treasured keepsakes. 'I'd like that,' he said.

Bert dipped his head in acknowledgement, and this time he went out, closing the door behind him.

Bing threw back the bedcovers and heard Bert shout from the stairs, 'There's a bathroom along from you. No hot water but I can bring up a kettle.'

'I know what I want,' Bing said. He could see the ferry was still tied to the bollards on the pontoon at the end of the gangway. A covering of frost lay over the grass on Ferry Gardens. He was cold. The early-morning air smelled of dust and cordite even though Gosport had been mostly free of night raids for a while. Bea was shivering and the tip of her nose was pink, despite the knitted scarf that covered her hair and was wound around her neck. Men pushing bicycles were streaming from the pontoon onto the ferry. He'd heard about the dockyard workers whose bikes were dumped unceremoniously on the ferries – sometimes it took ages to sort them out when the vessels reached the other side. Bing gave Bea a smile. His heart was cut in two at going and he didn't want to leave with her in tears.

'And what do you want?' Bea asked. Her hands were tucked into his pockets for warmth.

He'd insisted she leave him on the Gosport side. It had been cold enough walking the short distance down Mumby Road to the ferry and he didn't like to think of her facing the bitter journey back across the water from Portsmouth Harbour station.

'I want to kiss you,' he said.

He felt a shiver run through her but she answered, with a grin, 'I don't think that's a good idea . . . Could lead to all kinds of problems.' She fluttered her eyelashes coquettishly.

He felt the warmth of her breath as she stood on tiptoe and gently kissed him. Her lips, full and supple, moved on his for several moments. Bing put a hand on her neck, under her scarf and hair, and pulled her face towards his as close as possible. Her tongue met his and played inside his mouth. Her perfume filled his nostrils. His arms wanted to embrace her and his mouth to devour her. He forced himself to pull away and stared into her blue eyes. 'You are lusciousness itself,' he whispered.

'And you had better run or the ferry will leave without you,' she said, bringing her hands out from the warmth of his front pockets.

Bing looked down at the pontoon and heard the clang of chains as the deckhand began fastening the metal across the boat's entrance.

'Run!' Bea said, pushing him away from her. 'They'll wait if they see you running.'

'Gotta look after our servicemen,' said the warmly dressed ferry worker, as he made a circle on the decking of the rope he'd unwound from the bollard.

'Thanks,' said Bing. He was breathing heavily when he looked up to the railings high above where Bea stood waving at him. Already he felt as if a part of him was missing.

Chapter Six

'Get your big bonce out of the way! I can't see to put my lipstick on!'

Bea tried to push Ivy aside so she could look into the mirror but Ivy stood firm. Rainey, ever the peacemaker, shouted, 'Pack it in, you two! There's hardly room to swing a cat in here without you coming to blows over who gets to look in the glass!'

Ivy pulled a face. 'Well, it's her fault, and my head's no bigger than hers!' She stuck out her tongue at Bea, then composed her face into a smile and aimed it at Rainey. 'I know she misses Bing but do we all have to suffer her bad temper because she's not heard from him?'

'I am not in a bloody bad temper!' Bea's voice was practically a shout and, in the sudden silence, it echoed around the manager's office that the Bluebirds had been allocated as a changing room. Tonight they were appearing as guest vocalists with a big Portsmouth band, Mel Bond's Travellers, to celebrate the reopening of the Lee Tower Ballroom on the seafront. A bomb had demolished the pier and part of the building. Lee Tower was a money-making attraction, with a dance hall, picture house, café, ice-cream parlour and shops. The beach was covered with barbed wire to stop the Germans invading, but Lee Tower was a magnet for local people.

'Of course you're not,' said Rainey, and laughed. Ivy joined in and, within moments, all three girls were laughing.

'I'm sorry,' said Bea. When she looked into the mirror she saw that her mascara had run. Wiping the black streaks from below her eyes, she added, 'Now I need to do my eyes again as well as my lips.'

Ivy looked down into her drawstring make-up bag and took out a small blue box of cake mascara. She passed it along with its tiny brush. 'Here, use mine.'

Rainey was bent forwards and she was frantically brushing her hair. She threw her head back and shook her curls. 'You told me he was on some special operation so might not be able to telephone or write.'

'What special operation is that then?' asked Ivy.

'He couldn't tell me, so I don't know all of it,' said Bea, carefully coating her bottom lashes.

'Well, then, that's why he hasn't been in touch,' Rainey said. 'He loves you, and that's all you need to worry about.'

'I'm very lucky, aren't I?' Bea passed the mascara back to Ivy and took the lipstick Rainey handed to her. She pressed her lips together after applying the creamy red colour. 'Right, that's me done. I'll get out of the way now.'

'Thank God for that,' said Rainey, taking back the lipstick. 'You really do care for him, don't you?'

'Like I've never cared for any man before,' said Bea. She slid away from the mirror and twisted round to check her stocking seams were straight. The girls were dressed in identical short black dresses and black suede high-heeled shoes. Bea touched the double string of pearls at her throat. Ivy had a treble strand at her left wrist and Rainey a single around her waist as a belt. The remaining differences between them were, of course, their hair styles and colours. Bea, the blonde, was the centrepiece, Ivy to her right, with her glossy dark bob, and Rainey on her left, with her long red waves.

Bea watched Rainey outline her lips with the same lipstick she'd used, then fill in the colour. 'And how about you? I'm amazed at the way you seem to have bounced back after . . .'

'When I'm alone I have my bad days,' Rainey said.

'Sometimes the nights aren't so good either. But I thank God for the happiness I've had . . .' For a moment there was silence. 'Now I'm on an even keel with Mum again I feel so much more settled. I wouldn't have come through it without you two, and the singing, of course.'

Ivy's face appeared in the mirror. Rainey put an arm around her. 'You've both been the best friends anyone could have. I guess I went a bit mad because of everything that happened.' She smiled at Ivy. 'Anyway, now that we have dates for appearances, we're back together as the Bluebirds and still making records for Parlophone, I'm going to thank my lucky stars and take each day as it comes . . . It's your turn next for a baby, Ivy, and to get married, of course, to Eddie.'

Ivy said, 'I'm fine as I am, except . . .' she grew wistful '. . . there's no sign of a baby yet. Maybe if I was pregnant I'd feel the need to be married. But, like Bea and you, for the present I'm content to sing.' A smile crept up to her eyes. 'Remember when we were at school? All we ever wanted to do was sing.'

'A lot of water's passed under the bridge since then,' Bea said. 'I still want more. I want Bing and I want to be famous like Vera Lynn.'

'You still want to be in pictures?' Rainey asked.

'When did I ever stop wanting everything I could grab with both hands?' Bea grinned.

There was a knock on the door. 'Five minutes!' It was their pianist, Sammy, who did double duty for the girls, driving them and their dresses to venues. Because there was a band performing with the Bluebirds tonight, Sammy didn't need to be on stage but Blackie was paying him to look after the girls and keep them out of trouble.

'Okay,' shouted Bea, then urged the other two, 'Come on, let's get going. Apparently there's a big crowd out there tonight.' She turned to Rainey. 'I haven't seen much of your mum lately. Still, I suppose now she's married to Blackie and the business is doing really well . . .'

'They're fine together, just like a pair of turtle doves. He's still buying those gold charms for her bracelet – the latest is a tiny gold book because she's taken over so much of the book-keeping.'

Ivy chipped in, 'Married or not, I'd want more than a little bit of gold for doing all that paperwork.'

'And she gets much more, Ivy. They'd go through fire and flood to keep that business running. Love the bones of each other, they do,' Rainey insisted.

Bea laughed. 'As long as they're not so much in love that they forget to pay us for tonight.' She looked first at Ivy, then Rainey. 'Ready to go, you two? We've got an audience to make happy.'

'Ready!' they chorused.

Maximilian Muller gave the guard at St Vincent Barracks a sarcastic German salutation by clicking his heels together after he had been pushed quickly from the darkness of night into the lamplit Nissen hut situated on the bank of the backwaters of Gosport's Forton Creek. The burly guard checked his notes, then looked along the hut, making sure that blackout procedures were being upheld.

'Don't think you can escape from here a second time, Jerry. You won't be that lucky. There's been a great many changes since you were last here, including a double-strength perimeter fence that you'll never cut your way through.' The men in the hut looked towards Max and the guard with interest.

Max stared around the eighty-bed hut, vast, and smelling of dust, sweat and paraffin. The pot-bellied stove, its flue going through the steel roof, sat in the centre of the room, next to a pile of logs, and was giving out as much heat as it could on a freezing March evening.

'Brought us another one, Jonesey?'

The man who'd spoken looked up from the game of

cards he was playing with three other prisoners. Twenty or so men lounging about on bunks stopped whatever they were doing to stare at Max and his guard.

A dark-haired man slid out from his bottom bunk and ambled towards them. He was wearing the prisoners' attire of trousers with a large P imprinted down one leg. 'This is a surprise. Welcome home, Max,' he said. 'Never thought I'd see you again. Thrown you out of Winchester prison, have they?'

Max used his fingers to push back his white-blond hair. He grinned at the man then at the card players. 'Thought I'd visit you again,' he said. 'About a dozen of us have been taken out of Winchester and spread around the south, after an influx of new men. Where are you working, Dieter?' He could tell from Dieter Weber's healthy skin that he was working outside the holding centre. Dieter had once been assigned to help him in the gardens fronting St Vincent.

He, like Max, had flown fighter planes for the Luftwaffe. After being captured, both men had been incarcerated at the prison on the south coast of England.

Dieter gave a harsh laugh. 'You are looking at fellow countrymen who have earlier returned from repairing roads in Portsmouth and the surrounding areas. Roads that were practically destroyed by our planes,' he said, glancing at the

English guard. 'Some of the others in here work for Eddie Herron, the builder. The man who used to employ you,' he added.

Max noted Dieter's English had improved. Still not as good as his own but, then, he himself had been taught by an upper-class prisoner of war forced to work on his father's farm during the Great War.

'The bunk at the end is yours, Jerry.' The guard pointed towards the rear of the hut. 'Don't think you've got it easy in here. The rest of the men are in the canteen, eating. Pity you're too late for supper. You'll have to wait for breakfast.'

Dieter, ignoring the guard, stepped forward and slapped Max on the back, then took his cloth parcel of personal items from him and led him further into the room. He walked past the card players and deposited it on a bunk. 'This one's yours, Max.'

Max grinned and thanked him. He stared around the room and nodded in greeting at the other men. 'And Hans? Is he also in this hut?' The men who remembered him would also know of Hans, a young German he had befriended.

Dieter frowned. 'If you had to return to this holding centre, it's good you have come back now. Hans is in the sanatorium. He is not expected to recover. His lungs have finally let him down. He'll be pleased to see his old friend.'

Hans had had difficulty in breathing and had not been the strongest of young men but Max had thought the excellent care given by the English doctors might have cured him. Apparently not.

The guard was pulling back the blackout curtain covering the wooden door. 'See you in the morning, Jerry,' he called.

Max turned towards him. 'My name is not Jerry, it is Maximilian Muller,' he said.

The guard laughed. 'To me you're all bloody Jerry,' he said.

Maximilian clicked his heels in mock salute and grinned.

Chapter Seven

'Over thirty thousand acres have been cleared of people and their homes at Slapton Sands, from Blackpool to Blackawton,' said Si Cusack to Bing. 'American and British guards have been posted so that people can't return to their homes.'

'We're not supposed to talk about it,' said Bing. He sat up on his bunk and slammed his book shut.

'If we can't talk to each other about Exercise Tiger, who the hell can we talk to?' Bing could see his friend was distraught.

'That's over three thousand people and one hundred and eighty farms and village shops. Don't you wonder what will happen to those people?' Si asked. 'If my folks had to get off their property, like the people round here, I'd be worried sick for them.'

'We don't ask questions. Those above us know the

answers,' snapped Bing. 'We just do as we're told to try to win this war. All I know is our leave and mail have been put on hold. We're preparing for a D-Day rehearsal off Start Bay because the South Hams district of South Devon is the one place with its beach of coarse gravel fronting a shallow lagoon and backed by high steep ridges of sand that closely resembles the Normandy coast.' He paused. 'I expect the War Office will see that the villagers are recompensed for being moved.' Bing tried to take Si's mind off it. 'I saw you rereading that letter from home? Everything okay, back in New Jersey?'

Si had shown him photos of a neat wooden house on stilts at the edge of a bay. He still lived with his parents and a sister. He'd worked, before he joined the army, at a hardware store in the small nearby town of Hamilton.

'Maybelle sent me another photograph, taken on Fair Day, look.' She, too, worked in the hardware store. Si pushed along a snap of two pretty girls, one blonde, the other dark, eating enormous doughnuts. The blonde had shiny chin-length hair.

Bing studied the photograph. He was about to ask what it was all about when Si said, 'Every year we enter the doughnut chomping competition. Whoever eats the most of Hughie's gets them free for a year!'

Bing passed it back to Si with a smile. He knew all about small towns and their yearly fairs. 'You love her, Si?' he asked.

'I reckon so. Never thought much about it, just knew I was gonna marry her some day! I will when I get home!'

Bing thought about the photograph he kept hidden in his duffel bag, the one of the Bluebirds, which Bea had since signed with a more personal message. He kept it safe and away from prying eyes to escape the jealous ridicule he'd get if he pinned it up where it could be seen. He was suddenly overwhelmed with sadness that he hadn't spoken to Bea for a while because they'd been advised not to make phone calls. He put on a smile for Si. 'Yep,' he said. 'Your girl looks fun. You should snap her up when we get back home again.'

He guessed the secrecy had plenty to do with South Hams being occupied by more than thirty thousand US troops ready for the intensive rehearsal on Slapton Sands for Exercise Tiger. No one, it seemed, knew exactly what was happening, except it was to be a trial performance for the troops, ships and planes to land eventually on the beaches of France for D-Day.

'Where on earth did you get that?' Ivy asked, fingering the strawberry-pink material on the kitchen table at 14 Alma

Street. Bert had arrived a while ago with a small brown paper parcel. Ivy had just come in from the scullery where she'd been boiling some terry-towelling nappies in a galvanised bucket on the gas stove.

'Ask me no questions and I'll tell you no lies,' said Bert. 'But I reckon there's enough material there to make either a coat or a siren suit for young Gracie.' He pulled apart the square of soft warm fabric. 'You feel how nice it is. There's also a bit of parachute silk you can use for a lining, if you want.'

'Black market, Bert?' Eddie grinned. Bert looked smart tonight in a dark grey suit. After he had taken off his overcoat, Eddie saw the suit was on the tight side and shiny from wear. Bert had left the jacket unbuttoned because it didn't fit across his belly. Eddie thought Della must have bought it at a jumble sale.

The book Eddie had been reading had been abandoned on the arm of the chair when he'd gone to answer the door. It had slid to the lino and closed, losing his place.

'I prefer to call the material a present from a friend of a friend,' said Bert. 'And now it's a present to you.' He rerolled the cloth and left it on the table with the parachute silk, then took a few mouthfuls of the tea Maud had made for him. 'Maud can lay hands on a sewing machine – that's right, ain't it, Maud? I remember a lovely little dress you made for Gracie, out of a silk shawl one of the girls brought back from the desert.'

Maud was on her hands and knees with the dustpan and brush, sweeping up wood ash that had fallen from the grate. She put down the brush and pushed a stray bit of hair out of her eyes. Then she got up, wiped her hands on her apron and leaned across the table to feel the material. 'That's lovely, that is,' she said. Then, 'It's not my machine. It belonged to Gracie's mother, Sunshine. She was always sewing. Had a gift for it, she did. Made lovely things. The sewing machine's safe in a cupboard up at Lavinia House where Granddad lives and where Sunshine used to work as a cleaner. It's too heavy for me to bring home on the bus and, to tell you the truth, it's a bit of a trudge going all that way just to get some sewing done.'

Ivy sniffed. She didn't like anyone talking about Sunshine – Eddie had slept with her only once and got her pregnant, yet Ivy and he had been trying for ages. It irked her to be reminded that she wasn't Gracie's true mother.

'You only had to ask, Mum. I'd have collected it in the truck ages ago. Why didn't you say something?' Eddie looked put out.

Maud sighed. 'I know how busy you are, son, so I don't

like to ask . . .' Her voice tailed off. Then she said sharply, 'Bert's right, I haven't used the machine since I made that little dress for Grace out of silk that came from Africa when the Bluebirds were touring with ENSA. To tell the truth, making that little garment took me longer than it should have done because I only went into Granddad's room for a quick cuppa and once Gertie, his lady friend, knew I was on the premises she kept popping in to chat.' Maud gave a half-smile. 'She's a lovely old lady but a time-waster when I needs to get sewing done.'

'Tomorrow, on my way back home, if the lorry doesn't play up, I'll collect that machine, Mum. If it's here, you'll be able to use it more.' Eddie retrieved his book from the floor.

'You're a good lad,' Maud said, smiling at him. 'I can just envisage Gracie in an all-in-one siren suit.' She turned to Bert. 'Let me pay you for the material, Bert?'

Bert glared at her. 'God love a duck, I don't want nothing, except maybe another cup of tea. It makes a change to drink tea I haven't made myself.'

Chapter Eight

Sammy asked, 'You girls been to Ford airfield to sing before? I think it's called Yapton Number Eleven Group Fighter Command now, or some such new-fangled name, but Ford'll do for me.'

Rainey yelped and stopped herself sliding across the floor in the back of the 1939 Ford Panel van by grabbing the base of the passenger seat. The cushion she'd been sitting on had moved when Sammy had gone around a corner too fast. Bea, on a cushion next to her, caught hold of Rainey to stop the pair of them getting hurt. 'Take it easy, Sammy! Don't damage the goods before we get to the hangar!'

'Sorry, Bea,' Sammy shouted. 'In this blackout with my lights so low, it's difficult to judge the corners and this is a very twisty lane.'

'I'm all right,' said Ivy.

'Yes, you smug cow, you're sitting on a proper seat,' said Bea. 'Well, on the return journey you can make yourself comfortable in the back on the floor. One of us can sit in front. Are you okay, Rainey?'

'I think so,' said Rainey, then to Sammy she said, 'No, we've never sung at Ford before. In fact, I've no idea where it is – or where we are.'

'We're off the main road, going towards the beach in Sussex. We turned off the road near Arundel Castle.'

'Thank God you know the way,' said Rainey. 'It seems like I've been sitting on this cold floor on this skinny cushion for ages,' she said. 'It beats me why on earth Blackie of Blackie Wilson and Associates couldn't get hold of something with four proper seats to take us to venues!'

Sammy ran his fingers through his red hair. That was one of the things Rainey liked about their driver and pianist: his carroty hair. Her own red locks didn't look so unusual when there were other people around with hair of a similar shade.

'It's the war, duckies,' Sammy said. 'You can't get anything you want for love or money. Anyway, this is a good van to drive and that's what counts, reliable transport. You want to thank your lucky stars I don't have to cart a piano around with me, like Blackie did for ENSA when you was singing abroad. Imagine that rolling round in the back and sliding all over you.' He added, 'Ivy Benson's providing music for you tonight, isn't she?'

'Yes, her all-girl band's fresh from appearing at the London Palladium.' Rainey pushed away a suitcase of stage clothing that had slithered along the floor of the van and jammed itself next to her leg. 'We've sung with her band at the BBC,' she continued. 'They're the resident swing band.' She sniffed. 'I bet they got better transport than us. And the actor Jack Warner, he's appearing tonight. I expect he gets picked up by taxi.'

'Is he on the bill with you?' enthused Sammy. 'Cor! He's gonna be a big film star. He's only been in one picture but everyone reckons he's heading for the top. What's he going to do to entertain the English and American troops tonight, then?'

'Recite monologues,' Bea said. 'He opens the second half, then Ivy Benson comes on, and later we sing with her band.'

'Don't seem right to me,' Sammy said. 'I don't think girls is meant to be playing all manner of instruments in an orchestra.'

'Why not?' demanded Bea. 'Since the war started women have been doing all sorts of jobs that used to be done by men so why shouldn't there be an all-girl band?'

'It doesn't seem right,' Sammy said. 'It's not natural!'

Rainey knew Sammy had been turned down for the forces because he'd had rheumatic fever as a child. He'd wanted to drive for the army. Instead he lived with his widowed mother and drove for Blackie.

'So,' Rainey said, 'what you're saying is that there are men's jobs and women's jobs and they should keep it that way.'

'Of course they should,' Sammy answered swiftly. 'I don't agree with women bus conductresses either.'

Rainey was getting cross with his old-fashioned ideas. 'I bet if you got blown up by a bomb, Sammy, and a woman ambulance driver came and scraped you up off the road to take you to hospital, you'd be only too glad to get there as quick as possible so that a woman doctor could fix you up again!'

Sammy started to laugh. It was another of the things Rainey liked about him. He was rarely bad-tempered and he was never late in picking them up for concerts. He was narrow-minded but he could always take a joke.

From the front of the van, Ivy said, 'She's got you there, Sammy! She's got you there!'

'It looks as black as the ace of clubs outside,' Rainey said, sitting up straight to ease her back and trying to peer through the windscreen. She felt the van swing around and saw ahead some trees with their trunks painted white so they could be seen in the blackout. She could also make out figures wandering around.

'Looks like you've got a mob to greet you, girls,' Sammy said.

Clouds parted from the moon's surface and Rainey could now see the crowd of men standing in the darkened doorway of the hangar. She never grew tired of people telling her how eager they were to hear the Bluebirds sing. It was like a dream for her, and she was humbled that, as much as she, Ivy and Bea enjoyed singing their hearts out on stage, people also loved listening.

She sometimes wondered how she could sing sad songs without breaking down in tears when they reminded her so much of losing the love of her life, Charlie Smith, and their baby. Professionalism kept the smile on her face. She was like Bea in that respect. She could reach out with her voice, sharing her sorrow, and people understood. She'd never be able to forget that part of her life, and she didn't want to.

Rainey understood Bea's ambition to go one better and carve a solo career for herself. She didn't think it was dis-loyal of her to prove that she could make it on her own. After all, it hadn't been so long ago that the fate of the Bluebirds hadn't mattered very much to herself when the most important things in her life had been marrying Charlie and having his child.

Every morning now when Rainey woke up, she thanked God she had a second chance at life because He'd given her a voice.

Another thing that helped was sifting through the memory box that Jo had encouraged her to keep. Looking at photos and personal items connected to Charlie made her remember how much he'd loved her. She cherished the few articles she had that had belonged to him. In anticipation of Rainey and him starting a life together in the flat above his photographic shop in Stoke Road, Charlie had moved in and stored all his personal items and clothing there. The bomb had destroyed not only Charlie but the contents of the flat.

Maybe, she thought, she should encourage Bea to collect a box of bits and pieces from her and Bing's relationship that would help to keep him close if he had to return to America after the war.

Ivy, too, had taken time away from the Bluebirds to be with Eddie and Grace. She had moved in with him and his mum. A family with Eddie was everything Ivy craved. Being a Bluebird didn't seem as fulfilling to her as it was to Bea and Rainey.

Rainey remembered how resilient Bea had been when

she performed as a magician's assistant to Melvin Hanratty, a horrible, lecherous man. Her professionalism and determination not to let Blackie's business suffer after Hanratty had let him down resulted in her changing direction for a while. She was soon back on track. Now, not only was she a Bluebird she also sang solo for the BBC, using her own name. That was Bea all over, thought Rainey. A trouper and she'd never give in until she'd reached the very top.

The van had stopped and Sammy had wound down the front window. The smell of cigarette smoke wafted into the cab from the men outside. Rainey smiled to herself. 'Time to open the back doors, Bea. Let the brave airmen have a laugh and an eyeful at us clambering from the van!'

'Well, it's an excuse to fall into a bloke's arms,' said Bea.

Rainey marvelled that Bea, who Ivy called the Ice Queen, could say something like that. It wasn't long ago that she had been scared stiff of men, and with good reason after what had happened when she was younger.

Bea was tetchy because she hadn't heard from Bing in a while.

'That's what it's like when men are in the services,' Rainey had tried to pacify her. 'He'll be just as fed up that his letters don't reach you and that he can't ring you.'

'But what if I don't hear anything and he goes on this

Exercise Tiger before . . .' Bea had moaned. The plan was for Bing to meet her when the Bluebirds appeared at the Alhambra in Brixham.

Rainey knew how special that meeting would be for Bea. 'Then you'll be the first person he contacts on his return when all the heat's off.'

Bea's voice shattered her thoughts. 'Come on, it's time we got out.' As she spoke, the back doors were unlocked and Sammy stood ready to hand them down. Rainey heard Bea laugh at the gaggle of cheering airmen, who were also more than ready to help.

'I never thought it would be as warm as this in such a huge hangar,' said Ivy. 'Why is it so hot?'

'It's the Yanks – they can't stand the cold,' said Bea. 'Our boys grin and bear hardship but the Americans expect better things.' She stared through a peephole in the long velvet curtains that shrouded the stage area and admired the decorations.

The garlands that twisted around the walls made the hangar look more like a kiddies' party room. 'And thank God the Americans get better food, and don't mind sharing it. This gigantic place is full of blokes sitting on chairs, standing around, propping up the bar, drinking and smoking cigars,'

Bea said. 'Have you seen that magnificent table at the end of the hall? It's overflowing with food.'

'We've got an act to do before we can get stuck into it,' said Rainey. 'There's tinned pineapple! I haven't had that for ages.'

'Bing gave me a tin of peaches,' said Bea, with a faraway look in her eyes.

'See what I mean? He's American!' said Rainey. She suddenly grimaced. 'You might have had tinned peaches, Bea Herron, but I never had a taste of them!'

'Bert, Della and I ate them on a Sunday tea-time,' Bea said dreamily, then changed the subject completely. 'Wasn't that comic duo funny?'

Rainey said, 'I've heard them on the wireless. Gert and Daisy are favourites of everyone. Two Cockney neighbours always moaning about their men and the state of the country during wartime. One has a husband and one has a boyfriend, Bert and Wally.' She paused. 'You just wait till our Bert finds out we've been on the same bill as them. He'll be that envious.'

'Who'd have thought that a couple of middle-aged women wearing wraparound pinafores and talking about their families and everyday things could make this lot laugh so much,' Ivy said.

'That's just it. All these brave men want to hear about is what goes on back home and the Americans are just like us,' said Bea. 'Mostly what makes us laugh makes them laugh.'

'They're Jack Warner's sisters,' said Rainey.

'Get away!' Bea was clearly astounded.

'Honest!' Rainey said. 'Elsie and Doris Waters are Gert and Daisy and they're Jack Warner's sisters.'

'They ain't got the same name!' Bea persisted.

'They don't have to have the same name,' Rainey said scathingly.

Sensing an argument, Ivy broke in: 'Has the band got our music?'

There was a moment of silence, then Bea nodded. 'Yes, I made sure I handed it to Ivy Benson herself. Stop worrying. She knows her stuff.'

'Jack Warner's down there now, sitting in the front row with his agent.'

Rainey let the curtain drop back into place. 'I bet he's glad he's done his monologues and can sit and watch other people making fools of themselves.' She pulled up the front of her short blue sequined dress where it had dared to slip down a little and show the swell of her breasts.

Ivy and Bea were also in blue sequins. Ivy's dress was floor length, while Bea's touched her calves.

'Shh! Listen!' said Bea. 'Ivy Benson's talking to the audience. I think she's going to announce us.'

A woman's well-modulated voice reached their ears and the velvet curtain began to move. The audience was cheering the all-woman band and by the time the curtain had swung fully back the Bluebird Girls had walked to the centre microphones and were facing their audience. The smell of Brylcreem, beer, cigarette smoke and cigars hung in the air like mist.

The Bluebirds' welcome from the men practically raised the roof of the hangar.

Bea stepped forward and thanked Ivy Benson. Then she smiled warmly at the women nursing their instruments. Ivy Benson had shown the world that she could put together a professional and successful female orchestra.

Bea thanked the men for their hospitality and, as usual, won their hearts with a little saucy chat. Then she moved back, taking Ivy's hand, and the pair left centre stage to Rainey so she could sing 'That Old Black Magic'.

Foot-stamping and whistles accompanied her introduction and started up again as she finished the last notes. Ivy took her place at the centre and gave them 'As Time Goes By'. As her last notes rang out, Rainey felt the bubble of happiness that Ivy's smoky voice always produced in her.

Tonight she was overwhelmed at being on stage in front of such an appreciative audience.

Bea's solo was 'You'd Be So Nice To Come Home To'. The last time she'd sung it had been when she'd met Bing. The words were sentimental and special to her but she sang it because it was always a favourite with the men. Rainey could tell memories of Bing brought Bea very close to tears. However, professionalism allowed her to mask her feelings so that the audience concentrated on the meaning of the words.

The three harmonized in 'Taking A Chance On Love' and hammed it up to make the audience chuckle.

Ivy Benson's band led in next, with the Bluebirds singing 'All Or Nothing At All', a forces favourite, followed by 'You Are My Sunshine'. The last song for the evening was 'Coming In On A Wing And A Prayer' and the girls exaggerated limps as they sang the line 'limped through the air'. The audience loved it. Mostly airmen, they cheered, shouted and whistled.

Bea finally took centre stage and, with difficulty, waited for the audience to quieten so that she could thank Ivy Benson and her band for accompanying them, the men for being there and for the delicious spread they hoped they'd be able to join in eating. And then, to tumultuous applause, the three girls stepped off the stage to mingle with their audience.

'Jack Warner's agent couldn't take his eyes off you,' said Ivy to Bea, trying to sign photographs and autograph books, and chat to men all at the same time.

'I never noticed,' Bea said. Singing her solo had affected her more than she liked to let on. She hadn't been able to hide it from Rainey.

'He's making his way towards us,' said Rainey, 'but I don't think it's us two he's interested in, Ivy.' She could see the tall, thin man weaving through the throng.

'Tell us later what he wants,' said Ivy, as she was ensnared by an airman waving a photograph of a woman and a baby under her nose. The men, away from their families, were always eager to show photos and talk about the loved ones they missed so much. The girls felt the least they could do was listen to what they had to say and look at their pictures: these brave men were fighting for their freedom.

Ivy was whisked away by another American flyer.

'Maybe he's about to offer you a deal, Bea,' said Rainey.

'Maybe. Yeah! But what kind of deal? I haven't got over the last offer I had to get me into pictures,' said Bea. A frown crossed her forehead. 'It wasn't a film Basil Dean, the producer, wanted me in. He wanted me in his bed and only because I reminded him of Meggie Albanesi, a former starlet. She was dead but he was still obsessed by her.'

'Lightning doesn't strike in the same place twice,' said Rainey. 'And without Basil Dean there would have been no Entertainments National Service Association, or ENSA to you. And we wouldn't have travelled abroad.'

'That doesn't mean I should have been grateful to have him slobbering over me,' said Bea. 'If I can't make it to the top without having to share a bed with some bloke, then . . .'

Rainey patted her arm, hoping to silence her before she became angry about the past. 'You'll make it, Bea, I know you will. And you'll do it by your own hard work, not by giving out favours.'

Chapter Nine

Max could hear the snores and coughs of the sleeping prisoners in the hut as he lay thinking about Hans. He looked over at Dieter lying on his back with the thin blanket pulled up to his chin. The hut was chilly but Max had slept in colder places. He hadn't been quite honest with Dieter. He'd told him that chance had brought him back to Gosport. That wasn't quite true.

Servicing and repairing motors in the Winchester prison workshop had seemed like a heaven-sent job. But when Max heard that some of the inmates were to be transferred to a Gosport holding camp, due to an influx of new prisoners, he became especially 'helpful' to one of the prison officers. He hadn't rated his chances. After all, how many men get to return to the centre from which they had previously escaped?

Luck was with him as Officer Edgar Cole, a staunch family man, frequently had problems with his 1937 Jaguar 3.5 litre Roadster 3. He relied on Max for repairs and then on advice about upgrading to a model more suited to his needs.

Max had confided in him. 'I don't want to return to Germany when the war has finally been won,' he said. 'Before I was captured, I met an English girl and made her pregnant. I want to do the honourable thing and marry her, and work for my little family, if I'm ever released. She's a Gosport girl and I want to be near her and my child.'

Max smiled to himself in the darkness. It was easy to tell part of the truth and lie about the rest.

Making himself indispensable to Officer Cole allowed the two men to become close. They also shared a love of gardening. Max's knowledge helped Edgar Cole win several prestigious local allotment club competitions for the first time ever. In return, Max gained Cole's respect and was put on the list of Germans being sent to St Vincent or, in his case, returned.

Early in the war Max's plane had come down in an English field and he had been captured. At St Vincent he had worked, on day release, for a builder. He had deliberately conned an impressionable girl into believing he loved her, when all he wanted was her cooperation in helping him escape. Sunshine, pregnant by Max, began working in the kitchens at St Vincent so the affair could continue. She worked tirelessly, believing his lies that they would leave England together. He thought of the British soldier's uniform she had sewn for him, the passport and papers she had worked for so that he might leave the country. But before she could meet him to hand over the documents and some money, he had stupidly allowed himself to be caught by the police in the Central Café. He was immediately transferred to Winchester prison.

Hans was the only person who suspected the truth.

Max had heard no more of pregnant Sunshine. His son or daughter would be toddling now. Perhaps Sunshine no longer lived in Gosport, but Max knew that if he could return, it was possible that his young German friend might be able to tell him something to his advantage. Perhaps he might see his child. More importantly, perhaps Sunshine could be persuaded to help him escape again. After all, he knew the pitfalls this time.

Luck had been with him, and he was back in Gosport. He frowned, thinking of Hans in the infirmary.

He'd visit as soon as he could.

*

Eddie pulled up outside his front door, got out of his van and looked down Alma Street towards the main road. His truck shuddered, then died. It would be a devil to restart.

The darkness of the houses stood out against the yellow and orange glow in the sky. Flames from burning wood were billowing from the trees behind Dimon's cycle shop. The stench of acrid smoke stung his nostrils. He wondered, not for the first time, why the local council officials had decreed an evening meeting about local rebuilding works just when the bloody Germans had decided on another night-time blitz along the south coast. Above him, searchlights illumin-ated the smoke that rose in plumes towards the ferry and the Portsmouth dockyard. He heard the chilling scream of a bomb descending and made a grab towards the key hanging on a string behind the letter box. One of the loudest blasts he had ever heard caused him to stumble in the hallway after he'd slammed the front door.

The silence told him his family were in the Anderson shelter. Within moments he was running through the dark-ened terraced house, out through the back door and was on his way to join them at the bottom of the garden. After a loud shout and a quick thump on the metal entrance, Maud opened the door in the half-light provided by the paraffin lamp and Eddie practically fell in among the women.

'Thank God you're safe,' Maud exclaimed. She began to fuss over him, asking a million questions at once. 'You're not harmed, are you? Is the house all right? What's going on out in the street? Who's copped it?'

'Give us a minute to breathe, Mum,' Eddie said, breaking into her tirade of questions.

It was warm in the shelter and he quickly stripped off his overcoat. Ivy's pale face stared worriedly at him, and as soon as he had rolled up his coat and pushed it under the bench out of the way he leaned across the cot containing his sleeping daughter and kissed Ivy hungrily. The warmth of her lips and her musky scent fuelled his need of her.

'Am I glad to be back here!' he said, his eyes holding hers. 'It's like a night in hell out there. Are you all right?'

'Yes, we had time to fill flasks and mash food for Gracie when the siren went off. We've been worrying about you being out in this lot. I knew you'd try to make it home instead of going into a public shelter.'

'That's what I said to Ivy,' Maud told him. 'The daft bugger will try to get back instead of looking after himself.'

'You know me too well, Mother!' Eddie's eyes moved again to the Thermos flasks standing on the old rug near the cot. 'Any tea left? I'm gasping. That stuff they dish up at council meetings is like hot water.'

Maud was immediately fussing with the flasks and tin mugs.

'How did you get on?' Ivy asked.

Without taking his eyes from hers, he said, 'I got another contract to go on using reclaimed materials for rebuilding bomb-damaged premises and a promise!'

He took the mug from Maud and managed a gulp of tea. 'That hits the spot,' he said, and his mother nudged his arm.

'Promise? What promise?' Her blue eyes were flashing nosily.

'There's a new kind of semi-permanent housing being manufactured and Hampshire have put in a bid . . .' He put down his tea and fumbled in his inside pocket for his pen and a small notebook he'd been taking notes in. He looked down at the silver pen almost as though seeing it for the first time. It had belonged to Charlie and Eddie had coveted it as soon as he'd set eyes on it. Charlie had jokingly told him he'd leave it to him in his will when he died. The morning after the bomb had killed Charlie, wrecking his business and flat, Eddie had spotted the pen hiding beneath some detritus at the kerb. Eddie had loved Charlie like a brother. But that wasn't how he had envisaged becoming the new owner of the silver pen.

'Housing? Semi-permanent? What does that mean?' Maud asked.

'You just won't let it go when you want to know the ins and outs of things, Mum. If you stay quiet and listen, I'll tell you. I made a few notes at the meeting to remember the details.' He glanced inside the notebook. 'In America Sears, Roebuck have been selling these prefabricated buildings since 1908. They've sold thousands. They consist of dwellings manufactured in standard sections that can be assembled wherever they're needed. They'll last about ten years and come with hot-water systems, bathrooms, fridges, coppers for boiling clothes, two bedrooms, living room and kitchen. Each will have its own square of garden. The Burt Committee under Churchill's government has been looking into this since 1942.'

'Compact little houses? That sounds too good to be true.'

A huge explosion caused the shelter to shake on its foundations. Ivy jumped up and leaned over the cot to protect the little girl. Maud covered her head while bits of dust and earth fell from the rounded metal roof and swirled in the air about them. Eddie ducked, throwing his arms wide to protect Ivy and Gracie. Then there was a moment of silence and he looked from Ivy to his mother, making sure they were both unharmed. 'That was a bit close for comfort,' he said, letting out a huge sigh.

'I wonder who copped that,' Maud said softly.

'With a bit of luck it might have messed up a few back gardens,' said Ivy, 'and missed the houses.'

'Ivy, unwrap them sandwiches,' said Maud. 'Pass me back that mug, Eddie, and I'll pour out some more tea. Got to keep our strength up and show those soddin' Germans we can take it.'

Maud busied herself with lining up three tin mugs on the wooden stool she was using as a table, then unscrewed the large flask again. Eddie saw Ivy settle back on the bench. In her cot, Gracie had allowed her tiny hands to unclench and was once more breathing steadily. Eddie replaced the pen and notebook in his pocket.

'Your daughter'll sleep through anything,' Maud said. 'That reminds me. Did you fetch the sewing machine from where Granddad lives?'

'She takes after me,' said Eddie, smiling at Gracie. Then, 'What with the bombs, I forgot, sorry. I promise I'll pick it up as soon as I can.' She nodded and he knew he was forgiven. 'Now I'll take a look outside.'

'Oh no you don't. You'll let all that stinkin' soot in here. Whatever's happened outside needs to settle down. We're safe where we are.' Maud paused. 'Well, I hope we are. You finish tellin' us about these ready-made houses. Does this mean more work for you?' She emptied a couple of

97

little white saccharine tablets into Eddie's mug. 'They're for sweetness and shock,' she said, stirring them in. 'You can have a couple too,' she said to Ivy, who obviously had no say in the matter. She rolled her eyes at Eddie.

'Of course it means more work, Mum. People need homes and while this war lasts there's precious little in the way of new building materials to be got hold of. I've been promised a contract to get some of these cheap prefabricated houses up and running as soon as the war ends, maybe earlier if all goes well.'

Eddie stopped speaking. The all-clear siren was wailing. He passed a mug to Ivy, who took it and sipped, then pulled a face as she didn't like the metallic taste of saccharine.

'Thank Christ the raid's over until next time,' he said. 'I'll get out of here and see what the damage is . . .'

'So, this promise could be the making of your building firm, Eddie?' Maud probed further. 'Could make you rich?'

'Perhaps,' Eddie said.

Chapter Ten

Bea tried to sleep in the lumpy single bed pushed against the wall in Bert's cellar. She could hear Della snoring in the double bed near the door, and every so often Bert mumbled in his sleep. They were so far down beneath the café in North Cross Street that although she heard the bangs and blasts from the bombs the sounds were muffled.

The conversation she'd had with Jack Warner's agent at Ford airfield went round and round in her mind. The tall, thin man, smelling of a sharp lemon cologne and wearing an immaculately tailored dark blue suit, with spectacles that looked too big for his face, had elbowed his way through the airmen surrounding her and asked to speak to her in private. 'Somewhere, preferably, we can hear ourselves think,' he said.

Rainey had been at Bea's side and she'd answered for her.

'If you climb up onto the stage, you'll find it's quiet around the back. You probably won't be disturbed there.' Rainey had looked to Bea for confirmation that she agreed, but also stared straight back at the man and added, 'If I think you're starting something with our Bea, I'll send round a couple of fellers!'

To his credit Henry Lucas, at first taken aback by her outburst, had laughed as Rainey had swivelled on her high heels and left.

Ensconced among bits of unpainted scenery, discarded clothing and superfluous furniture, the revellers' voices were muted by the thick velvet stage curtains. 'I think you know who I am,' Henry Lucas said, with dignity. And before she'd had a chance to open her mouth, he continued, 'One of Jack's sisters seems to believe you might be just the right person for a part in a film that's going into production, possibly next year, with Jack starring.'

Bea remembered now that her mouth had fallen open and she'd quickly had to close it and swallow. 'I don't understand . . .'

Henry Lucas had smoothed a hand across his Brylcreemed hair and said, 'You're an extremely beautiful girl and I can understand your friend's reticence in leaving us alone together. But I assure you I'm only interested in my business, its profits and . . .' He smiled. Bea noticed how white and sharp his teeth were, like a shark's, she thought. Then he continued: '. . . and obviously the welfare of my clients.' He paused again. 'I also listen to my clients. Florence, that's Elsie, takes a big interest in her brother's career and has suggested you'd be ideal for one of the younger sisters in this film. Apparently both of Jack's sisters were quite taken with your adaptability when you sang for ENSA in the Libyan desert. They also travelled to Portsmouth and caught you doing a very funny magic act. With your permission I'd like to approach your agent, Blackie Wilson and Associates.'

Bea had taken in every word. She had tried to remain cool, calm and collected when inside she couldn't believe what was happening to her. 'Of c-course,' she'd stuttered, then managed to ask, 'What's the film called?'

'It's Robert Hamer's third film at Ealing Studios. A married woman shelters her ex-boyfriend who's escaped from prison. Googie Withers, John McCullen, Susan Shaw and, of course, Jack have already shown an interest. *It Always Rains On Sunday* is the title . . . You'll need to be screen tested.' Bea hadn't heard any more – her head was whirling.

She remembered him confirming Blackie's telephone number and then he had said his goodbyes and left. Bea had collapsed onto a broken chair to regain her senses.

She was still sitting there, when Rainey had come back to check on her.

'All alone?' she asked, confused.

'Well ... yes. You were right. That agent did want to make me an offer.'

'He didn't try anything, did he?' Rainey quickly asked.

'No. To tell the truth I don't think he's interested much in women. He smells too nice. He's all business!'

'That's not a bad thing. Well, come on, then – don't keep it to yourself! What did he say?'

Bea stood up from the sagging chair. 'He said I need to take a screen test for a film with Googie Withers in it.'

Rainey started laughing. 'Don't be daft!' she said. 'Googie Withers is a famous actress!'

For a moment there was relative silence, until Bea said, in a small voice, 'Honestly!'

Only then did she see that Rainey believed her. Suddenly Bea threw her arms around her friend and cried, 'Oh, Rainey, I want so much to get to the top. I'm not stupid, I know this might not lead anywhere, and until Blackie calls me in, I won't really believe any of it. I'm going to try not to think of what Jack Warner's agent said.' She let go of Rainey, stepped back and gabbled, 'Please tell me I'm not dreaming, though. Henry Lucas did come and talk to me a moment ago, didn't he?'

Rainey stared at her. 'Yes, he did. And if this works out, you deserve it. I knew you were more than just a singer when you saved Blackie's reputation by taking on Melvin Hanratty's magic show while he was in hospital. What did you do? With less than twenty-four hours to curtain up at the Coliseum you bullied our Ivy into appearing with you when she hadn't set foot on the stage for ages and allowed her to tell some of Bert's outrageous but utterly silly jokes that the audience loved! You've got enough talent to conquer the world!' And this time Rainey threw her arms around Bea and nearly crushed the life out of her.

Bert was mumbling again in his sleep. She heard him say, 'Two teas.' Even asleep he couldn't stop thinking about the café.

Blackie was her agent and he had to agree to anything she was offered, with her, of course. She decided to put it all from her mind and go on doing her very best for the Bluebirds. She'd almost forgotten that the three girls had been promised an appointment with the BBC in London to sing on *Music While You Work*, a programme that was broadcast daily on the wireless and beloved by factory workers. She also had a date for a recording with Parlophone under her own name. All in all, she thought, she wasn't doing too badly for a Gosport girl.

She thought about Rainey, who was coping well. She was throwing herself into stage work and was remarkably bright and cheerful. Several times, though, Bea had come across her sitting quietly. She admitted she thought Charlie's face was fading from her mind, which upset her. Her memory box and photographs helped to remind her. Bea thought she was becoming a master at disguising her true feelings. She had noticed that Rainey seemed closer to Ivy and Gracie. She'd volunteered to babysit Gracie so Eddie and Ivy could go to the pictures. She'd also started knitting again. She said it helped to soothe her nerves. The patterns came from *Woman's Weekly* magazines, courtesy of Della in the café. She'd even begun accompanying Della and Maud to jumble sales, scavenging woollen clothing, then unpicking, washing and reusing the wool to make fluffy toys.

And Ivy? Ivy was happy – you could see it in the way she moved, in the way she sang. She had Eddie and she adored Gracie. Only one thing could complete her happiness and that would be a child of her own.

Earlier this evening Bea had sat in the café writing a long letter to Bing. She would post it in the morning. She had no idea if he received her letters and she'd still heard nothing from him, but that was how things were, she thought.

Of course she worried about him. The date for the

Bluebirds to appear at the Alhambra in Brixham was nearing. The show was billed as *An Easter Extravaganza*. Easter was to fall in early April this year. Already the cold grip of winter had loosened its hold, and thank goodness, she thought.

The girls had elected to have Sammy drive them down rather than travel by train. They'd also decided to stop on the way a few times to change seats. Bea would have preferred to go down by train. 'That's because you love it when you're recognized by servicemen!' Ivy had said. Bea smiled to herself. Of course she did! She wanted to be so famous that everyone recognized her!

Bert gave a snore that was more like a bear's growl. For a moment Bea was lifted back to reality. It was quiet in the cellar, or as quiet as it could be with Della and Bert exploring the land of dreams. She realized she hadn't been aware of any thumps and rumbles for a while. Perhaps the Germans had given up and gone home . . . Bea slept.

Chapter Eleven

God, Max hated these places. Bleach and disinfectant that didn't quite mask the smell of blood and something much worse, like rotting flesh, he thought. Rows of identical iron beds with little to distinguish the patients as they slept. This wasn't a real hospital, though. It was an infirmary attached to the St Vincent holding centre where patients could recuperate. No operations were carried out there because there weren't sufficient qualified staff. The Royal Hospital, Haslar, situated on Gosport's waterfront, dealt with anything serious. Even so, he'd had to request permission from the officer in charge to see Hans and was relieved it was granted.

Apparently, Hans had few visitors.

Behind a large blue-curtained screen and propped up on pillows Hans looked more like a child than the once vital young Luftwaffe fighter pilot shot down earlier in the war. It occurred to Max that although he himself had been incarcerated since his capture, he had never worked at one job or in one place for long. Hans had spent all of his time here in Gosport practically unable to work. Smoke in his lungs from his plane crash had left him with violent coughing spells that rendered him useless in temperature changes. Working outside had become tortuous for him. In the early days, more out of kindness than for the use he had been, Eddie Herron, the builder, had allowed him to work at small but necessary jobs.

Max remembered the gratitude Hans had shown him, gardening on fine, warm days. He smiled thinking of the swastika of crocus bulbs they had planted at the entrance to St Vincent to welcome visitors. He wondered if Hans remembered.

Max now sat on a metal chair watching his young friend sleep. The place felt like a mausoleum, he thought. Hans's transparent white skin was stretched tightly across his face. The scar, another remnant of his plane crash, running along the young man's chin was raised and pink-looking. He was a shadow of his former self.

'They put the screen up because his outbursts of coughing upset the other patients. If they don't see it, they can ignore it, see? When he does sleep it's the sleep of the dead,' the male nurse had told him.

Max saw Hans's eyes open and a frown pass across his forehead almost as though he couldn't trust what he was seeing.

'Yes, it's me, my friend,' said Max. 'I'm not some kind of spectre.' He felt for Hans's thin, cold hand and held on to it. 'How long do you intend staying in this shithole then?'

Hans's mouth curved into a small smile. He gave a sigh that reminded Max of rattling chains.

'If you promise to cheer up, I'll come and visit again.' Max glanced past the screen to the centre of the rectangular room where the nurse sat at a table, writing. It was so quiet he could hear the scratch of the nib against the paper.

Encased in Max's hand, Hans's fingers moved.

'Can you talk, my friend?'

Hans took a deep breath. 'Heard you were caught . . .'

Max had had to lean closer to hear his words. 'Yes, they captured me and I've spent time at Winchester. I'm lucky to be here.' Max paused. He had to ask Hans some questions, and time was of the essence. 'I want to find Sunshine. You remember Sunshine, my Gosport girl, don't you?'

Hans inclined his head. Good, thought Max, he had not forgotten the wisp of a blonde girl. 'You were a good friend to me, then. Together we planted the garden at the entrance of this place with bulbs, remember?'

Again, a smile. Max could see that Hans not only remembered but also understood. 'The guards here saw you working diligently and never suspected for one moment that I was lying in the arms of a fresh young girl in one of the storage sheds near the creek. They were fools.' Max glanced into the middle of the room, where a guard was now leaning against a chair chatting with the nurse.

'She helped you escape,' Hans murmured.

Max gave a small nod and spoke softly, yet clearly. He didn't want to be overheard. 'We became separated. I did not see her again. She could not give me the identity papers I needed to leave the country . . . She was pregnant with my child. Did you know this?'

Hans took a deep breath that moved his entire frail body. He opened his mouth but nothing came out. He managed to nod. Good, thought Max, we're getting somewhere. He knows I'm going to ask where she and my child are.

Max couldn't tell him the truth – that he wanted to find the woman he'd wronged so that she'd take another chance on helping him to escape. She'd loved him once. She'd still have feelings for him, surely. He didn't want to rot in this place until the war was over and Germany's victory or defeat decided his future.

He said what he knew was expected of him. 'This war

can't last forever. I fear we shall not win.' He didn't want to depress Hans further by telling him that in the past few weeks the RAF had dropped nearly four thousand tons of bombs upon Germany. 'I wish to make amends to Sunshine. I have not been honest with the young woman. I need to find her and see my child. If the British will allow it, I would like to remain in this country . . .'

Hans's fingers slipped from Max's hand and his eyes closed. Max felt suddenly bereft. 'I must make amends,' Max whispered.

Hans's eyes opened suddenly, like small shutters, disturbing Max. His mouth moved slowly: 'Dead. Sunshine's dead.'

Max was shocked. He sat back quickly on the chair so that it squeaked across the tiled floor. The nurse glanced at him, then went on chatting to the guard. As if he'd been reminded that Max was still there, the guard put up five fingers telling him his time was almost at an end. A half-glass of water stood on the bedside table. Max wondered if helping Hans drink might ease his throat, loosen his tongue . . .

'Dead,' repeated Hans. Max had not misheard.

Hans closed his eyes. Weakness had overtaken him, and he was too far gone to continue. But Max could not leave without knowing more. 'And my child?' Anger rose within him. 'Tell me, where is my child?'

Hans opened his eyes. He looked startled. The breath rattled in his throat. 'Eddie Herron, baby,' he managed. Then with a supreme effort: 'Eddie . . . like to see . . . Eddie.' He closed his eyes again, exhausted.

The guard was at the bedside. 'Time's up,' he said.

As though in a dream Max nodded, staring down at Hans, who made barely a mound in the bed.

The guard turned, expecting Max to follow, which he did. Max was trying to process all he had discovered. Sunshine, dead? He felt no pain at her passing. The girl had been no more to him than a means to an end. She had served his purpose in helping him to escape. The baby was another matter. His child, a German, was being brought up by an Englishman.

Resentment roiled within him. Max didn't speak until they were outside in the cold, crisp air.

'My friend Hans, as I did, worked with the Englishman, the builder Eddie Herron,' Max said. He took a deep breath. 'I would like to volunteer my services again. Since I have just returned to this holding centre, I have no idea who is in charge.'

'Not a problem, mate,' said the guard. 'Eddie Herron still

picks up prisoners regularly. The officer who deals with all that is in his office today. I'll show you the way if you like.' He laughed. 'Your lot bombs our places down, only fair you should help put 'em up again.'

Chapter Twelve

'It's strange patrolling a village that's been evacuated,' said Si. 'One day it was full of folks going about their everyday business and now there's no local people – even if there were, we've been forbidden to talk to them. It's a ghost town, that's what it is, a ghost town,' he repeated. 'Except when we're shelling it and tearing the guts out of the buildings.'

'And when it's got thirty thousand American soldiers billeted nearby. But I guess that's the Admiralty for you,' said Bing. 'People have been told it's just for six months, and then the families can return.'

In the darkness of the April evening, the moon lit shattered roofs, broken windows, shell holes, doors hanging off hinges, gardens trampled and fences flattened. The smell of cordite and burning wood hung in the air, refusing to be swept aside by the fresh winds from the English Channel's Start Bay.

'If they believe that, they'll believe anything,' said Si. 'It'll take ages to get all the damage repaired. And thank God no one's allowed here to see the wreckage while we're still using it. Some of our exercises have been devastating. Yanks camped everywhere in and around the area of Slapton Sands. Still, it'll all be over soon.' He perched his backside on a stone wall that looked likely to crumble at any moment. 'What would ordinary folk think if they knew this place has been taken over as a prime site of interest just because it looks like the stretch of shore around France's Normandy coast? Utah Beach. I'm sure that's what the officials have codenamed it. I suppose they know what they're doing.'

'More than I do,' admitted Bing. 'Though you seem to be pretty clued up about things.'

'I keep my eyes and ears open, don't I? People round here would have to be nuts not to know about Exercise Tiger, what with all the roadblocks, night explosions, defence posts, gun emplacements and guys at observation posts,' said Si.

'But how can anyone know more about what we're supposed to be planning than we do? Officially we've been told nothing.' Bing sighed. He looked at his watch.

'We should be relieved of our duties soon,' he said. 'Then it's back to the canteen for us. I wonder if there are any letters from home.'

Bing knew Si was eager to hear from his girl. He wondered how long it would be before his own letters to Bea could be forwarded on to her. And when he would receive one from her. 'Suspicion and secrecy dominate this damned place,' he grumbled. He heard footsteps and hung back in the darkness, his rifle ready. Si was already hidden in the shadows.

He could hear and smell the sea. Waves rolled on the shoreline. Night sounds and footsteps disturbed his ears. It was relatively quiet tonight. The blackness out on the water hid many things. Who would know that many landing craft and anti-aircraft ships were moored close by?

Bing saw two of his countrymen walking mechanically towards them. He breathed a sigh of relief. When at last he returned to the canteen and the warmth of the mess hall his thoughts could once more be with Bea. Communication with the outside world was so limited while these exercises were taking place, and secrecy was all very well, but he needed to hear Bea's voice ... kiss her lips ... There'd been talk of a few days' leave before 27 April. If that was true, he'd make sure he could see her when she sang at the

Alhambra. But what if leave had been just a rumour? God, he hated this damn war.

'Where d'you want the sewing machine, Mum?' Eddie stood holding the heavy object in both arms. He kicked the front door closed behind him – the key on its piece of string jangled against the wood. 'Don't worry,' he called sarcastically. 'I can stand here all day carrying it!'

'What are you doing coming home at this time of day?' Maud, wearing a wraparound overall and a turban, walked through the open scullery door, then the living room and stood at the bottom of the stairs waiting for an answer. She was wiping her hands on a tea-towel.

'Never mind that! Where d'you want this?' he repeated. 'You've been on about it for long enough.'

'It's the sewing machine!' Maud exclaimed. Eddie raised his eyes heavenwards. 'You've been to Lavinia House and picked it up for me,' she said. 'Oh, you little love.'

'Yes, Mum, and I'd like to put it down before I drop it!'

'In my bedroom.' She pushed past him and opened the front-room door. Since Ivy had been living at Alma Street, there'd been a change-around of rooms. Upstairs Eddie and Ivy had taken over the bedroom at the back and Gracie was in the one at the front, facing the road. Maud preferred sleeping downstairs. 'Put it on the floor over there by the fireplace,' she said.

'Don't you want me to set it up for you on a little table or something?' His eyes roved over the shiny wooden top of the case concealing Sunshine's Singer.

'We can do that later. I'm just blooming glad to have it here,' Maud said. A broad smile transformed her face. 'Did you get any backchat from Mabel Manners? She's had this thing stuck in her cupboard since Sunshine died.'

Eddie set the sewing machine on the lino. He stood up straight once it was out of his arms and tried to rub some life back into his aching flesh. 'Not at all. She said she was glad it was going. It's a good machine. Bloody heavy, though.' Then he asked softly, 'Is Ivy in?'

'You're a treasure, Eddie. I can make up that lovely bit of material Bert got for Gracie. Sorry, love, your Ivy's taken Gracie to the shops. I heard there was oranges on sale at Watt's. You gonna wait for her?' She scratched her head where a metal curler was digging into her scalp.

'I'll wait long enough for you to make me a cuppa. I reckon I deserve one after collecting that.'

Bea was watching where she walked on the worn wooden planks of the Portsmouth ferry's landing stage. It was so embarrassing catching a high heel in the gaps. A sailor wearing navy bell-bottoms and a tight jersey gave a low wolf whistle and automatically Bea grinned at him. In a dark red fitted costume, showing the pussy-cat bow of her white blouse, she knew she looked good. Last night she'd washed her blonde hair with Amami shampoo and now it blew around her face, wafting its flowery scent in competition with the ozone smell from the sea.

The short crossing had been chilly. She, Ivy and Rainey had had to stand on the deck as the downstairs cabin was full. Not that Bea had minded: the cabin always smelled of cigarette smoke and sweaty bodies. With her back to the funnel, which gave off warmth, she could look at the ships moored in the harbour. There were tankers, and warships, dredgers and American destroyers waiting in the dockyard. Seeing those ships made her think of Bing. Where was he? What was he doing? There was still no word from him. It hadn't occurred to her that something might have happened to him because she knew the Americans were practising for something so important that silence needed to be maintained at all times. Nightly she wrote to him, telling him all of her news and about where and when the Bluebirds would be appearing, either to cheer up the troops or to cut another record in London. She hadn't written about her meeting with

Jack Warner's agent. That was something she would prefer to tell him in person. Besides, so far she'd heard no more and she didn't want to dwell on what might never happen.

It wasn't long now until they were due to appear in Devon at the Alhambra, which was probably why Blackie had summoned the three of them to his offices today.

'Are you cold?' Bea asked Rainey, as they went along the short walkway that spanned the murky waters where the mudlarks dived for pennies. It amazed her how fearlessly they climbed through the barbed wire strung across the beach.

Rainey was eating the remains of a currant bun bought from the Dive Café near Gosport's bus station. The café was famous for them. Her vibrant hair was almost hidden beneath a head-square. 'You don't expect April to be really warm,' said Rainey. 'Anyway, it's always cold crossing the water.' Bea watched the last bite of the bun disappear and Rainey swallowed contentedly.

Opening her black handbag, which was looped over her arm, and extracting a handkerchief to wipe her sticky fingers, Rainey said, 'I wonder why we have to see him in person.'

'Usually Blackie telephones,' agreed Bea. She watched Rainey replace the hanky, then untie her loose belt and pull it tighter to emphasize her small waist. 'You look nice in grey.'

'So nice that Ivy just had to have a new grey coat as well!'

Ivy didn't pause as she walked alongside them. 'My new coat is nothing like yours, Rainey. Anyway, Maud got it from her church jumble sale so what am I going to say to her? "Sorry, I can't wear that lovely duster coat because it's the same colour as Rainey's?"'

'I saved my coupons for nearly a year to buy this coat,' Rainey said.

'And stuff bought at jumble sales is coupon free,' snapped Ivy.

'The coats might both be grey but there the resemblance ends,' Bea said. 'Rainey's is fitted and belted and yours swings about with so much material in it you could probably make a second coat out of it.' Bea stopped walking.

Surprised, Rainey and Ivy paused as well, almost knocking into each other on the busy pavement. Bea glared at them. 'I wish you two would stop bickering. It fair gets on my nerves!'

For a moment the silence was broken only by the noise of traffic and seagulls crying as they wheeled above the mud near the harbour railway station.

Ivy put her arm around Bea's shoulders. 'You're worried that you're not going to see Bing again, aren't you?'

Tears formed in Bea's eyes. 'Is it so obvious?' she asked.

'Only to us who care about you,' Rainey said.

'But I was looking forward to—'

'We know what you were looking forward to,' Rainey and Ivy said in unison.

'You've got to believe in Bing and trust him,' Ivy said. Her dark eyes searched Bea's blue ones. 'He promised to take you to a hotel and that the night would be as special as he could make it.'

'But the date of the concert in Devon is getting nearer and nearer and I haven't heard from him.'

Rainey smoothed back the blonde curls from Bea's forehead. 'Bing's not the sort of bloke to let you down. A promise is a promise to him . . . But it won't be your fault or his if you don't see him in Devon. It's this bloody war. It's got to end soon.'

Just then the sailor who had wolf-whistled Bea stepped up behind them. 'What's this? A mothers' meeting? Get off the bloody pavement, girls! Some of us seamen have to get back to the dockyard. There's a war on or didn't you know?'

Chapter Thirteen

The polished brass plaque outside the door next to the bell stated, 'Blackie Wilson and Associates'. Bea, Ivy and Rainey looked at each other.

'I wonder why he wants to see us,' said Ivy.

'Now we're all on the phone, surely he could have telephoned if it's news about stage work,' began Rainey.

'Well, there's only one way to find out,' said Bea, and pushed the bell.

'I bet it's something to do with that other agent, you know, Henry Lucas,' said Ivy.

'But that only concerns Bea, not us,' said Rainey.

The shiny black door opened and Rainey's mother, Jo, said, 'Welcome, girls, Blackie's been expecting you.'

Rainey threw her arms around her mother and squeezed her. She was wearing a fitted grey skirt and a pink fluffy jumper with shoulder pads. 'You look nice,' she said, taking a deep sniff of her flowery perfume.

Jo kissed Rainey's cheek and said, 'Come on in before all the warmth gets out of this place.' She disengaged herself and closed the door behind them. Her gold charm bracelet jangled as she moved. Rainey couldn't stop herself grinning at her mother.

'Don't have to ask how you are, Jo,' said Bea. 'Marriage certainly agrees with you.'

Jo blushed.

Rainey said, 'Don't tease her.'

A door opened at the top of a flight of carpeted stairs and Blackie stood there, handsome and tall in a dark suit. In one hand he held a sheaf of papers. 'Come on up, girls. It's lovely to see you again.' Then he smiled at Jo. 'Will you bring us up something to drink? I'd like to suggest coffee because it's good manners now we've become used to the Americans drinking it. But . . . we haven't any, not even that dreadful chicory stuff . . .'

'Maud tried baking acorns in the oven, then grating them. It was a recipe she found in a book. She doesn't like that chicory substitute either,' said Ivy.

'What was it like?' Blackie sounded very interested.

'Like having a mouthful of grit. None of us could drink it.'

Bea said, 'Why didn't you tell me you've got no proper coffee? I bet Bert can get his hands on some decent stuff.'

'I worry about black-market food,' said Jo, her fingers on the handrail ready to go downstairs again.

'Well, it's never worried Bert,' said Ivy and Bea together. Everyone laughed.

Bea was the first to enter Blackie's main office. A fire burned steadily in the grate, warming the large room, which was decorated with elegant velvet-covered seating and floor-length curtains. Every time she saw the furnishings they took her breath away. Then she remembered Blackie had bought them with the premises after it had been on the market for some time. He'd got the place at a good price after inheriting money from Madame Nellie Walker and her husband. They'd been surrogate parents to him, but had perished when a bomb demolished their Southsea studios.

A large polished wooden desk sat in front of the window with Blackie's leather chair behind it, facing into the room. Around the walls hung photographs of past and present stage stars, who were Blackie's clients or Madame Nellie's. He'd not only inherited her money but also her considerable business.

Bea looked at the mantelpiece above the fire: there was the very first photograph the Bluebirds had ever had taken for publicity purposes. The double of Bing's photograph. She smiled. The three girls looked so innocent, so untouched by life. She couldn't help the smile that crept over her lips. Indeed, the Bluebirds had been untouched by life then!

Bea sat down on a squashy sofa and was joined by Ivy. Blackie moved towards his chair. Bea could see he was waiting for Rainey to settle. He set the papers he'd been carrying on the table and stood facing them. He watched them carefully, his odd-coloured eyes, some called them ghost eyes, settling on each of them in turn.

'I've called you in because I need to talk to you and clarify bookings. First, I'm not sending you or anyone else abroad again until we know which way the war has swung.'

Bea searched for Ivy's hand and squeezed her fingers. She knew Ivy, who hated being apart from Eddie and Gracie, would be cheered by that. Blackie went on: 'The next date you have in your diaries is the show at the Alhambra in Devon for three nights. If you wish to cancel it, that will be fine for all concerned.'

Rainey was frowning. Bea sat up straighter. What did he mean? He didn't usually allow them to opt out of singing at a booked venue.

'George Formby's wife, Beryl Ingham, who, as you know, is also his manager,' he took a breath before continuing, 'has sorted out her differences with the management and can now allow George to go ahead with the show.'

'Oh, no!' Bea almost shouted. 'I've been looking forward to that!' She saw Ivy look at Rainey.

Blackie frowned, then asked, 'Do all three of you really want to go to Devon?'

Silence reigned, until Ivy said, 'I've been looking forward to it.'

Immediately Rainey exclaimed, 'Oh, yes! I love Devon! You shouldn't let Beryl Ingham dictate where she wants George to be when it means messing other artists about.'

Ivy said, 'She's one bossy woman. And she's rarely sober, a nasty piece of work. You know full well Basil Dean won't visit the recording studios when she's there with George.'

Rainey broke in, 'Why should we step down from that booking? Why can't we both be on the bill? I'm sure the patrons would love that.'

'It's also about money, dear girls. The management won't want to pay both acts . . . Are the three of you telling me to put Beryl in her place and say you're doing the Alhambra?'

Bea didn't speak but Ivy and Rainey shouted, 'Yes!'

Ivy added, 'We want to go so much we'd do it for half the money!'

Rainey's mouth fell open, but she recovered quickly. 'You

know there's loads of troops in that area and they'd love to see our two acts.'

Bea looked at Rainey and smiled, then squeezed Ivy's hand so tightly that Ivy removed it from her grasp. Tears filled Bea's eyes. They knew how much appearing at the Alhambra meant to her.

Blackie nodded, then began writing in a large notebook. 'Fine,' he muttered. 'I'll see to it.'

Rainey foraged in her handbag, then got up. She'd found her handkerchief and stepped across the room, handing it to Bea. 'Don't you dare start snivelling,' she warned her.

As she returned to her seat, Bea sniffed. 'This is all sticky from that currant bun!'

Blackie finished writing and closed his notebook. 'I'd like you three to visit some of the local factories where war work is going on.'

'Like *Music While You Work*?' asked Ivy. 'What's on the wireless?'

Blackie nodded. 'Well, sort of. That's been on the cards for a while. I'm awaiting dates. Geraldo has said he'll back you, and Ivy Benson is eager to work with you again. Visiting armaments factories and other local venues doing necessary war work will give your profiles a lift. Get your pictures in the papers. The remuneration is good . . .' His voice tailed off. Then he was talking again, with more definition now. 'This is something new, Geraldo and His Concert Orchestra—'

Ivy stopped him. 'That sounds very good. But what about our recordings with Parlophone as the Bluebirds and Bea's solo recordings under her own name?'

Blackie turned the pages in his notebook. 'I've got dates in advance for all that, as long as they're suitable for the three of you.' He stood up. 'You've nothing to fear, there's plenty of work.'

'Why did you make us come over on the ferry to see you? All of this could have been sorted out on the phone.'

Ivy, Bea thought, wasn't going to let this rest.

At that moment the door was pushed open and Jo came in with a large tray that she set down on the edge of Blackie's desk, well away from the notebooks and papers. 'Tea's up,' she said, with a grin. 'Shall I pour?'

Blackie caught her eye and nodded. Jo went ahead clattering cups on saucers as Blackie spoke again. 'As I almost said, Geraldo has also come up with an interesting proposition.'

All eyes swivelled towards him.

'Have you heard of Geraldo's Navy?'

Bea shook her head. Ivy and Rainey frowned.

Blackie went on, 'I won't go into details but there's been

a ban for some time on our jazz musicians appearing in America and vice versa. Geraldo has a lot of sway in the music business and has been in meetings with Cunard liners. The *Queen Mary*, the *Queen Elizabeth* and other notable ships will feature all sorts of music, not only jazz,' he added. 'Geraldo has suggested you three might be interested in singing, on the high seas, as it were—'

'That's terrific,' Rainey interrupted, 'but I don't want to get blown up on the water!'

'Not now! He's thinking ahead to when the war's over but . . .'

'Does he have such faith that we'll win the war?' Bea stared at Blackie. Jo had finished pouring the tea.

Blackie sighed. 'Businessmen plan ahead and look ahead. This is a wonderful new venture, a chance for all of you to go on singing when the war is over.'

Bea opened her mouth to speak, but Jo weighed in: 'Let him finish, Bea.'

Blackie shot her a grateful smile. He ran his hand through his dark curls and said, 'Music hall is dying – the wireless is putting the nails in its coffin. People want music. I happen to think this is a good idea. It will also make money, which can't be bad. But ideally for you three, who have stated firmly that you don't want to work too far from home . . .'

Bea opened her mouth again, and Blackie put out his hand to silence her. 'Yes, Bea, I know you're not included in that. I know you'll travel.' He paused. 'Geraldo is willing to take one of the Bluebirds, two of you, or all three, just as you and your personal lives dictate.'

'So, on one voyage from, say, Southampton to New York, it might be Ivy and Rainey singing with the orchestra while I could be off somewhere else?'

Blackie nodded at Bea. 'He's willing to accommodate your wishes.'

'I couldn't ask for anything better,' said Ivy. 'It means I can spend most of my time with Eddie and Gracie.'

'Cruise liners go to really exotic places ...' said Bea, thoughtfully.

'I think it's a grand idea because it means we'll still be working after the war when there's bound to be so many changes,' said Rainey.

Bea added, 'We know what we're getting with Geraldo. After all, we've worked with him before at the Savoy in London.' She looked hard at Blackie. 'You'll sort everything out in our favour?'

'Bea, you girls will always come first with me. I have the three of you to thank for helping me on my way in this precarious business. Especially you, Bea. When I was let down by Melvin Hanratty, you devised a magic show with Ivy that had patrons laughing in the aisles . . .'

Jo chipped in, 'Let's drink our tea before it gets cold.'

Blackie nodded. He picked up his cup and made to toast them. 'I will always do my very best for you all,' he said.

Bea, despite the warmth from the fire, noticed a sudden chill in the room. She drained her cup and replaced it in the saucer. It wasn't only Bea who felt the change in the atmosphere.

'Now,' Ivy said, 'I suppose you'll tell us the real reason you needed to see us all face to face.'

Blackie gave a small cough to clear his throat. 'Always one step ahead, eh, Ivy?'

'I didn't want you to hear it on the grapevine or read about it in the newspapers . . .' The girls stared at him. 'You'll be familiar with Melvin Hanratty who I hired as a magician,' he said. ' I teamed him with Bea but he let us both down.' He didn't wait for a reply from any of them. 'You'll also remember that a young woman went missing after an ENSA concert in the desert during the time that you and he were there.'

'The police decided he had something to do with it, didn't they?' broke in Ivy.

Blackie nodded. 'Yes, he's been on remand in Portsmouth prison awaiting trial . . .'

Bea felt sick and put her hand to her mouth. But even after taking a deep breath, she couldn't stop her heart beating so hard she was sure they'd all hear it.

Blackie continued: 'A young airman apparently was also involved in her death. He, too, was remanded. The girl's body was discovered in a shallow grave. Both men were awaiting trial.'

Blackie, who had stood up to toast the girls, suddenly sat down heavily on the leather chair.

Bea couldn't help but remember how Melvin Hanratty had tried to put his hands all over her practically every time they were alone together. He wouldn't take a simple no for an answer. He had attacked her with rape on his mind in a doorway near the Portsmouth ferry. She had pushed him to defend herself and had sent him onto the road and beneath the wheels of a taxi. He'd spent a few days in hospital while she coerced Ivy to return to the Coliseum's stage, thus saving Blackie's reputation. Bea had had nightmares about Hanratty. Nightmares that had left her when she met Bing and discovered that men could be loving and kind.

'Hanratty was obviously worried about the impending trial,' said Blackie, 'and couldn't face its outcome. He tore up the blanket in his cell and hanged himself from the high window's bars.'

Only the ticking of the clock and the sparking of a log in the fire could be heard as each in the room digested the news.

Bea broke the silence. 'Don't feel any sympathy for him. You lot don't know the half of it. It was an easy way out for him. What goes around, comes around. I hope he rots in hell.'

'That's not a charitable thing to say, Bea,' said Blackie, frowning at her.

Bea tried to wipe away the tears that were now streaming down her face. Rainey's handkerchief was useless at its job. 'I know I shouldn't speak ill of the dead,' she said. 'But thank God you didn't know him as well as I did.'

Chapter Fourteen

Bert put three mugs of tea on the stained Formica tabletop and pushed one each towards Bea, Ivy and Rainey. Then he pulled out a fourth chair and sat on it, as if it was a relief to be off his feet for a while. From the wireless high on the shelf came the voices of the Mills Brothers singing 'Paper Doll'. Bea was busy looking at a large sheet-covered object pushed to the corner of the café. To her it looked like a piece of furniture he'd hidden from customers' prying eyes.

'Not a nice way to go, is it, stringing yourself up in a cell?'

'Don't talk about it any more now, Bert,' said Bea. What she really meant was 'Bert, stop talking about Melvin Hanratty because I don't want to hear his name mentioned ever again.' Unfortunately, his suicide was all over the front page of the *Evening News* so the talk in the café went on, and the conjecture would continue until it died a natural death. The three girls were discussing all that had happened in Portsmouth when they had been to see Blackie. Bert, of course, had to be kept up to date with all the latest news.

Bea received a huge wink from Bert. 'Did Blackie say anything about a screen test, ducks?'

She let out a sigh of relief. Thank goodness Bert and she were on the same wavelength at last and he was talking about a different subject. 'No. I'm keeping my fingers crossed, but until I have a contract in front of me to appear in that film, I'm just taking things with a pinch of salt,' she said. 'But the three of us have been assured there's work for us in the future. If there is a future. All we've got to do to be happy is win this damn war.'

'Mind yourselves,' said Della. 'This is hot.' She set down a large thick white dinner plate in the middle of the table that was piled high with sandwiches. The wonderful smell of cooked bacon cut through the fug of cigarette smoke from the customers puffing away on fags as they drank their tea.

'Don't talk daft, our Bea. Of course there's a future.' Della folded her arms and stared at her. 'The wireless said this morning the government promises that one of the first things that's going to happen after the war is that there's to be television for all.'

'Television!' Bert spluttered. 'Don't be daft, woman, us

ordinary folks can't afford televisions. It's bad enough trying to find money for the pictures!'

'Have you ever seen one, Bert?'

'Where would I see a television?' He helped himself to a sandwich. 'Come on, you lot, eat up before they get cold.' He gave a quick glance towards the counter, then smiled at Della. No one was waiting to be served. 'You take the weight off your feet as well, Della love,' he insisted. 'I'll get back behind the counter if anyone fresh comes in.'

Della gave him a huge smile. Bea could see the love shining between them.

She didn't bother to join in the conversation about the new-fangled television. She had also heard it being discussed while she was recording music at Broadcasting House in London. To have a small screen in the home showing pictures, like the big screens at the Criterion and the Forum, was practically beyond her comprehension.

Instead she said, 'What I heard on the wireless is that the government is banning all travel abroad. I reckon Blackie knew that.'

'I heard that as well,' said Della. 'I just wish this war would be over and done with. One minute the government is telling us the stuff of dreams, like television, is within reach, the next they're banning us from travelling to go and get it!'

Bea laughed before she took a bite out of a sandwich. In this smoky café she felt as far away from bad things as she could possibly be. Here she felt safe, cocooned with her loved ones around her. Most of them, anyway. Her brother Eddie was still at work. Ivy had told her he was taking on some more prisoners of war from the St Vincent holding centre as he had even more rebuilding work to sort out for Gosport's council. Maud was at home in Alma Street looking after Gracie.

Now Gracie was walking. Bea smiled. It was an ambitious word. What she did was fall over a lot trying to walk. Gracie and Maud had found a special place. Gracie loved the park, just a few moments away from Alma Street. She had been introduced to the delights of the swings in Forton recreation ground. She liked the slide as well. Maud didn't relish climbing the metal steps to the very top, then holding tight to Gracie, crowing with laughter, while they both slid down. Maud said she wished she'd never started sliding down the damn thing! She thought it was sad that some of the swings were broken, but the ones that were left gave the kids endless pleasure.

Bea thought about Jo and Blackie. They were good together. They were happy and working hard for their future and for the artists they represented. She wondered at the secret of their happiness. Blackie once told her that they spoke the truth to each other about everything.

As far as Bea was aware, Jo had kept her secret and never told Blackie about that trouble with the sailor. The three girls had still been at school then. The reputations of stars had to be whiter than white for them to succeed in show business. Revealing that one of the beautiful Bluebirds had practically lost her virginity at the back of a Gosport pub could have toppled them from the success they deserved.

Ivy and Rainey had pulled her through those dark days. They'd wanted fame as much as she did then. Bea, still focused on her future, sometimes wondered if Rainey and Ivy's priorities had shifted.

Bea worried a great deal about Jo keeping that secret from Blackie. What if Blackie discovered Jo had not been honest with him? Bea was in constant fear that Jo's promise to her could be the catalyst of bad feeling between Blackie and Jo. That she might be the cause of a break-up between them.

And just like she always did, especially when her fear caused her to wake up troubled in the night, she pushed it aside with great determination. And told herself, like Scarlett O'Hara, that she'd think about it another day.

Now, though, she was in debt to Ivy and Rainey.

'Thank you,' she said, 'for insisting we do the concert entertaining the troops in Devon.'

Rainey put down her mug. 'We know what it means for you to see Bing again. If he can be there, we know he will be.'

Bert, who knew the ins and outs of everything, put in: 'It's this bloody war, Bea love. That man loves the bones of you.' He got up from the table and went over to the bulky covered object. He pulled up part of the sheet and stood looking proudly at an upright piano. He lifted the lid and showed everyone the keys shining, like yellowed teeth. He let a hand very gently caress them.

The soft sounds reminded Bea of an angel playing a harp. 'That's the piano you told Bing you had upstairs,' she said. She knew then that Bert truly liked Bing. He wouldn't have gone to the trouble of getting someone to bring the heavy object down the steep stairs if he didn't.

'It is,' Bert said proudly, 'and I got a customer to tune it ready for when that boy of yours comes home again.' Bert let down the lid and began smoothing the sheet back over the instrument. 'You mustn't worry that he hasn't been in touch for a while. It's because he can't, not because he doesn't want to.'

Tears spilled down Bea's cheeks. Of course Bing loved her: everyone around her could see it. She knew it, too.

'We're going to have some good old ding-dongs and knees-ups when that lad comes home, and he's going to sing and play his heart out,' Bert said.

Suddenly there was a bang on the counter and one of the policemen Bea recognized from the station in South Street said, with a smile, 'What's up, Bert? You shut up shop for the evening?' He removed his helmet and put it down. 'If you haven't, I could do with a cuppa.'

Chapter Fifteen

It was cold, thought Max, waiting in the cobbled yard for Eddie Herron and his transport to turn up. He counted the men standing around, eight of them. Eddie must be doing well to be using so much German labour. Call-up had taken his regular young workforce – Max was aware of that from when he had worked for the builder before. He also knew that Eddie had had high hopes of rising in the ranks of the RAF. Sadly, he'd been unable to serve in the forces on medical grounds so instead he had concentrated on his building firm.

'Might be April but these early mornings are no joke,' said a fair-haired young man, stamping his feet to keep them warm. He blew on his hands then clapped them together to get the circulation going. 'I haven't seen you before.'

'No,' said Max. 'I arrived from Winchester only recently.

My name's Max.' He leaned forward to shake hands with the man, who held his fingers in a vice-like grip.

'Peter,' said the man.

Max liked the way Peter had kept eye contact with him throughout the exchange. 'I don't know why most of the residents in this place are content to stay here day after day doing menial jobs around the barracks,' Max said. 'It must make the time pass extremely slowly. And a shilling a day of wages is not to be sneezed at. First chance I had I put my name down to work outside.'

'Yes,' said Peter. 'After a day's work in the fresh air it's good to be brought back here for a meal and a cleansing wash or shower. It seems more normal to work during the day and relax with a hobby in the evenings.'

'You've something you like to do in your spare time, then?' Max was curious.

Peter grinned. 'In exchange for cigarettes or a few pennies I make peg dolls.'

Max had no hobbies. He liked to read. He was also rather good at calligraphy. He had been taught many years ago by the captured Englishman who had worked on the farm for his father. Max did not like to think he might spend his evenings holding a flat-nibbed pen at a forty-five-degree angle to produce copperplate writing, however good he was at it. He asked Peter, 'Peg dolls?'

'Yes, I whittle the wooden pegs the camp buys from gypsies. The British officers are pretty good about shopping for us. Stuff to keep us quiet, like pencils and pads, cards, games, papers and books ... When they can get hold of things, of course.'

'And you turn pegs into dolls?'

Peter nodded. 'Scraps of material for clothing, wool for hair. I'm good at painting faces,' he said. 'Many of the finished items we make are donated to schools for the kids. Some of the prisoners build ships and planes out of matchsticks. A friend of mine makes mugs out of condensed-milk tins. Very good they are, too.'

Jesus, the man liked to talk, thought Max. He guessed he, too, was a relative newcomer to the holding centre. There were few faces he remembered, even among the guards.

To drown out Peter's droning voice, he thought back to when he'd applied to work outside.

The Englishman who had quickly looked through Max's papers had laughed at his request. 'You want me to let you escape again?'

Max saw that he was still willing to hear him out. He defended himself. 'I have learned much from my stay in

Winchester prison.' Max knew there was a letter from Edgar Cole extolling his virtues, if he could only persuade the officer to read it.

Officer Hanley scrutinised his papers fully.

'Whatever happens, I wish to stay on in England when the war is over.' Max had continued with his patter. 'There is much I can learn from your way of life. If I can be of use working on rebuilding roads or housing now, I would be grateful for the chance to do so.'

Hanley had not given him his decision then. It had come a few days later. The delay had caused Max to spend nights tossing and turning in his bunk. The questions rolled around his brain, and only outside the prison could they be answered. Why was Sunshine dead? What had happened? Thinking about her reminded him of the feel of her slight body beneath him. And why did Eddie Herron have Max's child? None of it made sense to him. He couldn't see any man taking on another's child unless there were extenuating circumstances. If so, what were they? Max knew he could never bring up another man's child. He remembered when he had first met Sunshine while working on a renovating job at Bridgemary. She had been seeing Eddie, hadn't she? Max had known then that the girl could be very useful to him in his plan to escape. His charm, good looks and magnetism would serve him well. Before long, she was no longer seeing Eddie and was employed in the kitchens at St Vincent so she could be near to Max.

Promises of a wonderful life in Germany, along with his undying love, had been balm to Sunshine's ears. Growing up in foster homes where she had been ill treated had made her desperate to be loved. Her gullibility made her easy prey to a predator of Max's skill. Naturally they carried on their affair in secret: no fraternizing with the enemy was the law. The only person who had suspected the truth was Hans. During a period of light gardening with Max he had become a go-between.

Max had been told yesterday what time he should wait on the cobbles for transport to outside work.

Peter was still talking. He said he was from Cologne and went on in detail about how he had worked in a perfume factory when he was much younger. Max was trying not to show how bored he was with Peter's grating voice when the rumble of wheels from a Bedford thirty-hundredweight truck lumbered slowly into the yard and circled ready to face the exit. The driver didn't turn off the engine. Instead he kept it running by constantly revving on the accelerator.

Max saw Eddie was in the driving seat.

'Jump in the back, boys,' Eddie said. 'Make it quick – I daren't turn her off. You know she's a bugger to start.'

Max was speechless at the sight of the air-force blue truck with a torn blue tarpaulin tied to its sides with a frayed rope, 'RAF' printed on both cab doors. He watched as one of the men who had been waiting let down the tailgate and climbed aboard. Eddie revved the engine again and, with a stubby pencil and sheet of paper clutched in one hand, shouted, 'Give me your name as you climb in so I can mark you off my list.'

Peter, shouting, 'Peter Werner,' hoisted himself on board.

Max watched each man identify himself, and climb onto the wreck. Eddie marked his paper and glanced at the men. Some he chatted to briefly, others received a good-natured grin. At last only Max remained on the cobbles. He waited for Eddie to look at him properly. 'Hello, Eddie, Maximilian Muller at your service.' He stood as straight as he could before clicking his heels. And then he smiled.

'Max!' burst from Eddie's lips, like an explosion. 'I saw the name but didn't put two and two together! How are you, mate?' He was smiling broadly. 'You old devil! I thought we'd seen the last of you.' Just then the engine coughed and Eddie pumped the accelerator. The dying engine spluttered into throaty life once more. A cloud of oily smoke rose into the air. 'Get in the front with me, Max.' As soon as Max had pulled open the dented door and climbed in, Eddie yelled, 'Everyone aboard?'

Max saw him glance into the rear-view mirror, presumably to check the men were safely inside the truck. 'Well, Eddie,' he said, 'I remember you wanted to join the RAF to fight for your country but couldn't. Is this wreck of a truck the nearest you could get to the air force? Why are you driving this heap of shit?' Max looked scornfully around the inside of the cab. It stank of fumes and wires hung from the dashboard.

'Very funny! You forget we're at war? All the best vehicles have been requisitioned by the government.'

Eddie drove out of the main gate, nodding at the guard as he passed, without his papers and transport being checked. Eddie was obviously well known and respected, Max surmised.

'I bought the truck off a mate at Lee-on-the-Solent airfield.'

'You paid good money for this thing? That mate should have paid you to take it away.'

'What good's a builder without transport?'

Max put his hand in front of his nose and mouth. 'This stink can kill you while you're driving.'

'Good thing the boys got fresh air in the back, then, isn't it?' said Eddie. Max tried to wind down the window nearest him. It wouldn't budge.

'Don't worry,' said Eddie. 'This side's permanently open. Soon as we get up a bit of speed, the smell will clear.'

Max started laughing. It wasn't long before Eddie was chuckling along with him. After a while, Eddie said, 'I read in the *Evening News* some time ago that you'd escaped and got caught in town down in Bert's café. The article said you had no papers on you. Wasn't that a bit foolhardy?'

Max wasn't going to say that Sunshine was supposed to meet him with the necessary false identification documents for him to leave the country. He said, 'I was a fool, Eddie,' and left it at that. It was probably what Eddie wanted to hear. He sensed Eddie knew nothing of his involvement with Sunshine. If he had, he surely wouldn't be so friendly towards him. Hans had kept his secret. So, too, had Sunshine apparently. He breathed a sigh of relief.

'I could have a look at the truck for you,' Max said.

Eddie took his eyes from the road, glanced at Max and smiled. 'I don't think it's possible you can fix it. The bloke at the airfield told me to run it into the ground. I got it cheap because it's a wreck.' He set his eyes back on the road again.

'No offence, Max, but if a service mechanic reckons it can't be fixed, it can't be fixed, can it?'

'I've been working on Bedfords at Winchester,' answered Max. 'Let me have a go?'

Eddie didn't give him an answer. He took his hand from the steering wheel and gave Max a playful punch on his arm. 'It's so good to see you again, Max.' Max heard the sincerity in his voice. For a moment there was silence between them as Eddie drove along Forton Road. Eddie was the first to speak. 'I've been in to see Hans and I must go again. The authorities are not happy at any fraternizing with the enemy but sometimes a decent guard will turn a blind eye.' He frowned. 'I suppose you know he's frail?'

'Yes. He is very weak.' Max was thinking fast. Perhaps it might not be such a good thing for Eddie to look in on Hans. So far, his countryman had kept quiet about his relationship with Sunshine, but Hans was very ill. What if Eddie visited him again and the young man suddenly decided on a deathbed confession of Max's affair? He told himself there was no reason for him to think that would happen . . . was there?

But if Eddie visited Hans and mentioned Max was working for him again, might Hans, either wittingly or unwittingly, let drop secrets he had held for so long? That would spoil everything. One word out of place from Hans and Max's plans could be ruined.

'You are doing well, my friend?' Max asked. He knew Eddie would not brag about any good fortune hard work had brought him, but that he would be honest.

'I'm making a good living,' Eddie confessed.

'And have you married?' Max had already made it his business to find out about Eddie's circumstances. General chit-chat might give him better insight into Eddie's home life and ultimately tell him more about the child. To be forewarned was to be forearmed: was that not an English saying? For Max to be useful to Eddie Herron might benefit him when he decided to attempt an escape. Nothing must detract from that.

'No, but I'm living with a wonderful woman who's a good mother to my little girl.' Eddie's tone held such pride.

'Little girl?' Max pretended to be surprised. Eddie had fallen into his trap and was about to confide in him, just as he wanted. Perhaps now he'd find out how it was possible that Eddie had ended up becoming a surrogate father to the child that in all probability was Max's.

'Do you remember when we repaired houses at Bridgemary and I was friendly with a young woman who cleaned the lodging house, Lavinia House?'

Max shook his head and frowned. It was better to let Eddie think that the past and Sunshine were of no consequence to him.

'No,' said Eddie, 'I don't suppose you do.' He gave a small cough, then admitted, 'I got the poor girl into trouble . . .'

Again, Max allowed his brow to furrow. He knew quite well what that phrase meant but he wanted Eddie to explain himself, and squirm.

'I met her at the theatre, began seeing her and one thing led to another.'

'Plenty of lovemaking, eh?' Max tried to make light of his words.

'No, she wanted marriage and I wasn't ready. Besides, she was a virgin and determined to stay that way.'

Max sat back on the ripped seat. He knew it was expected of him to feign surprise.

Eddie sighed. 'It was only the once.' He glanced again at Max. 'Never think only once can't leave a girl with a baby. She kept it a secret, possibly because she knew I wasn't keen on marriage. Though naturally I'd have wed her to give the kiddie a name,' he added. 'Anyway, I'd stopped seeing her. The first I knew of the baby was when my mother, who'd been visiting Lavinia House, got caught up with the birth. Mum brought this tiny little scrap home to me and said that as Sunshine lay dying she confessed that the child was mine. "Take the baby to Eddie," were practically her last words. Unfortunately, she was too weak to survive the premature birth.'

Max almost felt sorry for him being taken in so easily. In a funny kind of way, he admired Sunshine for leaving her child in Eddie's care. And Eddie? Of course he would look after the baby. His was a caring nature.

Max had no doubt that Sunshine had never made love to Eddie all the time he, Max, was declaring his love to her. After all, it was unthinkable that Sunshine might have preferred the Englishman's fumblings to his own experienced lovemaking. Yes. Unthinkable! Max knew Sunshine had been a virgin the first time he had entered her. So, Eddie and Sunshine's coupling must have happened after Max had been caught while escaping St Vincent. Naturally, that was why Eddie assumed the child was premature. Yes, it all fitted together perfectly.

Sunshine, believing she would never see Max again and possibly knowing she could not raise the child, had done the next best thing in making sure the baby's future was assured.

Max then remembered the awful corset Sunshine had worn to hold in her burgeoning belly and to disguise her pregnancy. An unmarried, sinful woman due to give birth would have been dismissed from her job immediately.

What a woman, eh? Had she believed she might never see Max again and allowed Eddie to sleep with her so that she could pretend the child was his? What a clever, scheming little bitch she was!

And now, thought Max, it would be a shame to deprive Eddie of his so-called daughter, but the truth must eventually be accounted for.

Max's little girl belonged in Germany, with him, her true father.

To Eddie, driving towards the town and the destruction the Luftwaffe had wrought, he said, above the noise of the engine, 'You are a good man, Eddie Herron.'

'I'm glad you think so,' smiled Eddie. 'Of course it's terrible that Gracie lost her mother before she knew her, but that little girl is the light of my life. I'll tell you one thing, Max. I've never once regretted owning up to being her father. And Gracie's a pretty name, isn't it?' He smiled at Max. 'She's the light of my life. And I'm a lucky bugger to have the most gorgeous girl in the world as a mother for her.' He sighed. 'I've been blessed, Max.' Then he said, 'I'll show you a photo of Gracie in a minute.'

Max saw they had entered the heart of Gosport now and Eddie had slowed the vehicle near the bombed town hall and driven onto decimated ground that announced 'Gas Board'.

Eddie said, 'Keep your fingers crossed this vehicle starts again, else we'll be walking back to St Vincent tonight.' He brought it, with a shudder and several coughs, to a halt.

'We're on salvage work today, lads,' he shouted back, through his one open window. 'You know what to save and discard.' He automatically patted his top pocket, where Max decided Eddie kept the relevant papers. 'So, if any busybodies stop you working to ask what you're doing sifting through this lot, and putting stuff in the truck like looters, send them to find me. At dinner time I'll treat you to fish and chips from the Porthole.' There was a cheer from his men as they climbed or jumped down from the vehicle. Max knew fish wasn't rationed and the Porthole served the tastiest chips for miles around.

'Are you leaving the truck unattended?' Max looked worried.

Eddie started to laugh. 'It took me half an hour to start it this morning so good luck to anyone who tries to steal the old girl! Anyway, we'll be backwards and forwards carrying stuff.'

'This is our work for today? Sifting through burned materials?'

'Max, this showroom was hit a couple of days ago by a stray bomb that must have been meant for the dockyard or the munitions factory. The council sent for me to make it safe. This is a built-up area. These remains are a death-trap to kids or anyone else who has no business here. My boys know what to look for and what to do. Any undamaged wood, slates, bricks, piping, anything that can be reused, goes in the back of the truck. Whatever we save can be used for repairs—'

Max interrupted him: 'Is there a scrapyard hereabouts? For vehicles?'

'You thinking of trying to sort out the engine?'

'Unless you're worried I might escape while you're sifting through that lot.' Max nodded towards the tin sheeting that had been erected to keep people off the site. 'Believe me, I've been working on trucks like this in Winchester. All I need are spare parts that a scrapyard might have.'

Eddie looked at him. 'I trust the officer who signed the papers saying you could work outside for me today. Some officials make a point of coming around to check all is in order. I trust you, Max. If you think you can get this old girl running properly, I'll stump up for an extra bit of cod for you at dinner time.'

Max laughed. 'I'm flattered. My English is excellent so I can explain exactly what it is I am after.' He didn't add he would also get a spare key made and hide it, just in case, while escaping Gosport, he ever needed to steal the vehicle. 'But I will need a little money, if I have to buy . . .'

'You really think you have an idea of what's wrong?'

'More importantly I will not run away now. Eddie, you know I tell the truth. I have no identity papers to leave this island so how would I escape?'

Once down from the cab Max soon had one side of the bonnet pushed back and was examining the engine parts.

Eddie stopped him. 'Before you get oil all over yourself take a look at this photo of my little girl.' Eddie took a snap out of his wallet.

With hands that immediately began to tremble Max took it from him. The little girl's pale hair took Max's breath away. It was like looking at a picture of himself as a child. 'She's beautiful,' his voice croaked. One look at Gracie and the child had insinuated herself into Max's heart. He could see a family resemblance in her face.

'You cold, mate?' asked Eddie, as Max relinquished the photograph with shaking hands.

Max shook his head. He wasn't cold. But he had a lump in his throat. This child was his own flesh and blood, not Eddie's.

Chapter Sixteen

Rainey punched the cushion and put it back in exactly the same position on the sofa she had taken it from. She looked around her neat kitchen, freshly polished, newly swept and with not a single item out of place. She glanced at the clock on the mantelpiece above the range. Too early yet to walk round to Alma Street to ask if Ivy would like her to take Gracie for a walk in the park, much too early; Eddie might not even have left the house for work. She wondered if other people who lived on their own had too much time to fill with jobs that didn't really matter.

Lonely? Of course she was lonely. It was something she needed to address.

Last night the Bluebirds had sung at Alice Wilkes's birthday party at the Connaught Hall. Mentally, Rainey chastised herself. Alice Wilkes, once a music teacher at

St John's School, had married Graham Letterman, so she was no longer Alice Wilkes. To Rainey the woman who had breathed life into the Bluebirds would always be Alice Wilkes. Toto was there, her little white dog, yappy and bouncy as ever. But Rainey noticed the grey whiskers around his muzzle and that every so often he flopped, exhausted, beside Bess, Graham's Labrador guide dog.

It was emotional singing 'Where The Bluebird Goes'. This was the folk song they had practised in St John's Choir, which had netted them second place in the Fareham Music Festival. It had started their singing and their stage success. Graham Letterman had felt for and clasped Alice's hand all the way through the simple ballad.

'Where The Bluebird Goes' had been their final song of the evening. They had trooped onto the stage in their classic black dresses as the pianist began. Rainey's back had straightened as the notes were played. Listening to the words, she was exhilarated.

The Bluebird song was about love but, then, the most memorable songs were, she thought. Love and loss have many guises. Rainey had experienced some, and she felt every word she sang. She had lost the man she loved and the child she'd wanted. Her heart had been crushed, but the song urged her to carry on: love, it promised, would always win.

Next to her Bea was singing, and she could hear Ivy's huskiness telling everyone they didn't know what they were made of until they'd lost all they'd ever wanted. To Rainey it was clear that the beautiful words meant something different to each of the girls. As the last piano note faded the audience was clamouring for more. Rainey saw Alice Wilkes wipe a tear from her eye before she stood up and clapped.

She didn't want the fame that Bea craved. Rainey needed to be depended upon, useful, to give out some of the great love stored inside her. Not necessarily by and to a lover, although that might be nice, she thought. Charlie had been her great love; he had fulfilled her. To be the person she was before she had met him was impossible. Change was inevitable. One step at a time. And the more love she gave, the more she would gather back. The Bluebird song had shown Rainey the road to recovery, and last night she had slept the moment her head had touched the pillow.

'So where are you going, Maud?' Ivy grabbed the metal bowl full of wrung-out washing and put her hand on the scullery-door latch. She waited for Maud to answer her.

'To Watt's, the greengrocer's. Eddie phoned and said there was a queue a mile long. It's bananas this time, I know it!' Maud tied the headscarf beneath her chin, then stepped out of her pompom slippers and into her black lace-up shoes. 'Why are you bothering to hang that out? It looks like rain.'

'The wireless said it might rain later. Might, not will.' Ivy pushed the back door open and stepped out onto the concrete. 'And what's the point,' she shouted back into the house, 'of joining a long queue? By the time you get served whatever they had will have gone!'

'O ye of little faith!' yelled Maud. 'I've nearly forgotten what a banana looks like!' In any case, if Maud was too late for bananas, at least she'd catch up with all the local gossip. Ivy heard the front door slam.

The loud bang obviously startled Gracie for she let out a sharp cry. 'Two minutes, my love, and I'll be back indoors,' shouted Ivy. Gracie was safe in the playpen with her toys. She'd come to no harm. In no time at all the bowl was empty and the washing hung limply on the line in the weak April sunlight.

'Don't hurry yourself, I've got her,' called Rainey, from the back door. She had Gracie in her arms.

'I suppose you came through the front door as Maud went out?' Ivy said. 'She likes queues.' She tickled Gracie's tummy and the little girl giggled.

'Thought I could take Gracie to the park,' said Rainey, nodding in answer to her friend's question. 'Give you a chance to get on with something without having to worry about this little tyke.'

'More!' squealed the little girl, when Rainey set her back in the playpen and handed her the toy rabbit with an ear missing.

'I think you must be an angel in disguise,' Ivy said. 'I caught my heel in my black dress last night when we were on stage and I haven't had time to stitch it yet. I'll be needing it for Devon. Three nights, the blue, the silver and ending up with the black dress. That's what we decided, wasn't it?'

Rainey nodded. 'Mine are all hanging, ready, in the bedroom,' she said.

'I just don't have any time, these days,' said Ivy. 'I'm making tea. Want some?'

'Yes, please,' replied Rainey. 'I enjoyed being at the Connaught last night.'

'So did I,' admitted Ivy. She picked up the kettle, shook it, decided there was enough water in it and lit the gas beneath it. 'What d'you think about working with Geraldo's Navy?'

'I'm thinking it might suit me very well,' answered Rainey. 'Especially as some of the cruises may be quite short.' She was thoughtful. 'Bea will want more than that. But I'd certainly give it a go.'

'Bea will get more than that,' said Ivy. She set down two

mugs on the draining board. 'I'm keeping my fingers crossed that Bing manages to get to the Alhambra this weekend. If not, our lives won't be worth living.'

'He might get leave,' said Rainey.

Ivy went to the cupboard and took out a packet of Farley's rusks. She fumbled in the box and handed one to Gracie, who carefully laid the rabbit on the floor of the playpen. A big smile covered her chubby face and she put out her hand to take the rusk.

'What do you say? Listen, Rainey,' said Ivy.

Gracie said something that resembled, 'Fank ewe.'

'You darling girl,' gushed Rainey. Then she looked at Ivy. 'Expecting leave isn't the same as actually getting it, is it?'

'Bea will be hell to work with if she doesn't see Bing. That big exercise is soon, isn't it?'

Rainey took a deep breath. 'We're not supposed to know or talk about it . . .'

'We're allowed to talk about recording studios.' Ivy sniffed. 'Next week it's London for us, isn't it? Are you ready for it?'

'As ready as I'll ever be. "Sunday, Monday or Always" I like very much but that Fred Astaire cover, "I'm Old-fashioned", isn't one I'd have chosen.'

'Nor me,' replied Ivy. 'And we'll both have to wait around while Bea records solo . . .'

'What's she singing?'

'"At Last" and "I've Heard That Song Before".'

'They're both good songs for her,' said Rainey. She frowned. 'Have you forgotten all about making tea?'

Ivy touched her forehead. 'I'd forget my head if it wasn't screwed on.'

'Doesn't matter,' Rainey said. 'I can wait for a cuppa until I bring Gracie back from the park. Where's her little boots and her coat?'

Ivy pointed to the top of the sideboard where the child's coat, her knitted pixie hood and mittens were. 'Boots on the floor in the hall,' said Ivy. 'I'll get them.'

'Fine.' Rainey lifted the smiling child, with her rusk, from the playpen. 'Just don't forget to mend your dress.'

Chapter Seventeen

'Officer Hanley, I wish to beg for another visit to my good friend Hans. Yesterday, as you are aware, I worked hard in repairing Eddie Herron's vehicle and he is exceptionally pleased with me.' Max waited to see what effect his words would have on the officer, who went on writing. Max decided to carry on with his request. 'Hans is remembered with kindness by Mr Herron and I believe a short visit by myself will make Hans happy to hear how we spoke of him. I will not tire Hans or overstay my welcome.'

Max hoped his mawkish sentimentality sounded sincere enough to the officer. He kept perfectly still and stood to attention, showing the Englishman he awaited his verdict with respect. Today he was not working outside the centre. He had spent a sleepless night trying to work out the details of escape for himself and his daughter.

Victory for the Bluebird Girls

Hanley put down his pen. Max was well aware that Eddie had been more than happy to inform the officer that he was delighted by Max's workmanship in repairing the Bedford's faulty draw plug. The officer looked up at him. 'You are aware the patient is very ill and may be sleeping?'

'Yes, sir. If that is so, I will not wake him but will return at a more appropriate time to ask you again.'

The officer glanced once more at the papers lying on his desk, then at the bottle of ink and the metal-nibbed pen. He was a busy man. 'Five minutes. I will telephone the nurse and tell her that you are coming immediately.'

'Thank you, sir.' Max allowed his mouth and eyes to smile gratefully.

'You may go.'

Outside in the chill of the corridor Max took no hesitation in hurrying to the infirmary. Yesterday Eddie had told him he would visit Hans soon, but Max couldn't let that happen. He couldn't run the risk of Hans possibly letting slip that Max had been meeting Sunshine and had got her pregnant. So far Hans had kept Max's secret but . . . Max couldn't take that chance.

He was so deep in thought that he almost ran into the female nurse as she came through the open doorway with

165

two vases of wilting flowers clutched to her breast. 'I know you have permission. Five minutes. And only five. No more.'

Max had taken an instant dislike to the large Englishwoman. In Germany a woman would never have dared to speak to him in such a condescending manner.

As her footsteps echoed down the corridor, he looked carefully at the two sleeping patients several beds away from Hans. He took a deep breath and instantly regretted it. The stench of disinfectant and bleach made him want to vomit.

He walked quickly towards Hans's bed. The nurse had told him Hans was awake but he lay with his eyes closed.

Max picked up the spare pillow lying at the chair next to the bed and pressed it firmly over Hans's lower face.

There was no noise from his victim, only an almost imperceptible movement of Hans's frame. Just as Max thought all the air had gone from Hans's lungs, his eyes suddenly flew open. He was staring questioningly at his murderer.

Max adjusted the pillow so Hans's eyes were hidden and continued pressing. He thought it might be some time before he could rid himself of the memory of the sad, enquiring look in Hans's eyes. 'I'm sorry, my friend, but it's better for you to go like this than coughing your heart up one night in front of these strangers,' Max said softly. 'You and I understand each other, don't we, Hans?'

He set the pillow back on the chair.

Hans looked peaceful.

Max turned and left the room, walking quickly along the corridor.

He found the nurse at a stone sink rinsing vases. 'You must come quickly,' he said. 'Hans is not asleep. He is not breathing.'

Chapter Eighteen

'Bea? Bea Herron?'

Bea halted in the long corridor of Broadcasting House and looked behind her at the two women walking swiftly to catch up with her. Bea was hurrying to reach the designated café in London's Portland Place where she knew Ivy and Rainey would be waiting for her.

'Hello,' she said, gazing at the two middle-aged, very smartly dressed women, both wearing cheeky little hats. One had a huge glossy fox fur slung around her neck. Its beady eyes glared at Bea. Both women had smiles that stretched from ear to ear. For a moment Bea stared at them helplessly as their expensive perfume tickled her nose. Her head was still overflowing with the words from the songs she had just recorded for a new programme the BBC were promoting. It had taken more time than she had hoped and she was determined not to keep her friends waiting longer than she had to. Then everything fell into place. This was the celebrated duo of Elsie and Doris Waters, and she'd first set eyes on them, briefly, at Ford airfield in Sussex. A conversation she'd had with Henry Lucas, their brother's agent, had set her heart pounding that night. Yet now the possibility of a part in a British film seemed so far in the past that Bea had allowed it to slip from her mind.

'Are you going home, dear?' the shorter woman asked.

Bea had no idea whether she was Elsie or Doris. 'Sort of,' she said. 'I'm supposed to be meeting the other two Bluebirds and I'm already keeping them waiting. I've been recording songs for a separate programme.' Her words were tumbling over one another. She stopped talking and smiled, then began again. 'I do know who you are and I'd like to say how pleased I am to meet you.'

'Don't start on the silly chit-chat, Bea,' the taller one, the wearer of the fox fur, said. 'If we hadn't been so busy working abroad, we'd have been in touch with you before now, or Henry would have telephoned Blackie.'

'Do you have to get back to Gosport quickly, dear?' the shorter one asked.

'We came up to London by train. We can't leave it too late

to get to Waterloo. The trains can be crowded with troops either returning to barracks or going home on leave.'

They both nodded. Bea was about to insist that she and her friends needed to be on the train in time to catch the last Portsmouth ferry to Gosport, when the taller one said, 'It's fortunate Ivy and Rainey are with you. We must talk to you all, dear. Why don't we collect your friends and take you to our home in Steyning? It's much nicer than a café, and afterwards our driver can make sure you all get home safely, in comfort.'

Bea was stunned. All she could say was, 'I've no idea where Steyning is . . .'

'Fifty miles or so from Portsmouth, dear, and our driver will get us there in no time at all.'

Bea guessed they intended to talk to her about the proposed film, *It Always Rains On Sunday*. What else could it be? But hadn't they also stated they needed to see Ivy and Rainey as well? If she refused this invitation, it might seem as if she wasn't interested in appearing in the film and of course she was. Very much so. But how would Ivy and Rainey feel about not travelling straight home? Only one way to find out, Bea thought.

'It's very kind of you and I'm sure I speak for the three of us. We'd certainly love to visit your home,' she said. 'But

I have to make sure that the other two are happy with the change in plans. Can we meet outside the studios in, say, ten minutes?'

Both women smiled at her and nodded. Bea hurried down the corridor, almost at a run. Before she rounded the corner she turned and waved to them, then immediately felt a fool for having shown such childish excitement at meeting the two well-known stars. She was surprised to see them wave back.

It wasn't long before Bea pushed open the door of the café and stepped inside to the warm fug of cigarettes and stale perfume.

'About time too,' said Ivy. 'I'm on my third cup of tea already.'

'How did you get on?' Rainey asked.

'I did fine, I think,' answered Bea. She didn't sit down but hovered over the table. 'Look, I have a favour to ask you both. All three of us have been invited to Elsie and Doris Waters' home. They want to talk to us. I think in my case it's about that film business and, to tell the truth, I'd rather you were both with me.'

'Really?' Ivy couldn't believe it.

'Where do they live?' Rainey was interested. 'They're Gert and Daisy, aren't they?'

Ivy sounded a little peeved. 'I promised Eddie I wouldn't be back late.' She fussed with the collar of her grey suit.

Rainey ignored Ivy and asked again, 'Where do they live?'

'Brighton way, I think. They can take us in their car and drop us home afterwards,' she added.

'I'm up for it,' Rainey said. 'But it might be a good idea for Ivy to phone Maud, so she can tell Eddie where we are, just in case.'

'Just in case what? The two funniest and most loved comediennes in the world today decide to murder us?' quipped Bea. She laughed.

'Don't be silly!' Rainey snapped.

'I don't want Eddie worrying . . .' Ivy paused. 'If they want to talk to you about that film and you don't go, you might never get this chance again. Mind you, they might want to talk about work for all of us.'

Bea nodded. 'So, you'll both come, then?'

'You try and stop us,' Rainey said. A big smile had broken out on her face.

'I remember seeing a phone box about two doors up from this café,' said Ivy, rising from her chair. 'I won't be long. Don't go without me!'

Minutes later all three girls were sitting in the back of

the large black Wolseley that was purring through London driven by a young grey-suited chauffeur wearing a peaked cap. He had barely glanced at them when he was introduced as Timothy.

'This is nice,' said Ivy, who was sitting next to Doris, while Elsie, of the fox fur, or Florence, as she explained her real name was, sat in the front. 'In here it smells of leather and polish and expensive perfume. Definitely a step up from our usual transport.'

'And your usual transport is?' Doris asked, easing off her court shoes.

'The train. Or my brother's works motor, or Blackie has Sammy drive us in a small van, which means two of us – we take it in turns – have to sit on cushions in the back on the floor.'

Doris began laughing.

'Doesn't that take you back to when we first started?' said Elsie, to her sister.

'Oh, my, of course it does,' Doris agreed.

'You've gone very quiet, Bea,' said Elsie.

'So many things are going around in my head,' she said. 'So many questions I want to ask . . .'

'May I suggest you keep all your questions for when we arrive home at the bungalow?' Doris said.

'Oh!' Bea was slightly put out. She asked instead, 'Do you live together as well as work together?'

'Oh, yes. We've always got on. Too busy for marriage and children. We had a house before we moved to Steyning, but the stairs were beginning to give us both trouble,' said Doris. 'This place has such a wonderful view of the countryside.'

'One of our friends asked if we needed a higher roof but Doris said, "Definitely not. Just bung-a-low roof on it!"' Elsie began to laugh.

Someone gave a polite snigger but Doris warned, 'You're not on the stage now, Elsie. And that's a terrible joke.'

Bea began to feel easier in their company, and because they were all chattering constantly the time seemed to be passing very quickly. 'Is it far, now?' she eventually asked.

'No, and it's quicker when there's less traffic,' said Doris.

Bea put her head back against the seat and listened to the engine purring away and the hum of voices. She decided Elsie and Doris Waters were two of the nicest stars she'd ever met. Not that the Bluebirds had met many of their magnitude. Well, George Formby, perhaps.

Ivy asked about the two Command Performances they had appeared in. Bea looked at Elsie and the animal skin, its sharp nose and dangling paws. She shuddered. 'Ivy's mother is rather fond of furs,' she announced. 'Della once said she liked Madame Nellie's, and without a second thought, Madame gave it to her, just like that. Not that I'd want one – they scare the life out of me. I'd hate a dead creature hanging around my neck!'

'Nellie always had her clothes made by Norman Hartnell, as we do,' said Elsie.

Bea's mouth dropped open. Fancy that! But it made sense: Madame had always been impeccably dressed. Bea closed her mouth. She realized at that moment that these two were very familiar with the woman who had been their benefactor when the Bluebirds had first started. 'She was always impeccably dressed ...' admitted Elsie, as though she'd read Bea's mind.

'Hartnell? Isn't that the Queen's dressmaker?' exclaimed Rainey.

'Our money's just as good,' said Elsie.

Bea had such a lot to think about. She felt as if she was dreaming. She shut her eyes ... The next thing she knew the car was at a standstill and doors were being opened to allow them to step out. 'I'm so sorry.' She yawned. 'I must have slept.'

Doris was fumbling around in the footwell for her shoes. 'Don't feel bad about it. We often have a little snooze on the way home when we've been recording or filming,' she said.

Bea thought that, despite the differences between the sisters, it would take her ages to get their names right. Gert, Daisy, Doris, Elsie. They were also quite physically alike and did that trick of ending each other's sentences.

'Who plays who on the wireless?' Bea asked, when she was sitting on a comfortable sofa in a tastefully furnished drawing room. A fire burned merrily in the ornate fireplace.

Doris looked up briefly from the tea she was pouring. 'I play Cockney Daisy, who's married to Bert who's a bit simple. Elsie,' she waved the teapot towards her sister, who was busily putting scones on a plate, 'is Gert, who has a boyfriend called Wally.' She began filling another cup with tea. 'Our act didn't start off as a couple of ladies who gossip about their experiences, their men, the war and shortages. It sort of evolved. People fell in love with our characters, especially the nosy neighbour Old Mother Butler. I was told by a soldier in Burma that we reminded him of his mum and her neighbours swapping stories on their doorsteps.' She sighed. 'You can't get a more sincere accolade than that.'

'Praise indeed,' said Bea.

Elsie said, 'We were the first act to go to Burma, you know.'

Bea could see Ivy and Rainey were watching the two women with wide eyes, hanging on their every word. Neither sister had a Cockney accent. These were two exceptionally clever middle-aged, middle-class women, who knew exactly what their audience wanted and gave it to them.

Bea was reminded of someone else who had come into their lives and made a huge impression on them. As though she, too, could read her mind, Doris confirmed this. 'Madame Nellie Walker first told us about you, the Bluebirds, some time ago.' She paused. A look of sadness crossed her face. 'We were abroad entertaining with ENSA when we heard she was killed in a bomb blast. So very needless. So very sad.' She sighed. 'But I digress,' she said. 'One night sitting in her Southsea home, after we'd appeared at the King's and were drinking a glass of very fine port, she asked us to keep an eye on you all when you were "out on the boards", as she called it.'

Bea looked across at Ivy and Rainey, who were trying hard not to spill their tea from the delicate china cups with ridiculously small handles.

'My dear Bea,' Elsie broke in, 'for a start we apologize for not taking Nellie's promise seriously. This damned war has kept us on our toes.' She leaned towards Bea and, in a loud whisper, said, 'I'm sure you don't mind me talking personally in front of your dear friends here. Nellie followed and advanced all of your careers ... but experience had taught her you would all eventually take different routes to find personal happiness.'

Bea stared again at Ivy and then Rainey, who was frowning, then turned to Elsie.

'We've been through a lot together and there are no secrets between us. What do you mean, different routes to happiness?'

She received smiles from her two friends in return for those words.

'Very well,' Elsie said. 'Naturally, Nellie and we were speaking about show business. Nellie was a very straight talker. She told us she was going to use her influence and money to help you on your way. You all had terrific voices, she said, but only one of you had the certain something that equals star quality. The eldest, she told us – that's you, Bea, isn't it? – had had a nasty experience and it had sapped your confidence . . .'

Bea couldn't help it. Horrified, she allowed her mouth to turn into a straight line. 'She told you about that?' she spluttered. Her eyes were wide with disbelief. 'We were told if that incident got out it could hamper our chances of success so we three made a pact never to talk about it. The only other person who knew what happened that night at the Fox was Jo, Rainey's mum.'

'Quite so. I believe Jo had been hired as your chaperone,' Elsie said. 'But you must appreciate she was rather thrown in at the deep end, new to the job . . .'

'So, she asked Nellie's advice?' Bea guessed aloud.

'Yes, dear.'

Bea promptly burst into tears. 'All these years I've been terrified my secret would become common knowledge and I needn't have worried because it already was!'

Rainey put her cup and saucer on a small table, got up and went over to Bea. She pressed her handkerchief into Bea's hands, then sat next to her on the large sofa and put her arms around her.

'Not for everyone to talk about, dear,' Elsie consoled her. 'Your secret was kept by the people who mattered. This is what show business is like – often great sums of money are used to keep a star's private life intact. Especially when your mentor, Madame Nellie Walker, hoped to take you to the very top of the profession.' She suddenly peered at Rainey and Ivy. 'You two also came under close scrutiny,' she added.

Rainey looked affronted. 'What about?'

Elsie smiled at her. 'I repeat what was said earlier. Madame could sense when someone was destined for the top, or likely to wander in a different direction.' She stared at Rainey. 'We never knew her to be wrong. Of course, if she thought the change of path was the best way for the person concerned and she liked you enough, she did all she could to ensure your happiness. She pulled out all the stops, as it were.' She paused. 'You do realize that if someone like Madame was willing to invest a lot of money, she was definitely looking for a return on it?'

'I suppose so.' Bea sniffed. 'But I've been worrying for years that Jo and Blackie might have an almighty row when he found out about that sailor and my drunkenness and that Jo had kept it from him. The two of them set great store by telling each other everything.' Bea suddenly grasped what she was saying. It had never occurred to her before that Jo had kept her bond with her husband, Blackie.

'Why didn't you confide more in Jo, dear?' Doris asked. 'She could have saved your anxiety, especially after dear Nellie died.'

'I couldn't.' Bea sniffed again and wiped her eyes, this time with the handkerchief. 'Oh, my God, I've been worrying all this time about a secret that never was.' She gave a huge sigh and looked at Rainey. 'How big a fool am I?'

Rainey smiled. Bea shook her head. 'Well,' she said, 'I'm glad that's over and done with.' She turned to Elsie. 'It is over and done with, isn't it?'

'Unless in time you become so famous that jealousy

causes a nasty little journalist to dig up the past. Hopefully by then naughty rumours like that will be as water off a duck's back to your followers, Bea.'

Bea dabbed at her eyes again but this time it was happy tears. 'It's been like a weight around my neck.'

'Perhaps,' said Doris. 'But you overcame your fears and got on with it. Blackie also made a mistake in pairing you with that Hanratty fellow. Even so, you came up trumps for Blackie afterwards, didn't you?'

'So, he admits it was a mistake?' Bea asked. 'Making me Hanratty's assistant?'

'Only to himself and maybe to Jo. He's a good agent. But he's also human. He gave you your first chance, dear. Whatever happens in life makes you the person you are,' Doris said. 'You've suffered but you've come through it stronger than ever. Nellie, God bless her, believed in you. She was a damn good judge of character. She was sure you'd be the one who'd go through fire and flood to get to the top.'

'She'd do that all right,' Ivy said.

Doris smiled at Ivy, then continued, 'Madame was aware that singing groups rarely stay together. Even the best bicker and split up. She wanted to support you through alternative futures.'

'Really?' Rainey asked. 'And I was the first to let my heart rule my head. Did you know that? I turned my back on success for the love of a man.'

'She knew you didn't truly want what Bea strove for,' Doris answered. 'Even though your voice is your future.'

'She must have been a witch as well, then!' said Rainey.

Elsie said quietly, 'She wasn't the best in the business for nothing.'

Ivy looked uncomfortable. Elsie focused on her. 'She wasn't far off the mark when she said you . . . would undoubtably give up everything for the love of a good man and children.'

Ivy opened her mouth, closed it, and swallowed before the blush rose from her neck to sweep over her face. 'It's never been a secret that I've always loved Eddie . . .'

So, Bea thought, Madame had known each of them better than they knew themselves.

'You, Bea, unless something dreadful happens, will appear in *It Always Rains On Sunday*,' Elsie said.

'No one has been in contact with me about a screen test and I've not signed anything.'

'Blackie will take care of that, dear, when he talks to Henry Lucas. And all in good time . . . You do know that the book on which the film will be based hasn't yet been published?'

'What do you mean?' Bea was astounded.

'There's going to be an almighty furore about it when it comes out in print. The film rights have been snapped up already, of course.' Elsie was staring at Bea, who was confused. 'I can see you don't yet understand what goes on behind the scenes in show business, my dear, but don't worry. With overseas travel suspended, we'll be around to iron out any little worries you might have when shooting eventually starts.'

Bea felt as if her head might burst with all the information she was being given. But she managed to ask, 'What's the film about?'

'We'll start with the book, dear. This novel by Arthur La Bern is about to become a classic. Set in the East End of London, it's about a single day in 1939. Inevitably it will change the way people think about novels and films. For you to be involved in something of this magnitude is wonderful. Now, films aren't made in a couple of days, especially one that doesn't yet have a proper script. All will be revealed to you, Bea, in due course and then you'll sign a contract after a test.'

'What if the film test is no good?'

'Don't be silly, Bea. You have more charisma that Betty Grable!' This came from Doris.

Bea knew that Elsie and Doris had made films so she wanted desperately to believe them.

'Nothing gets done in five minutes in show business, and usually the shows or films that look like they've been cobbled together so easily have taken the longest time to prepare. There's no such thing as an overnight success,' added Doris.

'So why are you two telling me – us,' Bea glanced at Ivy and Rainey, 'all this now?'

'Because it's about time we put some effort into keeping our promise to dear Nellie.' Elsie stood up and began collecting crockery.

A thought occurred to Bea. 'Does this mean I have a chance of a part in that film only because Madame pulled strings or asked you two to keep an eye on me?' That was not what Bea wanted at all. She wanted to make it to the top on her talent.

'Oh! Dear me, no!' Doris smiled at her. 'You've proved by your own determination and tenacity that you're ready for bigger things, Bea. Nellie was a star herself, remember? She knew all about the casting couch and how some stars reach the top by sleeping with the trade's richest and most unscrupulous men. She'd had experience of stage-door johnnies with their offers of flashy jewels and dinners at expensive restaurants in exchange for sex. She wanted to protect you all, her investments, so to speak, and make sure no harm came to you. She was no longer active, out on the boards, and we are. Henry Lucas realizes you have what is called "a presence", and influential people are watching your career blossom. You are responsible for your own fates, my dears!'

Elsie set down the tray of used crockery on the table. 'Henry Lucas laughed at your naivety, Rainey, in trying to protect Bea. The dear fellow is in a loving and wonderful relationship with a young man who lives with him in his very nice Chelsea home.' She smiled broadly, knowingly. 'Trust me, my dears, there is much to learn about the entertainment business. Nellie cared so much for each of you, which was why she entrusted us to take over where she left off.'

Doris put in, 'What Elsie means is that we are here for the three of you, whether it's your public or private lives. Rainey, Ivy, you do understand that, don't you?' She paused in front of Ivy and studied her intently. 'What exactly do you want from life, dear?'

Ivy looked blank. She fidgeted, then opened her mouth to speak and, as though thinking better of it, closed it again.

Doris smiled warmly at her. 'Sometimes what we most desired isn't what we want, after all. You have a voice like melted honey and once upon a time, so Madame said, all you desired was the stage. She knew your heart rules your head, though. Her judgement was proved to be true when Rainey chose Charlie, and the Bluebirds briefly stopped performing. You, Ivy, were content to put your career on hold and be with that dear child, Gracie, and her hard-working . . . handsome father. I'm right, aren't I?' For a moment there was silence. Then Ivy nodded.

Bea could see Ivy needed to say something and the words suddenly tumbled out.

'I agreed to follow Bea's idea,' she nodded towards Bea, 'and together we came up with the comic magician's act at the Coliseum.'

'Yes, and admirably saved Blackie's skin,' broke in Doris.

'Bea persuaded you into that, didn't she?' The words flew from Rainey's mouth. Bea's face betrayed nothing.

'Well . . . yes,' admitted Ivy. She sat up straight. A look of enlightenment swept across her face. 'Oh, crikey! What you're saying is you think I haven't made up my mind whether I want a family or a career?'

Elsie smiled at her. 'There, you've finally admitted it to yourself! What Doris and I want to do is help you realize your true ambitions, whether they be monetary, the stage, making records or even perhaps homemaking in the future, of course.' Elsie looked at Doris, who nodded. 'We're both here for you, my dear Ivy.'

'Is my future coming under the microscope, next?' Rainey's voice was hesitant. 'Or would I do as well to visit Gypsy Rosa's tent near the pier in Southsea?'

'We've got a clever one here, Doris,' said Elsie, as she patted the waves in her hair. 'We've already heard that you're fed up with living out of a suitcase and that you want to be your own boss . . .'

'. . . and since you're as sharp as a tack, the pain you've already suffered will give you the strength to go for what you want in the future, Rainey.' Doris had finished Elsie's sentence for her. Then she said to Rainey, 'Come to us, dearie. For anything, for everything.' Then she picked up a small brass bell and shook it so that it gave out a jangle of notes. 'And now Timothy will take you three home.'

Chapter Nineteen

The conversation was stilted in the Wolseley on the way back to Gosport. Mostly due to Bea steering away any reference to the sisters with 'We'll talk about that later.'

She preferred complete privacy and Timothy, the chauffeur, was an unknown quantity.

When the car drew up outside the Central Café she said, 'Why don't you two come in for a cuppa? Bert would love to hear about Gert and Daisy.'

'Eddie'll be worried,' said Ivy.

Bea glared at her. 'You can phone him.'

Ivy gave in. Bea had known she would. She wouldn't want to be left out or miss anything that Bert had to add about their visit to Steyning. Rainey had no one waiting at home for her, so Bea guessed she wouldn't mind extending the evening at all. To the chauffeur as he got out to open doors for them, Bea said, 'You're welcome to come in for some tea.' But even as she said it, she knew he would refuse.

Bea pushed against the street door and almost fell inside as Bert unexpectedly opened it. 'I heard a car draw up and I guessed you three had come home,' he said. 'Ooh! Chauffeur-driven! You lot have fallen on your feet!' Bea smiled and nodded. 'I bet you all fancy a cuppa.' Then, 'Something to eat, maybe?'

Bert adjusted the blackout curtains, pulling them tightly closed once they were all inside. He set the kettle to boil.

'Where's Mum?' Ivy asked. Bert had brought some of his precious walking sticks down from upstairs and had been cleaning and polishing them. Brass handles gleamed and metal animal heads shone. Della didn't like him fussing with them when customers were about. When he was alone, he liked to listen to the wireless and think about the stories his sticks might tell. Bea noticed there was an absence of dirty ashtrays and the floor had recently been mopped.

'Della's in bed,' he replied. 'I thought I'd wait up for you. How did you get on with recording today?'

Bea had already taken off her jacket and slipped off her high heels. Rainey and Ivy followed her example. The smell of San Izal disinfectant hung in the air.

'You'll never guess who we've been with,' Bea said.

Bert's blue and white striped apron was grubby. His chin was covered with stubble. He looked tired, but before Bea could say anything else, he turned to Ivy. 'No doubt you'll tell me whose big car that was.' Ivy grinned at him and he went on, 'Eddie phoned a while back. He was worried. I told him I'd offer you all a bed if you came here first. So, if you want, that's what I'll do.'

Bea guessed Ivy would jump at the chance as she'd been yawning her head off in the car coming home, though she seemed to have perked up a bit now.

Rainey said, 'Yes, please.'

Bert looked pleased. 'So, who have you met?' he asked.

'Elsie and Doris Waters!' Their chorus was loud.

'What – Gert and Daisy?' Bert's faded eyes twinkled. The girls began telling him the joke about the bungalow and he nodded and said, 'That's a very old one. Older than some of mine.' But when he was told about the sisters being good friends of Madame Nellie Walker's, he said, 'Tell me something I don't know.'

He produced mugs of tea and before long Bea was asking him questions. 'They've said they'll keep an eye on our future engagements,' she said. 'It seems Madame Nellie had discussed and practically planned our futures for us! Funnily enough, Bert, it's what I think we want for ourselves. Or, at least, the way Fate is pushing us.' She paused. 'Did she ever share any thoughts with you?'

'Me and her had a few heart-to-hearts in our time. She was one of us, despite her money, you know.'

Ivy said, 'Remember when she gave that fox fur to my mum?'

Bert said, 'Della and the rest of us was in her posh house at Southsea and she calmly took off that expensive wrap and handed it to my Della, simply because she admired it.'

'Yes,' Ivy said. 'Later, when I asked Mum how she'd had the nerve to leave the house with that thing, she said if she'd refused to take it, Nellie would have been hurt. She'd given the fur out of friendship, not charity. My mum always said Madame had the ability to identify herself mentally with like-minded people.'

'She did.' Bert nodded. 'She had a special way of understanding folk, of bringing out the best in people.' He took a long slurp of his tea.

'Madame never expected to die so soon,' Rainey mused. 'Do you think she wrote anything down about us? Do you think she left instructions or told Blackie?'

'I doubt it,' Bert said. 'You never think you might die suddenly, do you? But she knew Blackie was capable of running the business she loved. She wrote a will leaving it all to him, didn't she?'

Bert was quiet now, mulling things over. The wireless, too, was silent, off the air for the night.

He stared at Rainey. 'I think when God closes a door, he opens a window. You, my girl, have tasted great sorrow early in life but there's untapped strength in you, mark my words.' He paused. 'I don't think you need to be told how to live your lives,' he said suddenly. 'The three of you look after each other well enough. But Nellie was a wise lady and knew the business inside out. Advice from Elsie and Doris Waters certainly won't hurt, will it?'

Bea shook her head. 'Madame worried unscrupulous people might take advantage of us.'

'Did she?' Bert frowned. 'And who might they be?'

'She meant the casting couch,' said Rainey, sipping her tea.

Bert spluttered tea, which dribbled down his apron. 'Fair enough.'

Bea saw the back of his neck begin to glow red, from his ears down to his collar.

After a minute or two, he asked her, 'Did you tell them about Bing?'

'Since falling for him, I feel differently about men,' she said quietly. 'He's part of my healing process. We love each other but we've no idea what will happen after the war. I somehow had the feeling that if I'd said I wanted to marry, they would have said, "Not yet awhile, dear. Taste fame first. When you're established, then think about it."' Ivy and Rainey fell about laughing. Bea had copied Elsie's middle-class voice to a T.

Bert put his hand on her arm. 'That young man cares deeply for you, Bea.' He was thoughtful. 'Anyway, aren't you supposed to be seeing him soon?'

'Next weekend,' said Bea. 'But, as I've already said, there's been no contact between us.'

Ivy set her mug on the table. 'I'm glad I don't want so much from show business. I never thought I'd hear myself say this but I actually prefer walking along the beach at Stokes Bay with Eddie and picking up shells, with Gracie beside us.'

Bea sat back in amazement. 'Really?'

'Yes,' said Ivy. 'And I do want to go on entertaining people, it's my job until my destiny for motherhood is ful-filled.' She added, 'But not at the cost you'll most certainly have to pay, Bea.'

'Oh, and what's that?' Bea's voice was sharp.

'Of people watching your every move, the newsmen ready to take photos of you and splashing every little thing all over the papers.'

193

Bea looked at Bert. He nodded sagely. 'Could you cope with that? Or would you prefer to settle down with Bing in America or here in England?'

For a moment Bea was quiet, thinking. Then she said, ignoring Bert's question, 'Talking to Elsie and Doris Waters today has certainly opened up a whole can of worms. I'm glad we're sitting here with you, Bert, thinking and talking about our futures. It seems now as if we all want different things.'

Bert scratched his head. 'It's good to get it all out in the open. That brings me to another question I've been thinking about. Bea, you, like Ivy and Rainey, should have a little nest egg put by. What are you going to do? Leave it to accumulate?'

'You mean am I going to buy a place of my own and move out?' Bea frowned. 'I like living here with you and Della. If I bought a house, I could share it with Bing. But we've decided nothing about the future.' Her eyes suddenly filled with tears. 'You and Della keep my feet on the ground. I'm never lonely here at the café because there's always something going on. You're not going to throw me out, are you?'

Bert put his large hand on hers. 'Never,' he said, and smiled at her.

'I know what I want,' said Rainey. 'I'll stay here in Gosport. It's my home. It's like a big warm overcoat and I feel safe here. Well, as safe as we can be with the war still raging on. I want to go on making my living by entertaining people but without being like Bea, right in the public eye.'

'What do you mean by that, Rainey?' Bert had finished his tea and pushed his mug to the centre of the table.

'You all know I want to stop gadding about,' Rainey told them. 'I'd like a place of my own, to be my own boss, but still sing because I love it so much.'

Bert was smiling at her as if her words made sense.

'Are you not going to ask me?' Ivy was wriggling about on her chair, like her knickers were on fire.

'I thought you'd already said you're happy with Eddie. Go on then, Ivy—'

Rainey got no further for Ivy blurted, 'Being on the stage now doesn't really mean as much to me as it did before. I want a baby with Eddie. I want a bigger house. I believe Eddie's work is going to take off after the war and hopefully he'll make a lot of money. I want eventually to be a wife with Gracie and a child of my own. I want to cook Eddie big dinners and maybe even have yet another baby.'

'For God's sake, shut her up,' said Rainey, with a laugh. 'She's making my head ache.' Then she yawned. 'I'm ready for bed. Is it all right if I sleep in your room with you, Bea? I'm on my own enough as it is in Albert Street.'

'I'll let you sleep in with me,' said Ivy.

'No fear! And have you chewing my ear all night about babies!'

Bert began gathering up some of the polished walking sticks. Bea knew he would carry them reverently back upstairs to the room that was their home. He stopped what he was doing. 'And if you ask me what I think, it's that none of you need any advice about your futures. You all seem to have worked out exactly what you want for yourselves.'

His last words were for Bea. 'Bing'll be there, if he can be, at the Alhambra, you mark my words, Bea love.'

Chapter Twenty

'She's a smasher, Bing. It's a bloody shame we're confined to base when she's going to be appearing on stage close by.' Si Cusack handed him back the photograph of Bea. 'I can see why you've never put it up where it could be seen, though. A beautiful girl like that going around with you! You'd sure get some stick from some of the guys.'

'You're supposed to be my friend, not do me down.'

'I'm only teasing you, man, you should know that.'

Bing looked at him, then took a deep breath. 'I know.' He laughed, a full-throated sound that was contrary to the way he was feeling. 'She'll be thinking I don't love her . . .' He turned down the page of the novel he'd been reading and slipped the photo back inside the last letter he'd had from Bea.

'You're not the only one fed up we've no leave and we're

being drilled and drilled, then drilled again for this damned exercise. You've just got to hold on to how it will feel later when it's all over and you can take her in your arms again,' Si said. He was watching as Bing slipped the envelope between the pages of Ernest Hemingway's *For Whom the Bell Tolls*.

'How did you get on with the chaplain?' Si asked.

'He said he'd see what he could do – he'd talk to someone else about leave, but I don't hold out much hope.'

'Oh, why's that?'

'Because I've begged everyone else to help me. He was my last resort. And his office was filled with other men asking him the same thing. I don't know who the hell is left for me to beg to get a few hours off to go and see my Bea.' He sighed. 'This is pretty serious stuff we're into here, I know that. And the only good thing to come out of it is that I've met the woman of my dreams. Even better, she's in love with me. Just imagine that!'

'I can't,' Si said. 'I can just about get my head around someone as beautiful as that even talking to you. No wonder you've kept her a secret.'

'Yeah! Just like it's supposed to be a secret that there's some thirty-two English cruisers waiting in Start Bay to take part in this exercise. Surely no one can ignore the night-time explosions and all this extra seaborne activity.'

'And imagine,' said Si, 'if every one of those troops broadcasts to their families and girlfriends what's going on.'

'We all know how to keep secrets!' Bing raised his voice.

'A few words in the wrong ears could spell trouble for everyone. Secrecy has to be the key.'

'And we all know this is Exercise Tiger, the rehearsal for the proposed landings on Utah Beach in France.'

'But it's more than just that, Bing. It's one hundred and fifty-six thousand men, including us Yanks. Over a thousand warships, guarding four thousand landing craft and almost two thousand ancillary and merchant vessels, supported by eleven thousand aircraft, with over three thousand gliders.'

'Trust you to know the exact numbers . . .'

'I listen and I take note of what's going on around me.' Bing could see his friend was getting hot under the collar. 'The intention is to simulate the real landings in full here at Slapton Sands because this terrain is most like that of France. This scene setting has to be as real as possible. We have to use live ammunition and have effective communication between all those concerned in the operation.'

'Effective communication? That's a joke! Nearly all the men are inexperienced. And how come, Si, you know more about what's going on than I do?'

'As I said, perhaps it's because I take notice of what's

going on around me and read bulletin boards, unlike you who always has his nose in a book.'

Bing laughed. 'Man, I think I've heard those words from you before.' His laugh grew louder. 'But I'm not the one whose forgotten we're supposed to go down and get booster tetanus jabs in preparation for the assault.'

Bing saw Si was laughing now. He glared. 'What's so funny?'

'The last tetanus injection I had put me in a fever and on my back for a few days. It's down on my notes that I get a reaction. But do they take any notice?' Si shook his head. 'No, they don't,' he said. 'The army knows best.'

'Cheer up, lad, you knew he was ill.'

Eddie swept back his blond hair with one hand. He glared at his mother, who was standing in the scullery doorway watching him. In the other hand he held his safety razor and was just about to break through the shaving soap on his chin to allow the blade to take off the day's stubble. From the wireless came the sound of his sister singing.

'I can't have a proper shave with you talking to me. I'll cut my throat,' he said. He put the razor down on the wooden draining board and turned to face her, using the flannel to wipe around his mouth. 'Yes, I've known the bloke a few years and I was aware he was never going to make it back home to Germany. But the last time I saw Hans I thought being in the infirmary was doing him some good. It certainly never occurred to me he was that close to dying.'

'But you hadn't seen him for a while . . .'

'True. Apparently, he died just before his mate Max got to see him.'

'Is that the blond feller used to work with you who run off and got caught?'

'It is.' Eddie looked into the small mirror hanging by the window on a bit of string. He used the flannel to wipe off more of the shaving soap. He looked at the shaving brush. He'd need to reapply the soap for a decent shave.

Maud continued, 'You said he does the work of two men. Wasn't he the one who got the truck running?'

'Yes.' He faced her. His mother was like a cat at a mouse-hole until she found out what she wanted to know.

'And it's him you've invited round for a bit of dinner on Saturday? Are you allowed to do that?'

'The bloke has saved me a great deal of money by fixing my truck. While he works for me, I feed him. That's standard practice. I thought him having a bite to eat with us would show him how grateful I am and that not all English people hate the Germans. He's a good bloke, Mum. How would you like to be in a hostile country without family? Ivy's all for showing him a bit of compassion.'

Maud was mulling over his words. 'Ivy shows everyone too much compassion! Fools rush in where angels fear to tread, my son. You don't really know the bloke, do you? He fixes your transport and you welcome him into our home with open arms. Still waters run deep, I say, and he's a German, not one of our kind.' She paused. 'But she's not likely to be here, is she? Ivy, I mean. Isn't she away doing a show somewhere in Devon?'

'She's leaving here on the twenty-second of April, the Saturday, or Sunday the twenty-third, depending on transport. What does it matter? All I'm proposing is we show a bloke who helped me out of trouble a bit of common courtesy. Now there's nothing wrong with that, is there?' Eddie tried to assert his authority by frowning at her while waiting for her answer. His mother had endured two wars with the Germans so she had every right to question his motives. But he knew her through and through and she wasn't about to let him down by not providing a bite to eat for a friend, even if that friend was a German.

'At least we've got a bed each!' Bea threw her cardboard suitcase onto the single bed nearest the window. The off-white nets with the daisies climbing heavenwards stopped people staring in.

'There's mould on the curtains,' said Ivy.

'And that dressing-table mirror has a crack right across the middle,' added Bea, looking around the dingy room

'You didn't break it, so you're not the one looking forward to seven years' bad luck, Bea.' Rainey, as usual, was the peacemaker. 'Look on the bright side. The Oakdene Hotel is only a few steps away from the Alhambra, so if it rains we haven't far to go. We've stopped at worse places. Remember when—'

Bea didn't let her finish. 'Damn Blackie!'

'For once I agree with you, Bea,' said Ivy. 'To get a phone call from him telling us we're doing a midweek show instead of our usual weekend slot is a bit much. I promised Eddie I was going to be nice to some prisoner of war he's invited round for a meal.'

'Good job you can't be there, then. I thought the English weren't allowed to mix socially with the Germans,' said Rainey.

'Apparently there's a difference between fraternizing and being hospitable,' said Ivy. She took off her suit jacket and opened up the large rickety wardrobe door. 'Would you look at this! Four bloody hangers between the three of us for all of our clothes!'

'The change isn't Blackie's fault. Bloody Beryl Ingham, being George Formby's wife and manager, decided not to play fair about the bookings.' Rainey set her suitcase on the middle bed and tried once again to make peace. 'George Formby's a huge star. He does what his wife says, and if she aims for the weekend houses that mean bigger audiences, who are we to complain? Anyway, she doesn't want us appearing on the same programme with him, in case he looks at us. She's jealous as hell!'

'He's a nice bloke but I don't fancy him, do you?' Ivy pulled a face. She didn't wait for an answer to her question. 'Blackie said we'd still be paid the original offer, maybe a bit more for our inconvenience. But Eddie's not best pleased with me because I did say I'd be there to welcome this Max bloke—'

'She's a champion clog-dancer is Beryl Ingham,' broke in Rainey. She pulled back the candlewick bedcover and inspected the sheets.

'Yes, well, if I had the chance and could do it, I'd clog-dance all over her.' Bea was not happy. 'This weekend is supposed to be when I'm meeting Bing . . .'

'*Supposed* to meet Bing. And supposed is the right word,' stressed Rainey. Now there was an edge to her voice. 'You've heard nothing from him and he might not even be in this country. This is bloody wartime, Bea, and Bing's a soldier . . .'

She said no more for Bea had suddenly burst into tears and now sat on her bed with her hands over her face, her shoulders heaving, as she sobbed her heart out.

'Well done,' said Ivy. 'Now look what you've done. You've made her cry!'

Rainey glared at her, then at Bea, and chucked the bed-cover back over the sheets. Standing up, she said, 'Bugger the pair of you. I'm going to find the landlady and ask about our evening meal and some hot water for a bath.'

She slammed the door so hard on her way out of the room that one of the three plaster ducks in flight fell off the wall.

Bea stood in her usual place at the side of the stage. Tonight, 26 April, was to be the Bluebirds' last night topping the bill at the Alhambra. If she could, she would leave Devon this very minute and go home to Gosport. But her pride wouldn't let her run out on Ivy and Rainey. She'd also signed a contract with Blackie and would never let him down.

Her heart felt like a lump of lead. Where was Bing? What was going on? She hadn't thought loving someone could hurt so much.

In a few moments Ivy and Rainey would be joining her and the three of them would go on stage. She would sing her heart out for the patrons who had paid for their seats in the splendid gold-painted Edwardian theatre. The show must go on. Wasn't that the mantra of every artist? She took a peep through a gap in the curtains and saw the tobacco smoke rising like a mist above the red velvet seats.

The first time she had stepped on stage in a theatre filled with people she'd thought she would never get used to the different smells. Now they were as familiar to her as the magic of what she did for a living. Every theatre held its own spell-binding charm, with scents of freshly painted scenery, old make-up and the blood, sweat and tears of everyone who had ever appeared there on stage. Momentarily she wondered how many other performers after disappointments or bad news had stood where she was standing now, and willed themselves to put a smile on their faces, go out and entertain, pretending their hearts were whole.

The three of them had, as usual, chosen their numbers with great care. Ivy was singing 'Stormy Weather' solo, Rainey 'Sunday, Monday or Always', also solo. 'You'll Never Know' was Bea's choice. Their other songs, well loved and emotional, had been chosen because the music would have sentimental meanings for the audience.

The auditorium was full. The hum of chattering voices filled the air. She stared up at the boxes high above each side of the stage. These were the most expensive seats in the house. All except one was filled to capacity. It remained empty, but she doubted it would stay that way. The Bluebirds usually played to packed houses, whether it was the general public or servicemen.

'Watch it!' Bea's voice was sharp as Ivy's high-heeled shoe grazed her foot. Luckily, unable to get hold of proper nylons, all of them were wearing fakes from a bottle. Bea knew she was being unnecessarily bad-tempered so she smiled apologetically at Ivy, who mouthed, 'Sorry.' She allowed the curtain to fall back into place.

Rainey, in a cloud of floral scent, stepped behind Bea, and positioned herself ready to lead them on stage when the orchestra began playing. Bea thought they all looked sensational. They were wearing full-length glittery black frocks dressed up with simple gold jewellery. A wide bangle for Bea, drop earrings for Rainey, which glittered when she flicked her red hair back from her face, and a thin gold belt looped around Ivy's tiny waist was all they needed to look similar, yet different.

Bea took another peep from behind the curtains. She saw that Sammy was standing at the rear bar chatting to a young woman. They were laughing, looking pretty pally. Perhaps, as he wasn't accompanying the Bluebirds on the piano, he was hoping to take her home after the performance. Bea wondered where he was sleeping tonight. It wasn't often he stayed in the same lodgings as them, though a bed for the night was part of his wages. Sammy had already said he'd be waiting with the van, outside their digs, at nine in the morning for the journey home.

The orchestra in the pit began playing. Then the musicians slowed and quietened for the announcements. At the Bluebirds' introduction the audience began clapping and the heavy curtains rolled back as the three girls sashayed towards the microphones at centre stage. Bea took a deep breath and composed her face in a welcoming smile.

Yes, she thought, this was what made her whole and truly happy. Performing. Giving people joy. Her eyes searched the eager faces of the patrons in the seats below the stage. Definitely a packed house. She glanced across and up to the boxes. Still one remained empty.

Ivy was welcoming the audience tonight, and giving out a little saucy chat. Usually this job fell to Bea but she'd begged Ivy to take over. As tonight's first solo singer, Bea was determined to give the people their money's worth. Just because she was desperately unhappy, there was no need for the audience to know. Her smile was her badge of courage.

At Ivy's introduction Bea took a single step forward.

'You'll Never Know' was her opening song. A movement in the empty box caught her eye and caused her to look across. The tall man sat down swiftly, took off his peaked cap and set it on the empty seat beside him. He looked towards the stage. At her.

"'How much do I love you . . .'" Bea's words were deep, questioning.

"'How much do I care . . .'" The second line came from her lips, which suddenly parted in a huge smile and a feeling of relief as she saw the man in the drab olive suit sitting alone in the box and smiling at her was Bing.

Chapter Twenty-one

'I thought I was never going to see you again.'

'Shh, honey.'

His face, shining in the moonlight with amusement, relaxed Bea. He knows how I feel because he's been feeling the same, she thought. His body was a warm, rich brown and hers looked startlingly pale beside it in the metal bed. She had willed herself to get past the shock of lying with a man for the first time in her life, for this was not any man, this was Bing, her man. The man who had dominated her every thought from the first time they'd met.

His chest was smooth with practically no hair, the muscles well defined. He smelled of fresh sweat mixed with cologne and she breathed him in before running her hand over his taut stomach and holding it there for a second. It really was her Bing, and everything was going to be all right.

Bea took a deep breath. She needed to gather her thoughts and try to understand why and how she was afraid of something she had longed for.

Bing kissed her then, at first gently, then harder, almost bruising her lips. She ran her hands down the length of his silky back.

'Mm! Bea, I could eat you all up.' His whisper was warm on her face. And then he was on her, making her moan as he began to kiss her body, lingering at her breasts, then over her stomach, down past the line of blonde hair that led between her legs.

Bea felt as if she was drowning in his kisses. She allowed her legs to fall open, and Bing said, 'I won't hurt you. Trust me, Bea.'

And she did. She trusted him with every fibre of her being. And she was lost to love's magic.

Later, she awoke. His lush body was sprawled over the bed across the rumpled blankets and he was breathing deeply. So that's what it's all about, she thought. That's what I've been missing all these years. And a smile touched her lips, blooming across her face. She felt calm and happy. She was remembering what had happened last night before they had arrived at the tiny village bed-and-breakfast in the jeep Bing had borrowed from his base.

She remembered his words as he had met her backstage, then pulled her into his arms. It was as if the detritus lying around from the previous acts, the performers and stage-hands milling about didn't exist.

'I have until seven in the morning. I was granted a twenty-four-hour pass,' he said, after his lips had left hers. 'Someone up there,' he nodded heavenwards, 'is looking after me. I've booked us a place. Can you come now?'

'I should change.' Bea shivered. Already there was a fall in the temperature backstage.

'Go quickly!' Ivy said. 'Before people start wandering around here to meet us.' She spotted a black knitted shawl, grabbed it and hung it around Bea's shoulders. 'Make sure you're back in time for Sammy to pick us up.' Bea stared at her. 'Go!' Ivy shouted.

Bing had driven the canvas-covered vehicle out into the countryside. She snuggled beside him, content. Sometimes they talked at the same time, touching and kissing as though they expected each other to evaporate into thin air. The road followed a small river to a village. The moonlight showed a water mill, and by its side a row of cottages. Bing halted the jeep outside one. He didn't need to ring the doorbell as a small, aproned, grey-haired lady already had the door on the latch and was waiting.

Bea was amazed at how she welcomed them inside, seemingly unbothered that a white girl in a revealing sequined dress beneath an old fringed shawl should be crossing her doorstep with a black American in the depths of a cold spring night.

'You got her, then?' was all she said, before lighting the way up the crooked stairs and opening a door.

'I did, Mrs Donnelly,' replied Bing. The woman's face crinkled into a huge smile.

At the top of the stairway in the confined space he picked up Bea and carried her into the chintzy bedroom. 'Carrying you across the threshold is an English custom?'

'Only if we're married,' laughed Bea.

'After tonight, we might as well be,' Bing said.

He set her down on the iron bed as the door closed behind them.

She scrambled to a sitting position. 'You told her about us?'

Bing pulled off his tie, threw it onto the floor and smiled at her. 'It's wartime and she can remember her own romance from the last war,' he whispered. 'Never make the mistake of believing it's only the young who have ever loved.'

'Let's not talk about her now we've got each other,' Bea said, pulling him close.

Later, much later, he explained about leave being cancelled. He stressed, 'After this exercise has been completed, I'm sure everything will go back to normal.'

'But I don't understand. Why is it so important?'

'I can't tell you, honey . . .' And then Bea no longer cared about the past or the future because she had this night and Bing, and he was kissing her and that was all that mattered.

Eventually they slept, entwined like the roots of a tree.

And now she could no longer stand it that she was awake and this lovely man was lying apart from her, asleep. Giant shadows danced happily on the walls as clouds crossed the bright moon shining in from the window. As if wishing made it so, she felt his body stir. He murmured sleepily, 'Come here, honey.' Then Bing slid across the sheet and pulled her close, breathing on her neck. The smell of his spicy cologne mixed with the muskiness of his body caused an overwhelming desire to rise inside Bea, spilling over, drenching her with its warmth.

His fingers traced the outline of her body, moving slowly down to her hips and stroking the insides of her thighs. And then she was drowning, his kisses smothering her, and she wanted the moment never to end. Bing moved his tongue between her teeth and she responded, feeling as if she was riding a wave that threatened to drown her, and she didn't care because she was loving the man who loved her . . .

'C'mon, sleepyhead.'

Bea opened her eyes to see Bing, fully dressed, standing over her. On the bedside table there was a tray with china cups and a matching teapot, steam curling gently from its spout. She smiled at him, remembering last night.

He winked at her as though he was reading her mind. 'You don't know how much I want to get back into bed with you,' he said. 'But I promised to be back at camp by seven and I have to honour that promise . . .' His voice tailed off as he looked at her with such love in his eyes that she wanted to cry. He took a deep breath. 'Mrs Donnelly left the tray outside our door,' he said. 'Don't let your English tea grow cold.' He smiled.

Later, sitting in the jeep driving back to the Oakdene Hotel, the early-morning mist had allowed thin fingers of sunshine to break through. Bea was cold, despite wearing Bing's jacket over the top of the shawl. She felt sad. There was none of the excitable chatter of the previous night. She struggled to find something to say that would lighten the atmosphere.

'Good weather's on its way at last,' said Bing, his hand covering hers as he drove.

She smiled. Even Americans talked about the weather when all else was said. 'Don't let this little bit of sunshine fool you,' she said, snuggling into the man she loved. 'English Aprils can be filled with storms.' As the words left her mouth, unease swept over her. She turned and looked at the profile of his head, nose and chin as he drove and knew she would remember that moment for the rest of her life.

Soon the countryside was lost to them and the town, with its shops and houses, appeared. He stopped the jeep outside the Oakdene and Bea scrambled out, closely followed by Bing. Bea didn't want the kiss to end but she forced herself to lean towards the window and scratch on the glass. Almost immediately a tousled, sleepy Rainey was pushing up the sash.

'I'll phone as soon as I can,' he whispered, taking back his jacket from her.

'I don't want you to leave me,' Bea said. She knew she must send him away with a smile. She'd had the most wonderful night of her life, but already tears were welling.

'Climb in here,' growled Rainey, her head now outside the window. 'You want the landlady to catch you?'

Moments later the sound of the jeep had disappeared and

Bea was sitting on her bed with Rainey and Ivy on either side of her. All she could say was, 'I love him so much. Now I know what it's all about. I never knew I could feel like this about a man.'

Chapter Twenty-two

He turned the hand-beaten mug around in his fingers. The condensed-milk tin had been polished until it gleamed. It seemed superbly made. It had cost Max one paper packet of five Wills Woodbines. It was a gift for Eddie. Another five cigarettes, Turkish this time, alas, had bought him two dressed peg dolls, a boy and a girl. He had thought to make sure there were no sharp edges on them as he had remembered that very young children put everything into their mouths. Max knew it was customary to bring gifts when invited to people's homes. However, there was little he could steal at the St Vincent holding centre to serve his purpose.

Now he was sitting with his gifts wrapped in newspaper in the front seat of Eddie's vehicle. Eddie had requested Max's help from the works officer at the prison and it had been granted for three hours.

As the van turned into Alma Street, Max was surprised that Eddie Herron should live in such a dilapidated area. There was a bombed-out house opposite number fourteen, and even though most of the rubble and rubbish had been tidied away, it would be a macabre sight to greet one on drawing back the curtains each morning. Much of the Gosport Max had seen looked run-down. However, the local people refused to be cowed. Lately, though, Hitler's assault on the south coast seemed to have lessened. Max wondered what new tricks the Führer had up his sleeve to win this war. Staring at Eddie's modest home, he decided that Eddie either cared little about what other people thought, or that he was happier staying true to his roots. Eddie Herron was certainly no one's fool.

'Welcome to my home,' Eddie said, smiling warmly at Max. He, of course, had no idea of the turmoil going on inside his German friend's head. He was unaware that soon Max would be meeting his own daughter for the first time.

Max followed Eddie down a darkened passage into a small kitchen that had a fire burning in the grate. He could smell fragrant cooked food. His mouth began to water. An elderly woman with a kind face sat in a comfortable-looking but sagging and dilapidated armchair. She rose to greet him. A table in the centre of the room was set with four kitchen chairs. It was covered with clean tea-towels, hiding what Max guessed were cold dishes she'd prepared. He was immediately struck by how peaceful the environment was, and felt humbled that the woman had gone to so much trouble to welcome him.

'Hello, Mum,' said Eddie. 'This is Max.'

Max stepped forward and shook the hand she proffered. He put his wrapped gifts on the white tablecloth and Maud gave him a smile. 'Hello, son, call me Maud. I was just taking a five-minute break. Our Gracie was a holy terror earlier, but she's having a nap outside now.' She waved her hand towards the window. Max could see a tall blue and white pram standing at the scullery's back door. 'She's been fractious lately,' continued Maud, 'more teeth coming through.'

Max knew what that meant: he'd been taught excellent English back home in Germany. He liked that Maud knew what ailed the child and could make allowances for her.

The blankets covering the pram moved. Max saw a tiny hand raised into the air. The child struggled into a sitting position and he had a clear view of a safety-harness strapped around her body to stop her falling from the pram. The little girl looked expectantly towards the kitchen window. Then she opened her mouth and began to cry.

'Someone's awake,' said Eddie, and went out of the

kitchen. Max saw the little girl put up her arms for him to lift her from the pram. He also saw that the cry died on her lips the moment she saw him and was replaced by a wide smile. Before picking her up Eddie kissed the child. It was clear to Max there was trust and love between man and child. A sudden dart of confusion, perhaps envy, pierced his heart.

Max couldn't help himself. 'She's beautiful,' he breathed. He saw the delicate features of her mother, Sunshine, etched on her face. And her blonde hair was exactly the shade of his own.

Maud said, 'She's the spit of our Bea when she was a kiddie.'

Max had to tear his eyes away from the window. Within moments Eddie had unbuckled Gracie's harness and was standing in the warm kitchen with her in his arms, looking extremely proud.

'A sleep in the fresh air does her good,' said Maud. 'But she always lets us know when she's had enough.' Max made himself look again at the food-filled table. It would be embarrassing for either Eddie or his mother to notice him avidly watching the child. Perhaps they'd comment upon him staring at her.

'Give her here,' demanded Maud. Eddie passed the child

to her. The little girl went happily to her, reaching out her arms just as she'd done with Eddie.

'You don't mind if I stay like this awhile, do you, Eddie?' Without waiting for an answer Maud settled herself back in the chair, Gracie on her lap, adding, 'As you can see, I've set the table. Welcome to our home, Max.' Maud began easing Gracie out of her knitted leggings and coatee, which looked warm and comfortable on the child, if a little grubby.

'Thank you,' Max said quietly. 'I have a gift for the little girl, and also for you, Eddie.' He smiled at him, then turned towards the packages. To Maud, he said, 'I apologize that I have nothing for you, Maud. Nor, sadly, do I have a gift for Eddie's woman who is not here, today. As you can appreciate, I cannot buy items such as you might find in the shops but I have these hand-made trinkets . . .'

Max put the mug into Eddie's hand; the crumpled piece of brown paper it was wrapped in fell to the floor. Max scooped it up and set it down on the sideboard.

Eddie turned the polished object in his fingers and stared at it. 'It's very kind of you. Look at this, Mum,' he said, showing her the mug and watching her smile, obviously admiring it, as Eddie himself did.

Max felt the emotion in Eddie's words, and wondered at Eddie and Maud's gullibility in inviting him into their home.

How easy they were making it for him to achieve a plan for himself – and his daughter – to disappear from their lives. He allowed hope to blossom once more in his heart. He'd been making tentative enquiries about the man Sunshine had worked for, who had provided her with his forged identity papers. Having escaped before from the holding centre, he could do it again. Of course he could. He would leave England, this time taking his daughter with him.

He said brightly, 'I have discovered no sharp edges on these.' He removed the newspaper covering the peg dolls. 'I know young children put everything into their mouths—'

'Eddie, put the kettle on,' interrupted Maud. 'And, for God's sake, take off your coats, the pair of you. You won't feel the benefit when you go out.' Max had already caught the glint of tears in Eddie's eyes as he had produced the dolls. He was a soft-hearted man, thought Max. He wasn't sure that his own countrymen would show such kindness to the enemy.

'Mending the van was good of you,' Maud said. Max could tell she was embarrassed by his gifts and was trying to put matters on a less emotional footing. 'Sit down, Max. Take off the tea-towels, and get started on the meal. It's probably not what you're used to back home but rationing . . .'

Eddie had already disappeared into the scullery to make

tea, so Max began to remove the covers from the bowls and plates. He stared at a dish of bright green leaves.

'That's watercress that is, fresh this morning from the watercress man.'

Droplets of water glistened on it.

'Go on, taste it,' urged Maud, Gracie lolling across her lap.

He picked off a small stem and put it into his mouth. 'It tastes peppery,' he said, chewing, then swallowing. He frowned at first but soon the frown was replaced by a grin. Max decided it was like eating peppery lettuce.

'Between slices of fresh bread, that's a right treat,' Maud said. 'Hampshire grows the best watercress. A man comes around selling it off a barrow but you have to be quick as it's soon sold out. There's fresh bread, baked this morning, from Peacocks, the baker's. And that lovely smell is a Woolton pie. Our minister of food came up with that. My Woolton pie is a little different, as a friend of ours, Bert, made me a present of half a pound of bacon.' She tapped her nose. 'Don't ask where he gets his bacon from, lad.' She laughed throatily. 'There's a syrup loaf and some scones I made this morning, too.'

Max sat up straight. 'You've gone to a lot of trouble for me,' he said. 'Thank you.' It had been a long time since anyone had held out a genuine hand of friendship to him.

Hans had been his friend, hadn't he? And look at how that had ended. But it had been necessary to cut short Hans's life for Max's own self-preservation. Surely the ease with which he had died had been better than a lingering painful death. Eddie and his mother would be deeply hurt to lose the child but he must not allow himself to worry about their feelings when it was important to him that he and his child leave England.

Maud's voice broke into his thoughts. 'It means a great deal for Eddie to have the truck on the road and you made that possible. So, thank you again, lad.'

Just then the little girl whimpered and opened her blue eyes. Maud struggled up from the chair. 'Take her for a moment. I'll help Eddie with the tea.'

Max now sat in the comfortable chair, awkwardly holding his daughter, while Eddie brought in a teapot and cups on a tray. From the scullery came the click of the oven door and suddenly Max welcomed the delicious smell of cooked food.

He looked down at Gracie, who stared openly up at him. Her soft skin was pink from being outside. Her blue eyes were clear, unblinking. She opened her mouth in a yawn and he saw the budded tips of white that were her newly growing teeth. A sudden rush of protectiveness flowed through him. This little girl was of his blood, of his body . . .

'Won't be a moment, Max, the top's nicely browning.' Maud's voice came from the scullery. Max realized she wanted the food to be as perfect as possible for him. Rationing in England meant food was in short supply. Yet Eddie and his mother had welcomed him into their home to share what they had with him. These were kind people.

He knew now why Sunshine had chosen Eddie to rear her child. Why it was necessary for her to sleep with the builder. She was an extremely clever young woman who, knowing that Max, imprisoned, would not be able to provide security for her child, had decided on Eddie as a surrogate father. A back-up father who would not shirk his responsibilities.

Today Eddie and Maud had unwittingly welcomed a serpent into their nest. Max looked down at his daughter and felt like crying.

Chapter Twenty-three

Bing, along with forty other men, boarded *LST 507* in the bay during the afternoon of 27 April.

'You'd have thought they'd give us instructions on how to put on these damned things,' he said. Wearing full battle-dress, backpack and carrying his rifle was bad enough, but the uninflated lifebelts were cumbersome and heavy.

'Yeah, we should have been shown how to wear them,' Red Simmons said, so-called due to his bright hair. He, like Bing and many of the others, found it easier to wear the lifebelt around his middle.

'In an emergency we gather at the designated muster stations,' Bing said. 'Then we listen to the loudspeakers for instruction. At least we know that much.'

LST 507 was the last of the convoy and was loaded to the gills with transport, equipment and army personnel.

The evening before, while in barracks, Bing had visited the sick-bay where Si, as he had prophesied, had had a severe reaction to the tetanus shot. A massively high temperature had put him out of action.

'All that practising and y'all don't get to go.' Bing had laughed at his friend and handed him Ernest Hemingway's book. 'You can read this and let me know what you think of it when I get back,' he said. After delving into his pocket he'd held a sealed envelope between his fingers and added, 'I'd like it if you could post this for me. As soon as I saw the bulletin board and knew we were off I wrote a short letter to Bea.'

'Not a problem,' said Si. 'I'll make sure she gets it.' Bing could see his friend was sweating and uncomfortable, so he hadn't lingered.

Since boarding the *507* and installing himself in his shared quarters, Bing had regularly checked the bulletin board for further assignments and discovered he was on guard duty from midnight to five a.m. There were no further instructions.

With another soldier he took a walk about the tank deck to gather his bearings and found it was loaded with land-trucks and amphibious craft, packed so tightly together that it was almost impossible to walk between them.

'Since this is only another drill, I guess it doesn't matter that we've never been told what do in a real emergency,' Red said. His brown eyes twinkled, giving colour to his pale face. He had been born in Oklahoma and frequently extolled the virtues of wide-open spaces. So frequently, that Bing longed for his bunk, a coffee and a book.

'I think we'd better get back to our sleeping quarters where there's sure to be a game of cards going on, or something similar,' Bing said.

Of course he was right, and after a shower and a coffee, Bing and Red played poker with a few of the other men. Some soldiers slept, some read, others sat on their bunks and chatted.

'This is a run-up to when we actually storm the French beaches,' one of the players, Alfred, said. He pushed an open packet of Hershey's cookies across the table towards Bing, who shook his head. 'That's D-Day, not an exercise drill.' He studied his poker hand.

'Are you worried about finally landing in France?' Bing asked.

'Piece of cake,' said Red. 'We've had enough dry runs.'

The words were hardly out of his mouth when there was a terrific bang and the room shook. Cards fluttered to the floor, followed by swearing from the men.

The door opened and a voice shouted, 'Torpedo! Get dressed and on deck!'

'Not another dry run,' said Red, a broad smile on his face as he scooped up cards and coins. The door swung shut again. 'If it was a proper torpedo, shouldn't it have blown by now?' He gave a mock yawn to show his unconcern.

'Get dressed,' Bing said sharply. He could hear frantic movements outside.

'Can't be bothered,' Alfred said, scratching his chin. 'You putting down a card or not?'

'Not!' said Bing, leaving his hand on the table. 'I'm on duty in a while.' He reached his bunk and began dressing again.

'That torpedo could have failed to explode,' Red said. But he didn't look so sure of himself now. He was hurrying into his clothes.

Bing moved as quickly as he could between the men scurrying about. He cursed the lifebelt about his waist. God knew what it would be like when it was fully inflated. He went out into the corridor and joined the noisy men rushing about like headless chickens. The sour-sharp smell of burning was in the air.

He'd just reached the designated assembly spot on deck when another terrific explosion felled most of the men about him to their knees. Flames appeared, shooting up from below and pouring from openings, doors and passage-ways. Men scurried, shouting, screaming, in all directions. Bing had sense enough to reclaim his dropped rifle. He found it difficult to move in the heavy clothing but he managed to grab hold of the metal railing.

'The electrics have gone!' someone shouted. Men were trying to extinguish fires that had broken out but there was no water because the electricity had failed. Some men were jumping into the sea, which was already catching fire due to the burning oil spills.

'Wait for orders!' Bing shouted. 'That's what we've been told.'

Men were now hanging over the side of the LST trying to drop into one of the launched lifeboats and falling instead into the icy water. The air was filled with smoke that burned Bing's lungs. He had no idea what was going on, only what his eyes could tell him, which was that *LST 507* was, incredibly, on fire.

'Fucking E-boats,' came a voice at his side. The man stared at Bing. 'You don't know, do you?'

Know what? Bing wondered. The man was in pyjamas and covered with oil.

Bing reckoned he himself must look pretty witless waiting

in the designated area for orders that were probably not forthcoming.

'E-boats, enemy boats, in the Channel. They've fired on us and the other craft. We're fuckin' sitting ducks.' Bing saw blood mixed with the grease in the man's hair. It ran down his neck and darkened his clothing. A shot thudded into the metal casing near Bing's head. Automatically he ducked, as did the other man.

'I thought Exercise Tiger was a secret?' Bing yelled.

The man had hunkered down. 'The fucking Germans had E-boats in the bay. The bastards were travelling at full speed. We've been hit!' He stared at Bing. 'Our men thought it was part of an exercise and have done fuck all! And there's no power, no light or communications between this LST, other craft and the shore. Even if they get that sorted out it'll be too late to do anything for most of these poor buggers. Just look at them.' He waved an arm expansively.

Bing gazed at the lifeboat hanging over the side of the LST. It was overfilled with men. Electric power was needed to lower it. Too many bodies in a small space and still men tried climbing down the side of the craft to get in.

Hanging unevenly by its ropes the lifeboat suddenly capsized, tipping all of the men into the now flaming water.

Most would go to their certain death, probably without knowing what had happened and why.

Men were jumping from the deck into the oily sea, wearing clothing that was dragging them down, on top of men already trying frantically to keep afloat, grabbing at floating detritus.

'We can't wait for fuckin' orders that aren't going to come,' said the man, wiping away blood that had made its way down his forehead past his eyes onto his cheek.

Bing knew this was true.

There was another blinding flash, followed by a gigantic deluge of seawater that swept him off his feet. He managed to grab hold of another twisted railing that halted him from slithering across the deck into the path of a moving amphibious craft. Some of the trucks had already disappeared into the burning water. He watched the craft slide beneath the sea. Only then came the garbled, indistinct order to abandon ship.

Bing managed to pull himself back fully upright to the relative safety of the broken metal railing.

'Help me, help me!' A soldier was dragging a petrol-driven water pump across the uneven deck. 'Got to get this below to the engine room!' he said. 'You can hear them screaming in there!' Foul-smelling smoke was pouring out now from every doorway and opening. Bing let go of the railing and stepped forward to help the man, but he was pulled back.

'You can't save them poor sods, now,' said a man who seemed to have appeared from nowhere. He was at Bing's side holding fast to the rail that was becoming hot to Bing's touch. 'Help yourself instead!' the man shouted over the noise.

It was pitch black, except for the multi-coloured fires on the ship. The heat was tremendous. On deck Bing could feel the boards sizzling through his heavy combat boots from the fires burning below. He touched the metal of the nearby doorway and it, too, was scorching.

'Jump.'

Bing felt himself pushed and then he hit the water. The sea was an ice-cold shock and his lifebelt and boots were dragging him below the surface. He tried to inflate it. A string, with a piece of metal attached, came away in his stiff fingers. He tried to take it off but the numbness in his hands hampered purchase on the straps.

He bumped into a corpse. He was aware now of other bodies floating in the sea about him, some burning where the oil had set light to them. A wooden raft nearby had men clinging to it. Men in waterlogged clothing struggling to stay afloat.

Bing thought the noise was incredible. Screaming,

shouting, crying men knowing they were going to die. He saw a man, face badly burned, eyes closed, let go of the rope at the side of the raft and simply slide away.

The *507* was sinking now.

Next to him, Alfred was struggling in the water. He looked exhausted. Bing managed to grab hold of the rope and when Alfred floated into view again, he caught hold of his clothing, jamming the man's arm up and around the raft's rope. Secured, Alfred could now float or be dragged along on top of the water. Bing was about to grab hold of the side of the raft when he heard, 'Get that nigger away from the fuckin' raft!' Hands pushed him below the water and though he struggled to keep afloat and to breathe, he was tiring.

As he surfaced again, a young man next to him floated away from the rope. Bing took his place. There were corpses everywhere. As the time passed Bing thought about his mother, their home. He was exhausted. Visions of Bea set themselves in his head. He loved her. He was grateful to God for the time they'd spent together. He wasn't afraid, he wasn't in pain. He wanted desperately to sleep, so he laid his head against his hands, which were still clutching the rope he could no longer feel, and allowed his eyes to close.

His last thoughts were of Bea smiling, singing to him from the stage with desire in her eyes.

Chapter Twenty-four

'Well, what did you think of Max?' Eddie called out, stepping into the passage and allowing the key to swing back behind the front door. He'd warned his mother not to go anywhere near the scullery until he came home from driving Max back to the St Vincent holding centre and signing him in. Eddie felt she'd surpassed herself preparing a meal for his German friend and he intended to wash up the dirty dishes himself.

'Here I am,' Maud said.

'What're you doing in here?'

Maud was in the front room, which doubled as her bedroom. She'd pulled out the sewing machine he'd brought back from Lavinia House and was examining it. The strawberry-pink material Bert had given her lay across the bottom of her bed.

'The needle's broken and the spool's empty.'

'I'll sort it,' he said. 'That's an easy job. Tell me what you think of Max.'

'He's all right,' she admitted, looking him straight in the eyes. He waited for her to add something, but she didn't. She merely went on digging in the tiny drawer that held spare spools filled with different-coloured cottons. 'Would you believe there's no spare needles in here?'

'You'll no doubt get them in Murphy's opposite Bert's café,' said Eddie, taking off his jacket and hanging it on the hook in the hall. 'That ironmonger's sells everything. Phone Bea and ask her to pop over the road and get some. Or when I'm next in town I'll go in. Anyway, what's made you decide to look at this machine?'

'It was that German.'

'Max, Mum. His name is Max.' He sighed.

'All right, Max. He kept staring at Gracie. Not just once or twice but constantly his eyes were on her.'

'What's wrong with that? I doubt he's seen many kiddies while he's been incarcerated in a prisoner-of-war camp, and you have to admit Grace excelled herself today. She doesn't usually like new people but she seemed quite taken by Max.'

'He gave me the shivers when he kept staring.'

'If you say so, Mum.' Now wasn't the time to be drawn into one of Maud's anti-German arguments. Eddie both liked and valued the Germans he had working for him, Changing the subject, he asked, 'Where's Gracie now?'

'I've given her a good wash and put her upstairs for a little sleep. I wondered if he thought she wasn't dressed as nicely as kiddies her age in Germany.'

Eddie stared at her. He hadn't noticed anything amiss the whole time Max was in the house. He was pleased the man had brought her the peg dolls as a gift. 'Don't be daft, Mum.' His mother was like a dog with a bone . She wouldn't leave it alone.

'I purposely dressed her in clean but old clothes because you know how she makes such a mess when she eats.'

'I'm sure Max thought nothing about what she was wearing.'

'Well, next time he comes he'll see she's got new clothes.' She picked up the pink material and shook it out. 'Lovely that is,' she said, caressing its softness. 'I won't have anyone sneering at my how my grandchild's dressed.'

'So that means you liked him enough to make another meal for him?' Eddie wanted her to shut up about his daughter's clothing.

His mother glared at him. 'I never said that. He's all right, I suppose, for a bloody German.' Maud refolded the piece of pink cloth and asked, 'You going to give me a hand with that washing-up?' As she walked along the passage to the scullery she said, 'There's another drawer beneath that machine, but it's stuck, I couldn't pull it out. Maybe that's where Sunshine kept the needles.'

'It's much nicer now that the weather's changed, isn't it?' Rainey said. The June sun was shining and Eddie had taken Maud, Ivy and Gracie to Stokes Bay beach so Gracie could pick up shells and perhaps have a paddle. 'You don't mind coming to the Criterion picture house with me?'

Bea answered, 'I haven't seen *Casablanca* and I know you've got a thing about Humphrey Bogart.'

Rainey tucked her arm through Bea's. 'He's so rugged. And he's good-looking in an ugly kind of way, like normal men are. That reminds me, have you heard from Bing?'

'Damn this belt.' Bea stopped on the pavement and thrust her white cardigan at Rainey to hold while she adjusted the belt of her yellow dress. 'It's one of those that doesn't have a tooth in the clasp so it works its way loose.' Belt tightened, she retrieved her cardigan and stared at Rainey. 'Not yet. I saw him in April, didn't I? That was when he went on that Exercise Tiger. I haven't expected any communication from him. I think the war's almost over. I'm sure we've got Hitler worried now we've landed on the beaches in France.'

'D-Day, it was,' said Rainey. 'We lost a lot of men on the sixth of June but so did the Germans.'

Rainey watched Bea fiddle with the narrow belt again. This time she'd slung her cardigan over her shoulder to get at it. 'W'Why don't you tie a knot and be done with it?' she asked.

'My waist looks bigger when the belt's not tight.'

Rainey glared at her. 'There's nobody around to see how big or small your waist is, except that family on the pavement way ahead of us. I doubt they'd care anyway!'

In the distance an elderly man, a couple pushing a pram and a little boy holding the man's free hand were walking past the playing field bordered by privet hedges.

'And they've all got their backs to us so how can they possibly see your tiny waist?' Rainey laughed at Bea, whose face coloured. She thought how sensible Bea was being about not hearing from Bing. The last time that had happened she'd been a nervous wreck. One night of passion in Devon had shown Bea that Bing would move heaven and earth to be with her. 'If the only thing you have to worry about is the belt to your dress, think yourself lucky,' Rainey said. She was glad that her lightweight grey trousers and white blouse weren't giving her any trouble, and suddenly thought of Elsie and Doris Waters and their smart clothing. She wondered if Norman Hartnell had been busy designing summer wear for them as well as for the King's wife, Queen Elizabeth.

They were about to walk past St Vincent, the holding centre for prisoners of war, when Bea grabbed Rainey's arm, 'Can you hear that?' she asked.

Rainey heard a whining sound that was getting louder. 'It can't be a raid – Moaning Minnie isn't screaming,' she said. 'And we haven't had an air raid for ages . . .' She looked ahead at the small family, who were now, like them, standing about and staring into the sky.

'We should take cover, just in case.'

'I'm not asking that guard at St Vincent if we can wait in there until that noise goes away,' Rainey complained. 'Doubt he'd let us in, anyway.'

'There's that bombed-out shop at the top of Mill Lane,' said Bea. 'It's not far.'

'Fair enough. Lightning doesn't strike in the same place twice.' Rainey grabbed her hand and began moving quickly across the road. 'I don't fancy the prison camp and the Germans,' she said. 'I don't even trust that Max bloke that our Eddie's so set on. Jesus, that noise is getting louder!'

Half running, half stumbling, they reached the derelict premises that had once been a sweet shop and tumbled through the doorway. Broken glass jars with screw-top lids crunched beneath Rainey's feet.

'Stinks in here,' complained Bea.

Rainey leaned back against the shattered counter. The sun was shining down on her through the destroyed roof and she could feel its warmth through her thin blouse. Bea cuddled into her as the whining noise grew louder.

'Oh, no! I know what that is,' said Rainey. 'It's a doodlebug! I've been hearing about them. It's a V-1 flying bomb the German buggers are sending over! They're new! Supposed to cut out and then fall!'

Almost as soon as the words left her lips the whine stopped and there was complete silence.

'Where's it gone?'

Rainey squeezed Bea's shoulder. She'd heard the fear in Bea's voice and, though her own heart was pounding, she wanted to comfort her friend.

'Wait for it to fall. Then you'll know where it is,' Rainey said. She clung to Bea and was praying that the damned thing wouldn't drop on them. A wall left half standing allowed her to see purple rosebay willowherb, which some called fireweed, growing through a rusted iron bedstead. Funny, she thought, she'd never noticed the plant until it started flowering on bombsites and now it bloomed everywhere.

The wait seemed interminable.

The noise of the explosion shattered the silence and made her ears ring. Debris was falling like hailstones, spattering through the shop's roof that was open to the sky. She was suddenly aware of Bea's fingernails digging into her flesh. Rainey clung to her like a limpet. Bea started coughing. 'Put your hand over your nose and mouth,' said Rainey. 'Try not to let the grit and dust go down your throat. We'd better get out of here quickly in case this lot falls down around us.' She hauled Bea out into the open air, and when she managed to clear the grit from her own eyes, she saw that part of Forton Road had disappeared. A huge crater had opened. Water was jetting into the air, probably from a broken pipe, and falling like fierce rain on an uprooted tree.

Bea said, 'That family would have been about there . . .'

'They'd have sheltered, like us,' said Rainey. 'Wouldn't they?' She felt panic rise within her.

'We have to see if we can do anything,' Bea said. She'd already started running along the pavement. Rainey followed her until the pavement was no more. The air was full of the stench of burning and black smuts flew about them, like dark snow. Rainey could hear voices now that her ears had stopped ringing. She and Bea weren't the only ones standing around the massive hole in the ground.

'Get back, ladies!' Rainey felt someone pull at her arm. A guard – she recognized him from the main gate of St Vincent – stepped in front of them, hampering their view. 'You don't want to see it!' His voice was gruff but kind.

Twisted wire hung, snake-like, from the trees. Rainey identified it as the temporary fencing put up when the majority of Gosport's iron railings had been commandeered by the government. Smoke was still rising from the earth. The mutilated body of a man – Rainey knew it was a man, for his legs were still covered with scraps of his trousers – lay spread-eagled on the ground.

'Don't look!' Rainey knocked Bea sideways, hoping she wouldn't see the body. Revulsion made her want to spew.

'Maybe someone needs help!' Bea shouted, angry at Rainey's intervention. 'This family . . .'

'Well, it's not a family no more,' came another man's voice, gentle, soft-spoken.

Rainey whirled about to see who was talking and almost fell into the arms of another guard from St Vincent. 'Don't look no more, girlies,' he warned. 'Get over to the holding centre and ask them for a cuppa. Leave this to us.'

'Rainey! Let's do as he says,' pleaded Bea. All the anger had gone out of her. 'There's been no all-clear, yet.'

And then there were more men milling about, searching, sifting through the hot earth.

'There was no warning either, love,' said another man.

Rainey asked the guard, 'Do you think they're all dead? It was a family.'

'I wouldn't be surprised.' Then he repeated, 'Why don't you both get over to the barracks and sit down for a bit in the guard-room? Leave this to us – you don't want the nightmares.'

Bea said, 'I want to go, Rainey. We can't do anything . . .' Her face crumpled and she began to cry.

'All right,' Rainey said. She knew without asking that her friend was thinking about the little family. She slipped her arm through Bea's, and her feet felt like lead as she began to walk away towards the main gate. A clanging noise was growing louder. 'That's an ambulance,' she said. 'Proper help's coming, now.'

'How did you know what kind of bomb it was?' Bea asked, as they reached the overgrown hedge opposite the holding centre.

'My mum heard it on the wireless. I read about them in the *Evening News*. We talked about it.' Rainey looked back at the scene. More people had arrived. ARP tin hats caught her eye, worn by men in dark clothing.

'Listen!' Bea stopped, pulling Rainey to a standstill.

At first, Rainey thought it was a kitten, mewing, lost perhaps. Bea saw it first, the pram handle wedged in the privet hedge.

'Don't look,' Bea warned. But it was too late. Rainey had yanked the handle and pulled the pram from the bushes. The hood was up and caught on a twig but was easy enough to free. Another cry came from inside the large old pram. Rainey saw that not only was the hood clipped up, possibly to keep the sun out of the pram, but the rain cover was studded in position. This time the cry was louder, more determined. She poked her head inside while her fingers were busy unfastening the cover. A lightweight blue blanket had been kicked off by a tiny red-faced baby in a long white cotton nightdress.

Chapter Twenty-five

'He's alive and there's not a mark on him!' Rainey had the baby in her arms, examining him, his head against her breast. 'He's wet, disgruntled and obviously not very old for his skin's got that mauvy whiteness of a new-born,' she said.

'How d'you know it's a boy?' Bea looked into the pram and discovered the sheet was wet. 'Oh, the blue blanket!' A few fresh twigs and leaves decorated the bedding. Bea began lowering the hood. 'Looks like this saved his life. He's got a really piercing cry, hasn't he?' Bea rolled up the cover and tucked it at the foot of the pram. 'We'd better get him somewhere so someone can feed and change him. It's a bloody miracle, that's what it is!'

'A miracle his family's been blown to bits and he's all alone?'

'Rainey, you don't know that for sure.'

'You saw what happened at that crater . . .'

Bea frowned. 'We have to take him to someone who can look after him.'

'Over to the holding centre?'

Rainey had poked her little finger back into the baby's mouth and he was sucking it. 'At least he's stopped crying.' Bea saw the brightness of tears in Rainey's eyes as she searched his face. 'My baby boy would have been older . . .' Rainey's voice was wistful. 'A little boy like you, though.' She bent her head and kissed the child.

A feeling of dread suddenly encompassed Bea. 'What are you thinking?'

'He needs someone,' was all Rainey said.

'Don't even think about it,' Bea snapped. 'He's not yours.'

'This is wartime. There's lots of kiddies end up with someone other than their true parents looking after and loving them.'

Bea stepped back and watched Rainey cooing and fussing with the child. She'd never had a child so she didn't know what it was like to lose one, but she'd been with Rainey after her baby died and she knew it had broken her. 'He's not a substitute for yours!' she said quickly, surprised at the harshness in her voice. Rainey was jigging the little one in her arms. That and the sucking of her finger was making the baby sleepy. That baby smell of milk and talcum powder was luring her . . . 'Give him here,' Bea demanded.

Bea saw the amazement mixed with hurt on Rainey's face as she reluctantly allowed her to take the child quickly into her arms. The shock of losing the dummy-like finger caused a scream of bewilderment. Bea clutched at the blue blanket and marched away, yelling, 'Bring that bloody pram with you!'

She didn't look to see if Rainey was following, but strode back along the burned grass to the myriad of people, the screaming baby in her arms. She saw what she was searching for and breathed a sigh of relief. From behind her she heard Rainey calling her name. She ignored her.

An ambulance, back doors open but empty inside, was parked on the grass. She walked to the cab, where a large man sat looking at a clipboard propped across the steering wheel. He wiped his face with his meaty hand, then stared at her.

'This little mite somehow escaped the blast.' She turned and faced Rainey, who had caught her up. Rainey had been crying. She hauled the large pram behind her. 'The pram protected him,' added Bea. Then, 'It was in the bushes.'

Now she returned the baby to Rainey, who took a deep breath and set him on the bare striped mattress, then quickly turned away. The wet sheet was hanging over the pram's handle. Rainey's shoulders were hunched, as if she was trying to make herself as small as possible. Bea's heart went out to her, but she said to the man, 'Can we leave him with you?'

The man studied Bea for a moment, then climbed down from the cab and stared into the knot of people, as though he was searching for someone. The baby, meanwhile, let out yet another lusty cry.

'The coppers, no doubt, will want a statement,' he said, picking up a notebook and pencil from the passenger seat in the cab. 'Just jot your names and addresses on here.' Again, he looked into the crowd. 'Jeannie!' he yelled, his voice like a foghorn from a boat in the harbour on a misty day. 'We got a live one here.'

Bea caught up with Rainey near the derelict house where they'd sheltered. 'Wait,' she said. 'We were on our way to the Criterion to see Humphrey Bogart.'

'You surely don't think I can concentrate on a film now, do you? Not after that?' Rainey stood in the middle of the pavement, her face red and blotchy, her eyes swollen.

'We can go in, in the middle of the picture, and sit there until it comes round to the bits we missed,' Bea said.

'I'm not bothered about missing the start of the film.' Rainey stared at her.

'What is it, then? I think you're still grieving for Charlie and your own baby,' stated Bea.

'It's not something that bloody disappears because you want it gone!' Rainey's shrill voice bordered on a shriek.

'You do realize what you wanted to do back there, don't you?' Bea's voice was hardly more than a whisper. Rainey stared at her friend. For a moment neither spoke.

Then Rainey took a deep breath. 'All right, you win. Just for a moment, holding that child in my arms, I wanted him to be mine.' She gave Bea a half-smile. 'Not one of my best ideas, eh?' Tears filled her green eyes.

'No,' said Bea. Now her voice held kindness. 'And if I hadn't stepped in, you'd have taken him home, wouldn't you?'

Rainey nodded. 'Probably,' she said, and hung her head. 'Yes,' she whispered.

'You'd have pretended he was yours? Tried to feed him milk. You'd have given him a name?'

Rainey shook her head. 'I didn't think about birth certificates and things like that. Or names.'

'So, you didn't think of anything except what you wanted?' She shook her head. 'You didn't think it through at all, did you?' She paused. 'Just out of interest, what name would you have given him?'

'Doodlebug!' said Rainey quickly. 'If it hadn't been for one of them . . .' She tried a watery smile at Bea.

'Honestly! Sometimes I truly think you've got a screw loose! Nice to know you've finally got your sense of humour back.'

Rainey shrugged. 'We've done the right thing. I know we have. And it's all because of you. That little mite will no doubt end up in the National Children's Home at Alverstoke while they search for relatives. He'll get the best of care and attention there. But I can't forget he ever came into my life. When the police contact us for our statements I'm going to ask if I can keep in touch with him, somehow.'

Bea was frowning.

'Look, I love living in Albert Street, but being on my own, it's not all it's cracked up to be.'

'Of course it isn't. But you have a home, Rainey. You also have the gift of a beautiful voice and you're certainly not without a bit of cash behind you. Why don't you begin to think about what you really want from life after the war? I just know we're going to win it,' said Bea. 'Do you remember Elsie Waters telling you the same thing? You even told Bert you didn't want to be a Bluebird forever, and you didn't like all the travelling. Charlie and the baby meant the world to you, so make your dream come true for them.' She smiled. 'Anyone can see you'll never be a housewife. Not like Ivy really wants.'

'I remember telling Bert I wanted to open a place where I could sing, where I was the boss and certainly never had to live out of a damn suitcase again.'

Bea was smiling at her. A funny know-it-all-smile. 'When I stayed with you, after your baby died, you were practically off your head . . .'

'All right, don't keep on about it.' Rainey kicked at a pebble on the pavement.

'Well, what's to stop you going after what you want, now?' Bea looked pleased with herself.

'Are you saying that because of the baby? Because I've made a fool of myself?' She looked back along the road to where an ambulance was on the move. Was the child inside?

Bea was still talking: 'I think if you started planning . . .' Her voice tailed off, then came back stronger as she saw she had Rainey's full attention once more. '. . . planning what you want,' she said, 'you won't have so much time on your hands to dwell on the past.'

Rainey took a long time to answer. When she did, it was because she had fully digested Bea's advice. 'Will you help me?'

Bea gave her a hug. 'Of course! We don't need to see *Casablanca* today – it's on for the rest of the week. Let's go to your house, put the kettle on and talk over a cuppa, maybe make a few plans, eh?'

'I'd like that. Better make sure I've got some paper and a pencil to hand, I don't want to forget any of the details . . .'

'You won't forget what you want to remember,' said Bea. She took out a handkerchief from the pocket in her dress and handed it to Rainey. 'Make yourself decent.'

Rainey sniffed, took the hanky, spat on it and began rubbing her face.

'Pity you forgot to keep tightening your belt.' Bea's dress was hanging off her like a sack. Rainey grinned. 'Well, you needn't worry about it now,' she said.

Bea looked down – to see that her belt had gone.

Chapter Twenty-six

Max blessed the day he'd applied to work for Eddie again. He still hadn't worked out exactly how he could use Eddie or his family in a further escape bid, but he knew sooner or later an idea would evolve. After all, he had a key to the lorry, hidden at St Vincent, so transport wasn't a problem. He would need papers, an identity card and a passport to leave the country. He'd made a few enquiries about the bloke Sunshine had worked for and who had, for a price, provided false papers. The police had collared him so he was now in prison, doing time for living off immoral earnings. Max had to rethink.

In the meantime, because Eddie had put in a successful bid to buy the bombed property opposite his house and rebuild it, in Alma Street, Max now saw Gracie every day while renovations to the property went on. He smiled to himself. It had been easy to win the little girl's affection. And why not? After all, he was her father, wasn't he?

'Do you want a sandwich?' called Eddie. 'Bloater paste?'

'How can I eat another morsel? We were both served a fine English delicacy by your good mother not an hour ago.' Max stretched out on the newly cut grass of Forton recreation ground, taking deep breaths of the fresh air and enjoying the feel of the sun upon his face. He knew he was lucky to be spending extra time with the builder who had applied for an extension to his working hours, something he didn't do for his other employees.

Eddie considered him a friend. Max had to admit that the more time he spent in Eddie's company, the more he appreciated Eddie's hard work in providing so well for his family. He also recognized that Eddie was lonely. He adored his beautiful Ivy, but she was frequently away. She was a singer, quite well known, by all accounts, and was often travelling around the country entertaining the troops. Eddie seemed content for her to have her career, or maybe he accepted it. Any German husband would soon have curtailed it. His countrymen preferred their women to be homemakers. Perhaps if Ivy had a child of her own, not that she neglected Gracie, certainly not, she idolized the child . . . but Max sensed that Ivy wasn't completely content with her lot.

Max looked across the short stretch of grass to where Eddie was pushing Gracie backwards and forwards on a wooden swing, cleverly designed so that the small child could not fall out. Max waved at her. She waved back, with a huge smile for him. In a little while he would go over and relieve Eddie of his duty. He would climb the steps of the tall slide with Gracie, sit her in his lap and slide down. It was a game she loved and he was happy to hear her crow with laughter.

'I brought the sandwiches because I don't think you enjoyed the winkles.'

Should he tell Eddie that the little grey snot-flavoured things picked from their shells with a pin had made him want to throw up? Or should he lie and say he had enjoyed them because Maud had travelled to Stokes Bay, gathered them from the rocks, brought them home and boiled them? 'I think they are an acquired taste,' he called back. There, Max thought. That answer would not hurt Eddie's feelings. It mattered to him that Eddie go on considering him more of a friend than just one of his workforce. The blond young man was one of the kindest people Max had ever met, and deceiving him was easy.

Unlike Ivy.

Max could feel her dislike for him. It rippled from her in

waves whenever they were near each other. She was beautiful. Her shoulder-length dark hair was so glossy it made him want to run his fingers through it. If she had been any other woman, he might have done just that. He smiled to himself. No doubt the cold bitch would like it. But she was Eddie's woman and he needed to keep Eddie sweet, until he betrayed him in the worst way possible.

He knew what was wrong with Ivy. Oh, yes, he knew. She was a young woman, younger than Eddie, and she wanted him all to herself. Jealousy was not a good partner in a loving relationship. Max could see she adored Gracie to distraction. But Gracie was Eddie's child by another woman – or so Ivy believed. Ivy could not bear to think of Eddie making love to anyone else, even though poor Sunshine was now dead. She did not dare show it, but Max knew her jealousy extended to him. If the poor cow only knew that he had murdered Hans to keep secret that he was Gracie's father, she might even come to respect him! He and Hans had had some good moments together. He felt a pang of regret. He pushed it away. The young man had been likely to cough himself into oblivion soon. Max had merely helped him on his way.

Rainey unlocked the street door in the middle of town and pushed it open. It went a little way, then stuck fast. 'Let me get my shoulder to that,' said Bert, parting the women waiting outside the empty Georgian building and shoving the door so that it swung back. He gave a mock bow, stood aside and allowed Elsie and Doris Waters to enter. Rainey remembered he had first met the comic duo at a dinner at Madame's Southsea house. He said he'd worn his best suit and when he'd spoken, Della had said later, he hadn't sounded like himself but as if he had a plum in his mouth. Now he didn't bother to put on airs and graces. Not since the two had sat in the café with him and Della eating bacon sandwiches.

'It's bigger than it looks,' said Elsie.

'You can say that about a lot of things,' quipped Doris. 'But it's certainly got a nice feeling about it.'

Rainey saw Elsie frown at her sister. 'That's what I thought the first time we were shown the place,' she said. She looked down the length of the hall to where the stage was falling to bits. Tattered curtains hung drunkenly at each side.

'Get rid of the seating,' said Bert, bending down and examining the floor. 'Polish and replace the parquet flooring. Keep the stage, but renew all the boards. Keep those chandeliers. God, they're beautiful! You're lucky someone ain't been in and pinched them,' he said. 'This used to be a theatre – did the agent tell you?'

'I think the girl could have worked that out for herself,' said Doris. She fumbled in her handbag, brought out a handkerchief and held it across her nose. Her handbag and shoe leather exactly matched her cream linen suit. 'What on earth is that offensive smell?'

'The place has been boarded up for years. It closed sometime in the nineteen twenties, if I remember rightly,' said Bert. 'It was, apparently, a very popular venue but there was some family scandal and the money ran out.' He gave Doris a tombstone-toothy grin. 'I'd think that stink is dead rats or cats. Animals of some kind got in here and died.'

'Oh, really, Bert, do you have to frighten Doris half to death?' Elsie walked down the central aisle, watching carefully for detritus on the floor to trip her. Rainey hoped her beautiful chiffon summer dress didn't get dirt on it. Elsie said, 'Nice view of the balcony. I'd clear that, Rainey. Put in tables, chairs, maybe booths at the sides.'

'That was exactly what I thought.' Rainey was glad she'd asked the sisters for advice. She could see that Elsie and Doris were as excited about her venture as she was. They were eager to help and seemed to know many people who 'owed them favours' that would result in offers of period furnishings. Above the balcony seats, there was living accommodation and an office.

'About money, dear. Can you afford it? I'm not asking if you like this place because I can see from the shine in your eyes that it's what you've dreamed of. However, you'll need a bottomless pocket to make all the necessary alterations,' shouted Elsie, from the orchestra pit.

Rainey didn't want to tell everyone that, with Eddie's help, the theatre had become hers for a knock-down price. The council had been more than happy to see one of Gosport high street's derelict eyesores become someone else's problem. 'Are you offering to lend me capital?' she asked.

'My dear, I can't be any more blunt! Of course we are. I thought we'd made it plain before that if any of you need help you must just ask. In fact, when you've got the place up and running, we'd like to book ourselves in to open it. By the way, what are you intending to call the club?'

Rainey blushed. 'I honestly don't know yet,' she said. 'But it gladdens my heart that you all approve.' Deep inside her she knew Charlie, too, would have approved.

Theatrically, Elsie raised her arms towards the heavens and said, 'Can't you feel Nellie's happiness? She's looking down and smiling. It's her wish you fulfil your dream. She has such admiration for you, dear Rainey!'

'What's not to approve, Rainey love?' asked Bert. 'Blackie

and your mother have access to artists and your voice will make the punters return time and time again . . .'

Rainey looked at each of them in turn. Yes, she was fortunate in being able to follow her dream, but she was even luckier that she had such good friends.

Chapter Twenty-seven

'Bea, come down, there's someone here who wants to see you, an American.' Bert scratched his head and said to the young man, 'She won't be long.'

No sooner were the words out of his mouth than one of the most beautiful girls Si had ever seen came quickly down the stairs. She stood in front of him and said, 'Do I know you?'

He watched as the expression on her face changed from joy to bewilderment. 'No, ma'am,' he said. 'But I feel as though I know you. Is there somewhere we can go where there's not so many people?'

Both he and the girl heard Bert move back from the door where he had been listening and return to the café where the wireless was playing and customers were eating. He gave a small smile. The old guy was only looking out for her. 'Follow me,' she said, walking down the passage towards the kitchen area. 'You don't mind sitting outside, do you?' He watched her flip up the latch and walk out into the late-July sunshine.

'Not at all, ma'am. It's very nearly as hot out today as it is back in the States.' Si thought that normally she'd be neighbourly and ask whereabouts in America he came from. But this young woman knew something wasn't quite right. She was being cautious. He followed her into the weed-covered area that was well trodden down outside the door. At the bottom of the garden, backing onto a high wall, was a whitewashed building that needed repainting. Of course it was the lavatory.

Bea pointed to a tall wooden stool near the back door and he perched on it. She sat on an oil drum with a bit of blanket on the top. 'It's to do with Bing, isn't it?' A flowery scent wafted across to him, young and fresh, like her, he thought. 'I know I should have heard from him by now.'

He took out a book from his drab olive jerkin. 'He left this with me to read. I'm not much of a reader and I thought you'd like it. Inside there's a letter he wrote you before going on that exercise . . .'

'He's dead, isn't he?'

They locked eyes. She took the Hemingway book and ran her fingers through the pages. As they fluttered a letter dropped to the bare earth. A photograph followed. She didn't seem bothered by either. She set the book beside her on the oil drum and looked at him.

'I came because he was my friend and I guessed if they were to inform anyone it would be his mother, as next of kin . . .'

Si didn't like it that she showed no emotion. He wondered if she was in shock. 'He idolized you,' he said softly.

'Was it on D-Day? I heard on the wireless it was horrendous.' She looked at him expectantly.

'No,' he said. 'I'm not supposed to talk about it. It was the biggest cock-up ever . . .' She raised her eyebrows at his use of the English expression. 'But I couldn't leave England knowing you were going to go through life never knowing what happened . . .'

'Why do you say that?'

'Because none of this will be published in the papers, ever. Ever.'

After a while she said, 'Is it to do with that secret exercise?' She didn't take her eyes from him.

Before he could answer, another voice said, 'I hope I'm not intruding. I wondered if you'd both like a cuppa.'

Si was about to say, 'No,' but the girl said, 'I would, Bert.' Bert stood in the doorway in his greasy apron.

Si waited until the elderly man had shuffled back inside, then said, 'Look, I came because Bing was a one-off. I valued his friendship. The guy was head over heels in love with you. I could be in big trouble for this. But he'd have done the same for me . . .'

'I understand. This visit of yours never happened. No, not at all.'

Si looked at her. It was hard for him to make her out. She wasn't like most bereaved women, who would have been screaming and shouting by now. But he wanted her to know how badly the army had screwed up. He swallowed his feelings. 'I'll tell you what I know. All of it. It's so painful I'd rather you let me speak without interruptions. Okay?' She nodded. It crossed his mind that, so far, those beautiful eyes had not blinked.

'Exercise Tiger was a disaster. It began as a practice for D-Day, with Slapton Sands chosen because the terrain was similar to that of France. Almost all the ships and artillery we got were in the harbour. A navy corvette spotted German E-boats. They were loaded with mines and torpedoes and shouldn't have been anywhere near. Warning signals about them never came. Some shortfall in communication, along with lack of preparation in what to do in emergencies, meant the men were sitting targets for the Germans. *LST 507* was the first to go down.' He watched her nod as he said, 'That was Bing's craft.

'The sea was on fire and our boys had no idea how to put on the heavy equipment. Bodies were discovered with lifebelts wrongly worn. The men died, face down, dragged under the icy water . . . As if that wasn't bad enough, when some of our boys managed to get back on Slapton beach, they were mown down with live bullets from our own men. More fuckin' confused communications.' He wiped his hand across his eyes. 'I beg your pardon, ma'am, for my language.' He was shaking with emotion. He knew he must not break down. He took a deep breath. 'Nearly a thousand men were killed. The E-boats got away. Bodies were taken to mortuaries, then quickly buried. Survivors were shipped out of the way, many to Wales. Everything's been hushed up. Morale had to be maintained, because Operation Overlord, the battle for Normandy, was still going forward as planned.' He took an even longer breath to stop his threatening tears. 'It did, and we landed on French soil.'

Bea was wrapped in her own thoughts, staring at nothing, her blue eyes like glass.

A movement startled him. A cough heralded a tray

brought by the old guy. There were three mugs, so Si reckoned Bert was there to stay. It was possible, Si thought, that he'd heard everything.

Bert's words 'You were there?' confirmed that he had been listening.

'Normandy, yes. Slapton Sands, no. I was in the sick bay.' He didn't want to elaborate. So, all he added was, 'I was sent back from France.'

He twisted his cap in his hands. Awkwardness had set in. He very much wanted to leave this quiet young woman. She couldn't possibly keep up this . . . What did people call it? . . . stiff upper lip facade for much longer.

He took a mug from the tray and drank the strong brew. It was too hot, but he didn't care. He muttered, 'Thank you.'

Bert put the tray on the ground. He picked up the letter and the photograph, slipping both inside the front pocket of his grubby apron. As he did so he caught Si's eye, and it was like he was telling him he'd completed his mission. Si could go now. 'Thank you for coming,' Bert said. 'I appreciate it. If you've something with your address on, I'd like you to leave it,' he said. 'Bea will want to keep in touch. You're a decent bloke.'

Bea was still sitting quite still, her eyes staring without seeing, her mug of tea, untouched, beside her on the ground.

In Bert's eyes Si could see infinite tenderness as he watched every flicker of her blue eyes. Si rose from the stool, glad to leave them to their grief. Bert was the man Bea needed now. As he walked away, he heard Bert's voice: 'I'll get rid of that bloody piano.'

Si was opening the street door when Bea's anguished scream followed him.

Chapter Twenty-eight

'Gosh! You gave me a start hovering behind the door like that!' Rainey stared at Bert, who was nervously stepping from one foot to the other as he waited just inside the door of the café.

'Made me jump an' all!' Ivy, a pace behind Rainey, closed the door behind her.

Above the noise of Judy Garland and Gene Kelly harmonizing 'For Me and My Gal' on the wireless and the general clatter of people eating and talking next door, Bert said, 'Thank God you've both come!'

Rainey saw Bert's forehead was creased with worry. 'I can't stop Bea cleaning! She's gone all busy like I've never known before.'

Rainey put her hand on his arm. 'If you telephone and say you're worried about Bea, of course we're going to get here as quick as we can. Maud's coming later when Eddie's home to keep an eye on Gracie. What d'you mean, Bert?'

'I didn't see her yesterday but she was all right the day before,' Ivy broke in, before Bert could speak. 'She was quiet, didn't want to talk about what happened to Bing but that's her prerogative, isn't it?'

Bert looked at her. 'I bloody well wish she would talk about him, Ivy. It's like he never existed. She's not shed one tear. It's not natural keeping grief inside her like that. Not natural at all. And she's on the go all the time.'

'Come on, Bert.' Rainey sighed. 'It's probably not normal for someone to go off their head after . . .' she slowed her voice '. . . after their baby died. But I did, didn't I?'

'You're different – that's different. You hadn't long lost your Charlie. Anyone would go a bit funny after that. But you're all right now, aren't you?'

Rainey thought he spat out the last words accusingly as though he thought she was a different species from Bea. But then, she thought, even Maud, Bea's mum, wouldn't let it rest that Bea was 'highly strung'. She took her hand from Bert's arm and pulled him towards her. He smelled of carbolic soap and bacon fat, so familiar, but she could feel him shaking. He was distraught and no wonder. Bea, was like a daughter to him. Rainey released him and when her eyes met his she could see he was holding back tears.

'What does my mum say?' Ivy asked. Rainey knew Della was a fount of wisdom. Having been through so many hard times in her own life, she trusted Della to do her best, and Bert, too, of course.

'Della says it's Bea's way of coping with what she can't bear to think about. I think she needs someone to shake her out of herself. Bea needs to come to grips with what's happened. She's always said she likes living here because it makes her feel safe. But she's not listening now to either of us. Five o'clock this morning she's up and washing down the stairs with disinfectant. She knows I do them last thing at night. I said to her, "Bea, why are you doin' this?" Know what she said? "When I'm busy I don't think." She's gonna wear herself out, collapse and be no good to anyone, least of all herself.'

Rainey digested his words. Then, 'Where's Bea now?'

'In the café polishing tables and chairs with Goddard's wax.'

'But you got customers in! Eating and drinking! They won't want someone fluttering a cleaning cloth around while they smoke and eat?'

Bert looked at Rainey. 'Course not,' he said, 'That's only

the half of it. When Bing's mate came and told us what had happened to his friend, he brought with him a letter as Bing had given him before he went on duty on the *LST 507*.'

Bert let air out of his body as though he'd been holding his breath. 'She won't look at the letter!'

'What do you mean?'

'I didn't tell you before but she was in a hell of a state after we heard about Bing's death. Della and me was so glad to get her quietened down, in her room and in bed. She'd been screaming, see?'

'That's natural, isn't it?' Ivy asked.

'Yes, I suppose it is, but what happened next day was peculiar. Me and Della shut the café that night so we could look after her, try to get her to quieten down, eat something, maybe, drink something—'

'We came as soon as you telephoned, didn't we?' Ivy interrupted. 'Eddie brought us down. He's worried sick, same as us.'

'Yes, and when you got here, she was asleep, wasn't she? Della had given her some Beecham's Powders, her answer for every ill, to help calm her down. I'd already asked if she wanted to read Bing's letter but she just ignored me, turned away from me, she did. I left the letter on her dressing table.' He shook his head. 'She ain't touched it.'

'She was barely awake when I was with her,' said Ivy. 'Very quiet.'

'I stood over her and asked her if she wanted anything,' Rainey said. 'She just shook her head and closed her eyes. I noticed the screwed-up Beecham's Powders papers and guessed she was tired, worn out with everything, and the powders were doing their job so I pulled the counterpane over her, kissed her forehead and crept out, leaving her to sleep.'

'You both did right,' Bert said. 'The next morning when you phoned, I said not to bother coming to see her because all she did was doze. Quite frankly I thought her lying in bed was doing her good. Well, sleep heals, don't it? Me and Della thought by the time she was ready for visitors, to talk to people, the rest would have done her good. What I never bargained on was the next morning she was up, dressed and sweeping dog ends off the pavement outside the café by the time I got up, and that was five in the morning, barely light and still bloody cold.'

Rainey frowned, then stared at Ivy as Bert carried on. 'I told her to come in out of the cold. I asked her if she'd read Bing's letter. She looked at me as if I'd asked her if she'd flown to the moon. So, I let it go and went on sorting out food for my early breakfast customers. She went upstairs

– I thought she'd gone back to bed. After all, the day had barely started.

'When Della came down a bit later, I took a mug of tea upstairs to Bea but her bedroom was empty.'

'Perhaps she'd gone out for walk,' Ivy suggested. 'Perhaps she went out to cry where no one could see her.'

Bert shrugged. 'Her room was tidy. Everything put away and folded up. I couldn't believe my eyes. It was like someone else was using her room.'

'Bea doesn't know what it is to clear up after herself,' said Rainey. 'She's the untidiest person I know.'

'She says why bother to put stuff away when she knows where everything is,' added Ivy.

'That's as maybe,' said Bert. 'But I'm telling you her room was spotless. I looked all over this place for her, upstairs, down and in the cellar, and guess where she was.'

'Where?' Rainey asked.

'Out in the back garden, gazing at the bloody lavatory!'

'What?' Ivy couldn't contain her amazement. Her mouth hung open.

Bert shook his head. 'Do you know what she said?'

'What?' Ivy and Rainey chorused.

'She said, "You never got around to whitewashing this place during the summer and being as all the stuff –" she meant whitewash and brushes that Eddie had got for me "– being as all the stuff is here, I'll make a start on it. It'll give me something to do."'

'The only painting she's ever done is to her face!' There was incredulity in Rainey's voice.

'You think I don't know she's never done no decorating in her life?' Bert snapped. 'Bea makes messes but she don't clear them up. Anyway, she asked me for an old apron so she'd not get too much paint on herself and said she was going to start later on this morning when she'd finished polishing!' Bert's face looked drawn and pale. 'Them café chairs and tables gets wiped over with a damp cloth! They've never had no Goddard's on them, never!' Another sigh escaped him.

'That's why I asked you both to come down. I don't know what to do with her.'

For a short while no one spoke. Then Bert added, 'Della reckons Bea's in some denial state, says she read about it once in *Woman's Weekly*. It's where people don't believe the telegram they've had about their loved one dying in the war so they go on believing their husband, relative, is still alive. Sometimes they even carry on writing to the dead people or believe they never existed . . . It's like when kiddies go on about imaginary friends, then later in life refuse to believe they made them friends up.'

'So, what d'you think me and Ivy should do, Bert?'

This time he couldn't help himself. He put a beefy hand up to an eye and wiped away a tear. 'Stay with her.' His voice was shaking. 'Talk to her. Make her believe Bing loved her and she loved him in return. You know what I think?'

Rainey looked at him expectantly.

'I believe she's scrubbed him from her mind as if he never existed, and as long as she keeps cleaning and being busy it stops her memories returning!'

'Maybe if we could get her to read that letter—' Ivy began.

'Will you stay with her?'

Bert looked so unhappy Rainey said quickly, 'Of course. We'll even help her whitewash inside that blasted lavatory if you think it'll do any good!'

Bert's face showed his relief. 'I'll get you some of my old aprons,' he said. 'Not much point in spoiling your good clothes.'

Half an hour later the three girls were surveying the dusty, flaking walls inside the large brick-built outhouse, containing the lavatory used by Bert, Della and the café's customers. The building was big enough to house a family.

'Bert mops this place out every morning,' said Rainey. 'Doesn't he, Bea?' She looked at Bea for confirmation.

Anything to get her friend to join in a conversation. Bea nodded. She was breathing heavily having dragged the bag of builders' lime down the garden from the cellar, flattening the grass on the way. The sack, Rainey could see, was heavy, yet Bea had refused her help. It wasn't like her to do that.

At least the lavatory bowl and its wooden seat were well scrubbed. Bert might be a bit rough around the edges himself, but where cleanliness was concerned, he was often heard saying, 'Cleanliness is next to godliness.' Even the lavatory chain was wiped every day and fresh newspaper hung in squares from a piece of string.

'I don't like the look of them cobwebs behind the tank on the wall,' said Ivy. 'Are we going to paint over them?'

'No, we're not!'

Ivy and Rainey stared at Bea. Her voice was forceful. Rainey was glad to hear her speak. So far this morning she'd hardly said a word. It was like she was there with Rainey and Ivy but, at the same time, far away.

Rainey winked at Ivy when Bea had turned her head. If they could get her talking, that would be something, wouldn't it?

'We'll sweep the walls down first with the yard brush,' Bea said crisply. 'Bert said that would loosen the flaking bits of the old stuff and get rid of the creepy-crawlies.'

'Sounds good to me,' said Ivy. 'Whitewashing's not so easy as you think it is.' She had a large handkerchief of Bert's knotted in the corners and had pinned her dark hair out of the way underneath it. 'I've had a bit of experience, what with Eddie being a builder . . .'

Rainey was happy to see the corners of Bea's mouth turn gently upwards in a smile at Ivy's boasting. 'Have you ever put paint on a brush, and slapped it on a wall?' asked Rainey. She hitched up Bert's apron, which hung almost to her knees, and then adjusted the tea-towel tied around her red hair to keep off splashes of whitewash.

'Well, not exactly . . .' Ivy blushed.

'When Mum and I moved into Albert Street,' Rainey said, 'the place was so filthy we were whitewashing and painting day and night.'

Bea tucked a few strands of her blonde hair beneath the small white towel wound round her head into a turban. 'We need salt and water to mix it to a sort of batter . . . like pancake batter.' Bea's voice was determined.

Ivy was wide-eyed. 'How d'you know that?'

'Bert told me,' Bea said. 'We'll mix it in a galvanized bucket. Then if we put it in the middle of the floor, we can all dip our brushes in.' She stepped out into the sunshine, picked up half a brick and jammed it under the wooden door to prop it open. She turned on her heels and disappeared down the path towards the back door.

'What do you think about Bea, then?' Rainey asked Ivy, who was using the long-handled brush on the walls and stepping back sharply when any little insect fell to the concrete floor and attempted to run away.

'Well, we're not talking about Bing, and neither is she. But I don't like to see our Bea all workmanlike, not one little bit. Usually when we get time off, she stays in bed, listening to her gramophone, doesn't she?'

Rainey didn't answer. Instead she touched her forehead as if she'd forgotten something. 'Of course,' she muttered. She smiled at Ivy, who frowned, mystified.

Bea came back, carrying a bucket and a block of salt. 'Scrape some of that onto a bit of paper,' she said to Rainey, handing her a knife from her apron pocket. She dropped the large brushes she'd also brought onto the floor. 'Just going back for water.' She disappeared again.

A short while later Bea was advising Rainey. 'Not too much water! It's got to be a thick paste, remember, and don't let any of the lime splash on your skin – or mine, come to that. Bert said it'll burn like beggary!'

'Fair enough,' said Rainey. Then, as Bea stirred the mixture, she asked, 'You are glad we're helping?'

'Yes,' Bea said. She stood up straight, leaving the stick she was using to stir the mixture in the bucket.

'Don't stop now,' said Rainey. 'Let's get on with it.' She chucked a handful of salt into the mixture. Then she began singing, '"You're my sunshine . . ."'

Ivy joined in as she swept a cloud of discoloured powdery bits and unmentionable dirt out of the door: '". . . my only sunshine . . ."'

'Come on, Bea, don't be a spoilsport! Join in!' Ivy said.

Bea began to sing, at first hesitantly then louder to keep the beat running smoothly.

One song followed another. Rainey's heart lightened as the whitewash splashed from the large brushes onto the walls and the cleaning process started. As it began to dry the colour grew brighter. Song followed song: 'Wish Me Luck As You Wave Me Goodbye', 'Over The Rainbow', 'Pennies From Heaven'. On and on they sang, on and on they waved wet white brushes up and down the grubby walls. They sang their solo songs alone. Neither girl joined in, except to start the soloist off. They just went on painting and remembering the places, the times, the songs that had all been sung before. So many songs, so many times, so many places, so many memories.

Rainey knew exactly what she was doing when she started singing 'You'd Be So Nice To Come Home To'.

Ivy, who had automatically joined in, halted: it was Bea's special song for Bing. She went on painting and listening as Bea and Rainey sang. Then Rainey's voice stopped, and Bea carried on singing alone. "'You'd be so wonderful to love . . .'"

So that they didn't interrupt Bea's concentration on the song that reminded her of Bing, Ivy and Rainey worked purposefully, covering the walls with the fresh-smelling whitewash and listening. Bea's voice was clear and sweet. Rainey stopped mid-brushstroke and looked at her friend. At the tears running from Bea's eyes, making channels in the dust on her cheeks and dripping onto Bert's whitewash-spattered apron.

As the last verse ended, Rainey put down her brush and gathered Bea into her arms. Ivy took Bea's brush from her and, when her own hands were empty, she enclosed both Rainey and Bea in her arms.

'Makes you cry, doesn't it? I always said you gotta be careful of whitewash!' Bert's voice cut into their tears.

Ivy released Rainey and Bea and, smiling, took the tray containing mugs of tar-like tea from Bert. She didn't say anything, not even, 'Thanks for the tea,' but she could see from his face that he was happy as he shuffled away.

Bea said only four words as the three of them sat on the lavatory step drinking tea. 'He's gone, isn't he?'

Chapter Twenty-nine

'There's an air of festivity in Priddy's armaments factory tonight, girls,' Rainey said, with just a hint of irony. She could hear music as she looked up into the star-studded night.

'D'you reckon it's because of us?' Ivy asked, as usual a little slow on the uptake.

It had been Rainey's turn to sit in the front seat of the van. Having crawled out of the back and let go of Sammy's clammy helping hand, Ivy now waited until Bea stepped down. The last few months since she had heard about Bing's death, which had nearly sent her over the edge, she had refused to cancel bookings. She'd told Rainey that when she was on stage it was like she was in a different world and nothing could harm her.

'No! It's because it's New Year's Eve,' said Bea, glaring at

Ivy, then brushing imaginary specks from her skirt. 'What do you expect? Lights always blazing for the Bluebirds?'

'I just don't expect to see this place lit up because we're on the coast and we're still under orders of a partial blackout,' snapped Ivy.

'Have you been here before, Sammy?' Rainey had already decided she wouldn't be brought into any argument between them. Talking to Sammy might help.

He shook his ginger head. Rainey said, 'We have. We all did a stint here filling shells. Bloody hard work. Mind you, that was long before Gosport knew who the Bluebirds were.' She glanced towards the main doors where a large woman in blue overalls and a white turban was waiting to greet them. She would probably have to search them for anything that could cause a spark and send the whole factory up in smoke. This was standard practice, as Rainey knew.

The van and Sammy had already been looked over by a guard at the entrance gate. And he'd been questioned. 'Appearing New Year's Eve, One Night Only, The Bluebirds,' announced the poster pasted on the wall near the door.

'I would have thought there'd be more people to meet us,' said Ivy. She was checking that the seams were straight on a pair of nylons she'd saved especially for tonight.

'What d'you want?' Bea wondered. 'A brass band playing outside, lights everywhere and a big sign telling Hitler to send his doodlebugs this way?'

'She's right, you know,' Sammy chipped in. 'We're not out of the woods yet. Them V-2's is like hell on earth. Day and night they come over.'

Rainey started giggling as the woman stepped forward to greet them.

'What's so funny?' There was an edge to Bea's voice.

'We decided on black high heels to go with black peplum suits. We all know the importance of wearing suitable clothing at Priddy's Hard. But what happens if Beefy Bertha here decides our shoes are too dangerous and gives us those awful rubber boots everyone has to wear instead?'

Bea laughed – Rainey thought how good it was to hear that sound. Bea said, 'Can you imagine us standing in the canteen, singing our hearts out, in tight skirts and heavy regulation boots?'

'Good to hear you so happy!' the large woman interrupted. 'We've got a huge audience waiting for you.' She began to pump enthusiastically at each of the girls' hands in turn. 'I already know who you three are. I'm Susan and while you're here, if you need anything at all, just ask. I'll be with you at all times.'

'Not up on the stage, I hope?' Bea was looking at the woman straight-faced.

Susan's flat countenance creased like a used paper bag. 'You three are like a bloody breath of fresh air!' In the middle of a chuckle she turned and looked at Sammy. 'Is your driver coming inside the factory as well?'

'He'd better – he plays the piano!' Bea told her.

'Come on through, then,' Susan said, the smile still fixed to her face. 'I heard you say you once worked here, so you know I have to give you the quick once-over.' She waited for the girls' agreement. 'You're performing in the canteen so you're well away from dangerous objects.'

'You must have a different cook from the one who was here for us,' said Bea.

'Very funny!' muttered Susan.

Rainey was happy to hear Bea chattering. It meant that for tonight, at least, her sense of humour was on form. The surprising thing was that she still refused to talk about Bing.

When Rainey had lost Charlie, she couldn't stop going on about him. But Bea had behaved like she'd never known Bing. She'd acted strangely. Strangely for her, at any rate, remembered Rainey. Cleaning up and putting things away had never been Bea's strong point but she'd become obsessed about making things nice. Bea said later that no man had loved her before Bing and she simply couldn't face remembering that she and he had shared such a deep love. Keeping busy had been her way of coping. Thank God Bea was back in the land of normality now, Rainey thought.

In the locker room, Susan asked questions about smoking materials. Cigarettes and matches were banned inside the factory. Their bodies were lightly searched. Rainey knew that if they had been singing near machinery or explosives the searches would have been much more stringent.

The Bluebirds were to sing at Priddy's for an hour. The workers were being treated by the management to a special New Year's party to bring in 1945.

'We didn't have to go through all this searching for *Workers Playtime* or for *Music While You Work*,' Ivy said, again checking the seams of her stockings. 'Mind you, this is the first time we've sung in an armaments factory and we do know how careful of accidents the management and labour force have to be.'

'Programmes for the BBC are a different kettle of fish, as well you know,' said Rainey. 'Many are recorded out and about, then put together in the studios. Some are wholly recorded at Broadcasting House. Anyway, I think it's lovely being invited back to this place.'

'Brings back happy memories, does it?'

Rainey didn't answer Bea. She'd let her think her sarcasm was wasted on her.

As they were following Susan towards the canteen, Rainey looked at the posters on the walls. One said, 'Always Carry Your Gas Mask', and another was captioned, 'God Help Me If This Is a Dud' below a picture of a soldier throwing a hand grenade. And then there was the one that had always been her favourite, a woman standing in front of a factory, saying, 'Women of Britain, Come Into the Factories.'

She couldn't help but turn to Sammy, who still maintained women should stay at home, and say, 'Good thing we women helped with this war, eh, Sammy?'

Of course he glared at her. There were some men whose minds would never be changed, she thought.

Rainey could hear the hum of voices grow louder the nearer they walked to the canteen. She wasn't a woman who was often nostalgic but she couldn't help feeling a certain pride when she remembered the dangerous work the three of them had done: the bomb cases travelling along the conveyor belt, filling them and tamping down the powdered substance. She certainly didn't miss the itchy skin, the chest complaints and the hair loss. Those bloody turbans were meant to protect their hair from turning yellow, but they had made their scalps itch. And the noise, the everlasting noise, mixed with the sound of the wireless to keep the working women happy.

Who would have thought that one day the Bluebirds would be visiting the factory to help keep the workers' spirits up? She turned to Bea. 'Remember when the front of your hair was discoloured?'

Bea glared. 'Yes, and I remember when your skin turned a lovely brown shade and everyone asked if you'd been lying in the sun!'

Their eyes met and they smiled at each other. That look said that both of them had suffered, but had come through it. Bea winked at Ivy. That wink reminded Rainey of the good times and of how lucky the three of them were to have each other.

The clock outside the canteen said it was five to eleven. The Bluebirds were topping the bill and a local comic had already warmed up the audience. Susan pushed open the swing doors, then stood aside so they could enter. She put out her arm to deny Sammy's entrance. 'Let them go in first,' she said. 'They're the stars.'

They walked together down the central aisle to cheers and whistles.

The noise made Rainey's heart swell with pride. All the tables had been removed and instead there was row upon row of chairs filled with workers cheering and yelling.

The stage had been set up with a central microphone; for the solo songs they'd have to change places. That didn't matter – they were used to assessing quickly what was available for use on stage. After all, they'd sung in the desert standing on oil drums, so this was perfectly acceptable.

Rainey raised her hand to check the yellow hand-made flower was still pinned above her ear. Bea's was pinned to her waist and Ivy had hers, brooch-like, on her breast.

On stage, Sammy seated himself at the piano and sorted out his music. Then Susan introduced them, saying they needed no introduction. Once the crowd stopped cheering, Bea stood in front of the microphone. 'Hello, everyone,' she said. 'A few years ago, I could have said, "Hello, fellow workers."' Bea then had to calm the enthusiastic audience to make herself heard again. 'We want to say a big thank you for everything. Without an audience we would be nothing, and you, the people of Gosport, have backed the Bluebirds every step of the way. I'm not going to ramble on because we've not long to show our appreciation for the way you looked after us when we worked alongside you, and for the grand job everyone here is doing to stop the war. Hitler won't win! Not when Gosport people stand united against him!'

Her last words were lost in cheering and foot-stamping from the audience.

Sammy began with 'I'll Be Seeing You', and the Bluebirds harmonized together. Rainey then moved centre stage and began 'I'll Get By'. It was, she thought, very emotional singing to faces she recognized. She had eaten lunch with them in this canteen, and sat in the pub with them after their shifts. As the words poured from her, Rainey felt she knew and loved all of these people who had been part of her past.

Ivy sang 'Five Minutes More'. Her husky voice held the audience spellbound. Rainey knew how her words affected the people listening. One or two hankies appeared dabbing at eyes. So many of the local people had husbands, lovers and sons fighting abroad. So many had lost loved ones. So many were still waiting to find out what had happened to their men.

As Ivy finished, Bea stepped forward and began 'You'll Never Know'. Rainey hadn't wanted her to sing that song because she knew it reminded her of Bing.

Bea stood quite still, her feet planted on the wooden stage. Rainey felt the shivers run up her spine. She wasn't singing this song for the audience, though Rainey was sure each person felt the words were meant especially for them. She was talking to Bing. The effect on the audience was magical. To tumultuous applause Bea stood with tears running down her face. Then she blew a kiss to the audience and smiled first at Rainey, then at Ivy. When Bea's eyes met hers, Rainey knew her friend was whole again. She and Ivy moved beside her.

'Sentimental Journey' was their last offering. When it ended the three girls made sure Sammy received his share of the applause. The manager of the factory gave his appreciation to them all, then chairs were pushed back and the countdown to the New Year began. There was no celebratory beer: many of the factory workers were on shift that night and due to return to their machines. Rainey, Bea and Ivy jumped down from the stage to join hands with everyone as Sammy played 'Auld Lang Syne'.

Bea squeezed Rainey's hand, grinned at Ivy and whispered, 'Happy New Year, and thank you both for being my friends.'

Chapter Thirty

'That Bert's right,' said Max. 'Now the seating's been removed you can see where the wood needs repairing. This parquet flooring is superb!'

Max didn't like Bert: he blamed him for his recapture in the café. Bert had reported him to the police when he noticed that several aspects of Max's behaviour were not consistent with that of a real English soldier. Luckily, he and Bert weren't often in each other's company and Max preferred it that way. But Eddie looked upon Bert as a surrogate father so Max never said a word against him. Just the opposite. In all the months he'd been working for Eddie he'd taken every chance to praise Bert. However, he could feel that Bert neither trusted nor liked him.

Eddie followed Max's gaze to the decorative wooden blocks. 'You're right, Max. That'll save Rainey some money for the renovations,' he said. 'It's just a shame that the roof couldn't keep the rain out.' He put out a hand and touched the marbled brown of the wall where the damp had seeped through. 'We'll have to strip and re-plaster after we've sorted out the slates,' he said. 'There's a lot of ruined wood down here. The front of that box's balcony is a positive danger.' He gestured towards one of the two elegant boxes high at each side of the stage.

Max looked around the cleared space that had once been the auditorium, then back at the two boxes. He nodded. 'You're right. Can't save them. One's all right but it'd look daft on its own. Both must go. You can smell it's rotten.'

Eddie agreed with him. 'Still, we can work inside here when the weather's bad and outside repairing bomb damage for the council when the sun comes out.'

'You expecting a lot of sun in February?' Max smiled at him then raised a questioning eyebrow.

'Dunno what to expect. I didn't bargain on any more bomb damage when it all went quiet, but them blasted V-2s keep coming, so anything can happen,' Eddie said.

'And the house in Alma Street?'

Work had slowed on Eddie's recently purchased property opposite number fourteen. 'That'll get finished eventually. No great rush, I need to bring money in to pay expenses, not spend it on personal stuff,' he said.

The door fronting the high street banged open. 'Those chimney pots want taking down before they fall,' warned Ol' Ted. He was rubbing his hands to put some warmth back in them.

'Another labourer who knows what he's talking about.' Max grinned. Ted had been with Eddie for years. He spoke as he found and was never late for work.

'Should do, I've been in the building game long enough. You can see from the other side of the high street that those pots are a bloody hazard.' Ted took off his flat cap, scratched his sparse grey hair, then stuck it back on his head. 'You should trust my judgement.'

'Course I trust you, Ted,' said Eddie. 'I've seen those pots, they look drunk. Wouldn't trust 'em in another raid or a bout of bad weather . . . You got your lad with you?'

'You want young Peter to get up a ladder and have a proper look?' Ol' Ted had anticipated Eddie's thoughts.

'I don't want him breaking his neck. This is a Georgian property, higher than most . . . No, I'll wait for the scaffolders and get up there myself.'

'He'll be back in ten minutes or so. I sent him down the Dive Café for some of Tom's currant buns. He's like a bloody monkey. Never mind waiting for the scaffolders. He can tell you today how bad it is up there.'

Ted was too old for the services but, wanting to be indispensable to Eddie, he would now go outside and wait for his grandson, a sixteen-year-old who liked getting his hands dirty to earn a few bob. He'd take the extending ladder from the truck, climb up, and have a proper look at the roof.

Eddie frowned.

Max knew he'd given Rainey a rough estimate of the cost of renovation. He needed to know exactly what he was going to have to fork out himself, if he could get hold of the materials. Luckily, a lot of the period stuff had ended up in scrapyards, second-hand shops and builders' yards. It was available, at a price. 'I'm making little enough profit on this job, but I don't want to be out of pocket. I've got a business to run. The sooner Rainey knows the worst, the better.' Then Eddie's face split into a smile. 'I hope Ted told Peter to get currant buns for us!'

'Can Rainey afford all this?' Max had met the red-headed girl only a few times. He knew that Eddie, through his contacts, had helped her buy the old theatre at a very reasonable price. He also assumed she had savings from her stage work. He wondered how she'd manage to borrow enough cash to pay for everything else when there was no man to sign as bank guarantor. She was a resourceful young woman, thought Max.

'What she can't afford, the Waters sisters are helping her out with,' Eddie said. 'I believe I'm right in saying her agent, Blackie Wilson, the bloke with the odd-coloured eyes, offered her a partnership on this place. He's her stepfather, inherited quite a nice windfall just before he married Jo, her mother.' He shook his head. 'Rainey's got a head on her shoulders. She's not just a version of Rita Hayworth. She's determined to own this place lock, stock and barrel. She wants to do it her way. She will an' all.' He smiled knowingly.

Eddie moved to the orchestra pit, and looked up again at one of the boxes, studying it from beneath. Max walked to his side. He ran his fingers through his blond hair. 'Are all the three girls . . .' he was searching for what might be the right English word to use '. . . loaded?'

Eddie laughed. 'Not really. They've worked hard. My sister Bea wastes money. She has clothes and shoes she's never worn, despite ration books and coupons. But what's decent to buy during a war? Frivolous, Maud calls her. She's different from my Ivy. She'd never see us without, but I wouldn't touch a penny of what Ivy's got put by . . .'

'Why ever not?' Surely, thought Max, there was no 'yours and mine' in marriage, only 'ours'. But, then, Eddie and Ivy weren't married, were they?

Proudly Eddie announced, 'I'm the mainstay of my

family.' He put his hand on Max's shoulder in a brotherly gesture. 'When those three girls started singing, they were kids and they had sod all. A lot's happened since the early days. Each of them had a dream, though. This is Rainey's dream, a place of her own. And we'd all move heaven and earth to get it for her.'

The street door opened again and Ol' Ted came in with buns in a bag and a wave of icy air. 'My lad brought you these,' he said.

Eddie peeped inside the bag and licked his lips. He took out a bun, then handed the bag to Max. 'I'll settle up with him later,' he said. 'Did you ask him about the roof and the chimney pots?'

'He said he'd get on it straight away.' Ted gave him a toothy smile. 'Probably up there now,' he added, looking up at the ceiling, then along to the myriad drops of glass. 'Them's lovely chandeliers,' he said, walking to the centre of the large area and staring heavenwards again. 'Could be made into electric with no trouble at all. Rainey don't want to be fiddling with all them candles. You'll need a bloke who knows what he's doing to get them down safely so we can carry on with the renovating, though. All that glass needs looking after.'

'More cost,' said Eddie. 'I agree with you, though, be an

eye-catching treat to walk through the doors of the club and see all that glittering crystal.' He swallowed the last of the soft buttered bun and wiped his fingers on his work jacket.

It was the loud crack that made him look up. Max's eyes followed. He saw the ceiling above them split, bulge, then sag downwards. Eddie leaped forward and shoved Max so hard that he flew backwards and stumbled into the orchestra pit. The bun he was eating shot from his hand. Then Eddie jumped, practically on top of him. '*Gott im Himmel!*' shouted Max, feeling the full weight of Eddie Herron squeezing the breath out of him.

The red chimney pot had crashed through the two soggy ceilings above the auditorium in a hurricane of laths, plaster, rotten wood, pipes and dust. Max could see the wooden stage vibrating with the weight of the debris. His ears hurt, and he thought his ear drums must have burst. But he was in one piece. He sat up, pushing Eddie's body away. He felt movement at his side as Eddie struggled to a sitting position. Eddie's fair hair was grey, and so was his face. Even his eyelashes were coated with dust.

'All right, mate?' asked Eddie.

'I wouldn't be if it wasn't for you,' Max said, unsteadily rising to his feet, then putting out a hand to help Eddie up. All around them it was still snowing dusty gobs of fluttering wallpaper and musty plaster. A large clay chimney pot lay smashed among the rubbish.

'Jesus Christ! Are you two all right?' Ol' Ted was wide-eyed with fright. He didn't wait for an answer. 'Look at that!' He pointed to the theatre's box that had earlier sat above them at the side of the stage. Now the velvet and cast-iron seating lay among the rubble, the wooden balcony rail split, rotten with damp, and lying atop the wood and bricks.

'I think so,' Eddie said, brushing himself down. He kicked Max's half-eaten bun. 'You won't be wanting that now, will you?'

From on high came a small voice: 'I'm really sorry. Is anyone hurt?'

Max looked up. He could see the blue of the sky. A scruffy-haired youth was blocking part of it and staring down at him. His face was pasty white and he looked worried.

Eddie took a deep breath. 'Don't need no bloody bull-dozers about, with you around, do we, Peter?'

Max felt a smile crease his face. He heard Eddie say to Ted, 'Get me some tarpaulins from the truck. And tell your kid we're all right. Get him down from that bloody ladder.' Then he turned to Max. 'I knew I'd have to climb up there myself. Can't leave the roof open to the elements.'

Max, speechless, watched him brushing himself down. Then words burst from him. 'If you hadn't pushed me, I'd be beneath that lot.' He pointed at the rubble. He stared at Eddie's dusty face, his heart full of admiration for him. 'You saved my life. I'll never forget you did that.'

'I'm sure you'd have done the same for me, mate!' said Eddie.

Chapter Thirty-one

'Max, would you bring in some logs from the shed?'

Max looked at the rain running down the kitchen window and smiled at Maud. He put the *Evening News* on the arm of the chair and picked up the coal scuttle from the fireplace. 'Is that what you call April showers?' He jerked a thumb towards the window. Why should he mind saving Maud from becoming drenched by the bad weather? After all, he was the one sitting by the fire, wasn't he?

In the shed he picked up lumps of sawn-off timber and filled the brass scuttle. Eddie was allowed to scavenge wood for house repairs and anything that was unusable was saved for burning. Even in the shed he could smell the sausages in the oven, keeping warm for when Eddie came home for tea. He took a deep, satisfying breath. Back in the kitchen he asked, 'Shall I fill the range?'

Maud nodded and went on with washing a very grubby little girl, who sat in her knickers and vest on the edge of the table. Gracie was leaning into the large bowl of soapy water and flicking bubbles as Maud tried to scrub her. The wireless played Glenn Miller music.

Max used the special tool to lift the round metal cover and drop in three pieces of wood. Job completed, he stood up, moved to the table and stood near to Gracie, poking her with his finger. She, of course, was now wriggling and giggling.

'Stop it, Max! You'll have her slide off the table. Then there'll be tears. How can I quieten her down for bed when you tease her so?'

A big frayed towel was thrown over the child and Maud began drying the little girl. The sound of giggling came from beneath the towel.

Max sat down on the armchair again. It was lovely, he thought, watching how his daughter interacted with Eddie's family. It was plain to see she was cherished. He picked up the newspaper again, and listened to 'A String Of Pearls' playing. 'It was a shame about Glenn Miller,' he said.

'I thought it was your lot that brought him down!' Maud snapped. She gave him a funny look.

'Not everything bad that happens is down to us

Germans,' he said. 'Some of us love his music just as much you do. The newspapers said it was a mystery how his plane disappeared.'

'A mystery that will no doubt be solved one day,' Maud said. She picked up the wriggling child and handed her to Max. 'Hold on to her. I don't want her falling off the table and hurting herself. I've to go upstairs for clean night clothes for her.' The music from the wireless changed to 'In the Mood'.

Max looked down into Gracie's blue eyes, which reminded him of his mother's, and whispered, 'This is the song many of us danced to during the war. Maybe one day you'll dance to it, too.'

He got up and began to jig around with Gracie in his arms. She was loving it, making all sorts of silly sounds as he sang the song in German to her.

'How am I supposed to calm her down for bed, you playing silly beggars with her?' admonished Maud, coming through the doorway with a white flannelette nightgown in her hands. She wasn't really cross, though; Max saw she was smiling.

She took the child from his arms and said, 'Get back to reading that paper. Eddie'll be home soon. It shouldn't take him long to drive to St Vincent to take back the rest of the workers.' She sat Gracie on the table and began to thread her arms through the sleeves of the nightdress. 'Did he say which pub you were going to tonight?'

The paper rustled as he picked it up again. 'I'm only signed out for an extra couple of hours, so we'll not be going far. Maybe the Alma at the end of the road.'

Maud now had Gracie cocooned in white flannelette. She stared at Max and said, 'You're not keen on Ivy, are you?'

Her forthright manner disconcerted him. He took a deep breath. 'I fear it is Ivy who does not like me.' He refolded the paper and looked at her.

'You don't want to take too much notice of our Ivy. It's just that she loves Gracie like she was her own and she can't abide anyone who tries to take over with her.'

'I have no wish to "take over" as you say. I have deep gratitude that you allow me access to your family.'

'I know you do, lad. But there's no need to tell her every little thing that happens when she's not here. She can't help having a jealous nature.' Maud stood in front of him with Gracie in her arms. 'When you tell her what's made you two laugh during work, I see her eyes darken. She wants to be with Eddie and Gracie more, and doesn't know how to tell him. It'd do her good to have a baby of her own, you mark my words.'

'But Gracie is a very little girl, why doesn't she just stay at home with her?'

'In the beginning Ivy wanted it all, a home life and to be recognized as a singer.'

'Oh, I see,' said Max. 'Sometimes when you get what you want, you find it isn't what you wanted at all.'

'Exactly,' said Maud. 'That jealous streak shows she doesn't have as much confidence in herself as she should. Eddie understands because he loves the bones of her.'

Max settled back in the chair. Maud had reached the bottom of the stairs. She turned and said, 'There's another job you could do for me.'

Max turned to her. 'Yes, of course.'

'If you go into the front room, near the fireplace you'll see a sewing machine. I'd like you to lift it – it's heavy, mind – and put it on top of the small table. If Madam here,' she looked at the child, 'will give me five minutes' peace while you and Eddie are out, I've got a lovely piece of material to make something for her. I've been meaning to do it for ages.'

'Your wish is my command.' Max stood up and clicked his heels together in a mock salute. Maud laughed and disappeared up the stairs. He walked down the passage, opened the front-room door and switched on the electric light. He looked around Maud's room. Out of habit he moved to the window and closed the curtains.

He heard Maud call and he went out and stood at the

bottom of the stairs. 'If you take off the wooden cover,' she said, 'you'll see a tiny drawer, where the broken needle is. Forget that drawer. If you lift the machine and push it back – keep hold of it, mind – underneath there should be another drawer space. I believe there's a packet of needles in there. There are spare spools and cottons so I can't believe Sunshine wouldn't have kept needles.'

Max saw Maud's arms were empty now. Gracie was probably in her cot. He nodded and returned to the front room. He stood in the doorway, thinking, his heart beating fast. What had Maud said? This sewing machine had belonged to Sunshine?

His mind went back to the slim blonde girl who had loved him. Gracie's mother.

Max couldn't help the sudden remorse that spread through him at the way he'd taken Sunshine's love for granted. He'd had many women before his plane had been shot down on English soil, but no German girl had loved him or done as much to show that love for him as Sunshine. She had helped him escape from the St Vincent holding centre. Sadness and regret flooded him.

Maud's voice broke into his thoughts. 'How you getting on? I told you it was a heavy machine. My Eddie promised to go into Murphy's and ask if they'd got needles but he hasn't yet. Mind you, he's got such a lot going on in his head . . .'

Max tuned out her voice and picked up the machine. She was right: it had a fair old weight to it. He sat it on the little table. After removing its cover, he pulled aside the hinged top and saw spools of coloured cotton. Then he lifted the machine and pushed it back, holding his hand at the rear to take its weight.

Pieces of paper tucked beneath confused him. A half-folded identity card, a passport. A scrap of material he recognized immediately as being similar to that of the British Army uniform Sunshine had made for his escape. He removed everything from the drawer, including a paper packet of needles, and let the machine fall gently back into place.

He dropped the needles onto the table. His heart was thundering as he unfolded the cardboard and the papers. He knew instantly what he was holding. The false papers Sunshine had promised him. Worked for and paid for with the sweat of her body. Of course he had never seen them before. He had been caught in Bert's café before she could meet him and hand them over. The passport photograph might even have been of him. A good-looking blond male with a strong jaw. He could quite easily have passed for the man if he was in a queue of people whose papers were being examined by rushed authorities.

He felt a lump rise in his throat, felt the sting of tears against the back of his eyelids. He hadn't cared about the girl who had truly loved him. Instead he had used her. Sunshine had kept to her part of the bargain. She had been ready to leave the country to be with him. At the time his contempt for her infallible love had made him enjoy watching her lose weight while the child grew inside her. She was destroying herself by working at several jobs so she could provide money for his escape, buy his passport and essential papers and make his disguise of an army uniform. All of this he had taken for granted. He remembered his own plan to disappear at Portsmouth Harbour station, to run away, abandon her, once she had handed him those necessary papers. He knew he'd be more likely to escape the country without a pregnant woman in tow. Her use to him would be well and truly over by then.

All he could feel now was disgust. Disgust at the way he had treated her.

Disgust for himself.

'You found them needles?' He heard Maud's voice, along with her footsteps clacking down the stairs. Max stood up. Where to put the papers? He wanted to look at them properly, but there was no time now. He didn't want to return them to the base of the sewing machine. Now that the lower drawer had been opened, it could be opened again, at any time, by anyone.

But neither could he put them into his pocket and take them back to St Vincent. If he was searched on the way in, as so often he was, they'd think he planned to escape in the very near future. He'd be taken from Gosport, sent to another camp! It didn't bear thinking about. He bent towards the fireplace, noting the folded newspaper fan in the grate. Obviously, this fireplace was not used regularly.

Quickly he shoved the papers up the chimney. He could feel a ledge at the side and trusted it was large enough to conceal them. Soot tumbled from his fingers onto the tiled hearth. He leaned forward, pursed his lips, and blew the black dust away.

'What you doin' down there?'

Max thought quickly. 'I thought there might be a few pins with the needles, I'm checking none fell out. Might be dangerous to Gracie . . .'

He needn't have bothered to think up an excuse because Maud wasn't really listening. She was far more excited that he'd found the replacement needles and that she could use the machine. 'Get up and out of the way.' Her face was wreathed in smiles. 'I want to put in a new needle.'

Max got up from where he was kneeling on the rug in

front of the fireplace and Maud immediately sat on the edge of the bed facing the machine.

Just then the street door opened and Eddie stepped in. He looked bemused to see Max and his mother in her bedroom. Maud spoke first. 'Max has found the spare needles so I can replace the broken one. I know you keep forgetting, but now you don't have to go down Murphy's!' She looked at Eddie. 'I'll be busy here for a while. You can dish up sausage and mash for the pair of you, can't you?'

'Looks like if we want any tea, I'll have to.' To Max, Eddie said, 'You're a good mate. I reckon you deserve a pint after sorting out that machine!'

Chapter Thirty-two

'How on earth can you explain singing the wrong song when Sammy's already started playing the tune?' Bea barked.

Ivy put her hand to her head. 'I don't know. My head's all over the place.'

'That's no excuse for getting well into "You Are My Sunshine" while we're singing "When The Lights Go On Again".' Bea stamped her foot. 'It's so unprofessional of you!' She pulled her dress off over her head as if she was trying to shut Ivy out.

The dressing room at the King's Theatre was old and shabby and smelled of stale sweat, but at least they'd been given somewhere private to change, Rainey thought. Not that she cared where they undressed. After working for ENSA, taking her clothes on and off in the jungle and the desert, it was satisfying just to have a door on their room.

For once they weren't the headliners; George Formby was. He deserved the star dressing room, of course he did. His wife, Beryl, had insisted it be newly whitewashed and cleaned thoroughly before he set foot in it, let alone took his ukulele inside!

'Do you really think the men minded my mistake?'

'Not a great deal . . .' began Rainey, but Bea rounded on her.

'Don't you make excuses for her, she's like a wet weekend just lately . . .'

'With the news before the show that Hitler's dead, I don't think anyone would have noticed if she'd taken off her clothes and run around the stage naked!' Rainey was cross.

Ivy thought that was funny and grinned. 'George makes loads of mistakes,' she said, 'because he commits everything to memory. He's not very good at reading and writing,' she added, 'so maybe it's just as well Beryl looks after everything.'

'So, what's your excuse, then?' Bea snapped. Then she looked at Rainey, and for a moment Rainey thought she was going to criticize her as well.

'Get it right, Ivy!' Bea shouted.

Rainey wasn't happy at Bea's ranting. During the past year she'd watched her friend go from a nervous, crying wreck to a powerhouse, always wanting to get things done. Sometimes

Rainey couldn't keep up with her – she had problems of her own to solve.

Rainey's club was getting closer and closer to completion and still she had no idea what to call it. And she was worrying because everything seemed to be costing twice as much as she'd thought it would. In a way it was for the best that Bea was eager to take on any singing job that was offered them, but Rainey was beginning to feel a bit ragged round the edges. 'We're working too hard,' she said. 'Don't go on at Ivy. It's not her fault.'

'If you think this is hard, just you wait until the parties start,' Bea said.

'What parties?'

'For God's sake, Ivy. Hitler's dead. *Dead!* He blew his stupid brains out with a gun! How d'you expect the Germans to go on fighting when their leader has shot himself?' Bea was almost shrieking now.

'What she means, Ivy, is that we'll all be celebrating that the war's over.'

'Of course!' said Ivy. 'So we'll be asked to sing at more venues?'

Rainey looked at Bea and smiled. 'Ivy, you got it!'

'We'll not be asked to sing anywhere if we let our standards drop.' Bea was determined to have the last word.

'If this war really is almost over, does that mean Geraldo will be able to go ahead with his Navy?'

Bea dropped one of the shoes she was putting on and stared at Ivy.

Rainey stopped brushing her hair and said, 'Fancy you remembering he was aiming to take orchestras and singers on cruise ships?' She nodded. 'I suppose so. Travel to the continent's going to go ahead after the war.'

'Blackie will let us know if Geraldo wants us,' said Bea, slipping on her shoe and standing up.

Rainey looked at Ivy, at the dark circles beneath her eyes. 'Are you all right, love?' She didn't want to mention that Ivy had been acting quite strangely lately. 'It's not that Max fellow upsetting you, is it? I thought he didn't have much to say to you, nowadays.'

Ivy shook her head. 'Even my Gracie loves him. But . . .' she stopped getting dressed and stared at Rainey '. . . when I first set eyes on him I didn't like him. There was something not quite right about him. I still don't trust him but the sun shines out of his backside for Eddie and Maud and that's all there is to it.'

Rainey walked over to Ivy and held out her arms. Ivy walked into them and put her head on Rainey's shoulder. Then the tears fell. Bea, Rainey saw, was watching them.

Rainey allowed her to cry, patting her back as if she was a child. Eventually, Ivy sniffed and said, 'I feel so tired all the time and I can't seem to do anything right.'

Bea was standing there with a creased but clean handkerchief. She handed it to Ivy. 'I'm sorry for being so snappy,' she said. Her voice sounded like a sulky child's. 'But . . .' there was always a 'but' with Bea, thought Rainey. '. . . I only want us to go on being as good – no, the best we possibly can be.'

Ivy lifted her tear-stained face. 'I know,' she said. 'I'm sorry. I don't mean to forget things.'

Bea put her arms around the two of them. They stood silently, each, thought Rainey, with their own worries but as united as they had always been throughout everything that had happened in the past.

Ivy was the first to break away. 'I forgot,' she said, going over to a brown paper bag with string handles. She foraged inside it. 'I remembered you told us that the book of *It Always Rains On Sunday* wasn't out yet . . .' Ivy's eyes were shining brightly in a face made pink by crying. 'Well, I saw it in the bookshop's window, so I bought you a copy!'

Chapter Thirty-three

Eddie constantly used the condensed-milk-tin mug Max had given him, which Max liked. He was also surprised that his first visit to the pub, the Alma, at the end of Eddie's road had been fairly uneventful. Not so his second. He had played a game called 'Shove Ha'penny'. Two teams competed against each other to shove half-pennies along a board to fall between horizontal lines. At first it had looked to be a simple game and there was much laughter. That was, until a flabby, red-haired man became belligerent. Eddie and he had ignored the first jibes, but the more beer the man drank the worse the remarks he made.

Eddie, well respected and as polite as ever, had refused a second game for the pair of them.

'Just don't let that German bugger near the arrows,' was

317

the last comment the man made. Max had been watching a darts game in progress.

Eddie said, 'Drink up, mate. We've got an early start in the morning.'

The barman had nodded knowingly and wished them goodnight. Once in the truck, driving back to the holding centre, Eddie added, 'Not all the English are as pathetic as that. Just you wait and see how many English girls marry your countrymen and settle down here.'

Max had not spoken. What was there to say? It would have been easy for him to fell the man with a single punch. But what good would that have done?

Now Hitler was dead, and effectively the war was over. Britain would not want to keep her prisoners of war. Repatriation would come next. Max was now among the workforce helping to put back together a country that his fellow men had tried to destroy.

What would be his next step? He realized he was happy. Happy to be working with Eddie's English and German team. Happy to be almost one of Eddie's family. Happy to be near his daughter. But now that would change. People were already dancing in the streets. Free from the fear of bombs and of oppression. You could almost smell the happiness in the air, he thought.

His plan had been to escape St Vincent and return to Pulheim in Germany, but to what? His family might be gone. Wiped out just as the Germans had annihilated families here in England. He had no way of knowing what had happened to them in the time he had been incarcerated.

Trusted prisoners, and he knew how lucky he was to be among those, would be granted even more freedom. He had read that Clement Attlee was eager for repatriation to start as soon as possible and that it was his goal to send home fifteen thousand prisoners a month. He thought of the fake papers hidden in Eddie's fireplace and sighed. What use were they to him now? Sunshine's sacrifices had been for nothing.

Ivy sat in bed hugging her knees and watching Eddie soaping beneath his arms as he washed in the basin before coming to bed.

'You sometimes wash downstairs in the scullery,' she said. 'Not that I don't like seeing your muscles move when you stretch!'

'Mum's sorting out coloureds from whites for tomorrow's big wash. You can't move in the scullery, so I thought I'd come upstairs and give you a bit of a floorshow!'

Ivy laughed as he pulled a towel from the hook on the side of the wash-stand and, holding it in front of him, started to wiggle his hips suggestively. 'You'd make a good fan dancer, I don't think!'

'Spoilsport,' he said, and continued washing, then wiped himself dry.

'You won't think I'm a spoilsport when I tell you a secret I've been keeping for the past few weeks.'

The words had hardly left her lips when Eddie threw down the towel and practically bounced onto the bed next to her. His arms went around as he said, 'There's only one secret I want to hear from you! Is it? Are you?'

Ivy pushed him away so she could look into his eyes. She gave him a slow smile. He was looking at her as if he wanted to swallow her whole.

'Despite you not being able to articulate a proper sentence, the answer is . . . yes!'

'Ivy!' He said her name again. 'Ivy, are you sure?' He beamed a grin that went practically from ear to ear.

'I waited until I was sure before I said anything to you.' She threw her arms around his neck, breathing in the Imperial Leather soap on his skin.

After a while, he disentangled himself and his lips found hers. Ivy felt as if all the bones in her body had turned to jelly as she allowed herself to revel in his joy, his passion, his kiss. This is what real love is, she thought.

Being able to make someone else so happy. Eddie pulled away. Suddenly he leaned forward and kissed her quickly on the tip of her nose. Then he was off the bed and she heard him call back from halfway down the stairs, 'Got to tell Mum! She'll be as pleased as Punch! my darling, darling girl . . .'

Maud held Gracie in her arms and jigged about in the kitchen with her. On the table the breakfast things were waiting to be gathered up and washed in the scullery. 'It's finished!' she sang tunelessly. 'The war's over! It's all over now!' She gave the surprised child a smacking kiss. 'And your mummy's going to need all the help Gracie can give her.' Another kiss followed. 'You are going to be a big sister to a baby girl or boy!' Gracie giggled and a piece of the chewed rusk fell from her chubby hand to the floor.

Eddie stared around the club, which was at last beginning to look less like a theatre and more like a place where people could enjoy themselves with a meal and a drink and watch a floorshow that would be worthy of the entrance fee.

His next job was to put up the flock wallpaper Rainey had insisted on. Gold and red fleur-de-lis. Ever one for a bargain, she had telephoned him one night and said, 'A manager of a theatre we've appeared at has a shed full of flock wallpaper. He's practically giving it away. What shall I do?' Eddie had driven to Southampton the next day with Rainey and bought the lot. 'There's enough there to paper the Criterion picture house,' he'd told her.

'You don't think red velvet curtains and red seating will be too much, do you?' Rainey had asked.

From Portsmouth, a man and his son had come and performed magic with the chandeliers. Now they could be electrically lit from a switch in Rainey's office. The outlay for that had been worth every penny. When she hadn't been on stage singing and earning, Rainey had been on the telephone, writing letters and enquiring about drinks licences, music licences, and making arrangements for firms to commence deliveries in September.

Eddie was proud of the renovations he'd made to the old theatre. Luck had been with him all the way. Buying new materials during wartime was impossible but he found reconditioned, renewed and period pieces in the strangest places. Elsie and Doris had come up trumps with antique furniture. And a farmer at Lee-on-the-Solent had contacted him about framed windows containing, wonder of wonders, bullseye glass that would make the Georgian windows a talking point. He told Eddie he had them stacked in a barn. Rainey was thrilled that the many small paned frames would be used on the front of the club. The farmer was much more interested in getting his barn cleared, and sold the lot to Eddie at a knock-down price.

Eddie felt as though he was walking on air. Things could only get better from now on. The first of the prefabricated houses would be arriving before Christmas. Gosport Council had already allocated land at Bridgemary, Elson and Clayhall as sites for them and the ground was being cleared. Future work for him was assured. That he could provide well for his family in the future was of paramount importance to him.

But more important than anything else was the news that Ivy, in the new year, was expecting his baby. He felt like he wanted to wrap her in cotton-wool. He felt ten feet tall.

'Come on in, Bea,' said Blackie. Momentarily she'd forgotten how good-looking he was but he had eyes only for his fair-haired wife.

Jo said, 'Settle yourself down. I'll go and put the kettle on.' On her way up the stairs she had shown Bea a new charm Blackie had bought for her gold bracelet. She was surprised to see a tiny gold replica of London's famous clock, Big Ben.

Jo had explained, 'Since he's presented me with charms from every country we've visited travelling with ENSA, he's now decided a few from our own wouldn't go amiss!'

They'd chatted briefly about Rainey's club and the excitement it had engendered. Bea could see Jo was extremely proud of her daughter. At the top of the stairs, she'd paused before she'd opened the door to Blackie's office. 'I know you're wondering what this is about and why it's only you he wants to see . . .' for no reason Bea could think of, Jo had enveloped her in a perfumed hug '. . . but I think you're going to be very pleasantly surprised and I'm thrilled for you.'

And now Bea sat, more confused than ever, on an upright chair in front of Blackie's large wooden desk while Jo was making tea somewhere else in the building.

Bea's stomach felt as if it was full of butterflies. She sat, clasping her hands to stop them shaking.

'Are you well?' Blackie asked.

'Perfectly,' said Bea. 'But I'd rather skip all the chit-chat and get down to why you've asked me here without Rainey and Ivy.' She knew she'd been manic lately about making sure the Bluebirds gave the very best of themselves at every venue they appeared at. Might someone have written a complaint about her aggressive attitude? Rainey had been, as ever, conscientious in all her dealings on stage and off. However, her mind was almost entirely fixed on the proposed opening of her club. Ivy? Now that Ivy's doctor had verified her pregnancy, the change in her was enormous. Gone was that annoying forgetfulness. Why on earth hadn't she or Rainey guessed the surge of hormones had made Ivy so completely out of touch with everything? A smile lit her face. At least now Ivy simply said, 'Whoops! Excuse me,' and dashed off to be sick, returning minutes later as though nothing had happened.

Blackie tidied the papers in front of him on the desk. 'We'll get on, then,' he said.

Bea took a deep breath and listened.

'You need to be at Ealing Studios next Monday. The screenplay has been written and work is starting on filming *It Always Rains On Sunday.*'

Bea's heart was thudding and she was sure Blackie must be able to hear it. But, no, he had steepled his fingers with his elbows on the desk and was watching her. She stared into his hypnotic and beguiling odd-coloured eyes. 'They want me?' Her voice sounded cracked and hoarse. He smiled. She coughed, putting her hand to her mouth. She felt herself slump and fall into herself as though the chair couldn't hold her.

'Don't look so surprised, Bea,' he said. 'It was a foregone conclusion.'

He continued to talk but she couldn't take in his words. Her head felt as if it was full of bees, happily buzzing but shutting everything else out. Her attention was disturbed by Jo setting a tray on the desk-top. She wore a smile a mile wide.

'Tea?' she asked.

Bea wanted to leap up from her chair, grab her and dance around the room. Instead, she smiled and answered, 'Yes, please.'

Blackie was talking again and reading from one of the sheets of paper he'd taken from the desk. 'It's not certain whether they're testing you for Vi or Doris Sandgate – they're the daughters,' he said. 'Rose, the mother, is Googie Withers. It's a J. Arthur Rank picture and when the cutting's finished it will run for approximately one and a half hours. You're very lucky to have Michael Balcon producing it, with Robert Hamer directing.'

Blackie was reeling off names Bea had never heard of so she sat and stared knowingly because she felt that was what he expected of her. 'Where's it going to be filmed?'

'London locations. Petticoat Lane is one, I believe. It might be better if you stay in London – seems senseless to travel up and down every day from Portsmouth.'

'I can't believe it,' Bea said, looking at Jo as she poured the tea. 'I don't know how I'll feel about leaving Della, Bert and the café. But what if the test isn't right?'

'Don't be silly, Bea. They wouldn't be offering you a part if they hadn't done extensive checks on your stage ability. This picture is going to be a turning point in films. It will also change your life forever. Now, what else do you want to know?'

Bea looked at Blackie. She looked down at the tray with the poured-out tea. She looked at Jo. Her eyes watered.

'Drink your tea,' Jo said. 'Blackie wanted to celebrate with something bubbly but I told him you never touch the stuff.'

Bea got up quickly from her chair, went around the desk and threw herself into Blackie's arms. These two people knew everything about her and they only wanted what she had wanted all her life. Now it was within her grasp. Then the tears of happiness fell.

Chapter Thirty-four

Gosport was still celebrating VE Day in September. Bunting hung above the shops to stretch across the high street, and music poured from accordions, gramophones and barrel organs. Public houses kept their doors open and couples danced in the streets well into the night.

Celebrations were under way in Rainey's club. In the orchestra pit the music was light and popular. The stage, hung with red velvet drapes, was enticing but empty. Couples danced on the glossy parquet. Small tables were placed around the dance floor. These, along with matching chairs, were made of scrolled metal and painted white. Overhead, the glass chandeliers twinkled, sending rainbow colours onto the heads and bodies of guests.

Outside, the smart white-painted Georgian building was a classy asset to the middle of Gosport. So, too, was the green-eyed, red-haired young woman standing at the balcony above the lower floor watching the dancers. Dressed in a slinky gold lamé dress, she seemed to be in a world of her own.

'Pleased with yourself?'

Rainey turned at Bea's voice. Bea had on a long black fitted lace dress that was a perfect foil for her golden hair. 'Yes, I think I am,' Rainey said.

'So you should be. It's taken you a lot of guts and hard work to own this. A lot of sorrow, too.'

'If anyone knows about sorrow and hard work, it's you, Bea.'

Bea laughed. 'That's got the mutual admiration out of the way,' she said. 'It's been a horrible war and I'm glad it's over. Are you happy?'

Rainey said, 'Yes. It's like opening a Christmas present and finding exactly what you want. I've already booked some class acts to appear here and sometimes I'll sing for the patrons, too. When the flat is finally finished on the top floor, I intend to move in. Of course there are still black days when I'm consumed with thoughts of Charlie and our baby, but in this business we have to put smiles on our faces, don't we? Hide the heartache. I've told Blackie I'd like to try the cruise ships, short trips to fit in with my business here, and from time to time I'll appear in public for him. He's been a wonderful agent and I see no reason to part from him now.'

'So you've got it all worked out?'

'I wouldn't say that, but it's my plan. And you? I haven't seen much of you these past weeks now you're hobnobbing with the film people.'

'Hobnobbing? What kind of word is that?'

'A good old-fashioned word meaning getting familiar with!' Rainey smiled at her. 'Just as long as you don't get too big for your boots!'

'I'll never do that,' Bea said. 'I'm a Gosport girl at heart and that's the way I'll stay.' She stood beside Rainey and watched the dancers below.

'Bert's dancing with Alice Wilkes!' Bea giggled. 'He'd better watch out – Della won't like that.'

'I shouldn't think she's too worried. Can you see her over in that far booth? She's drinking brandy with Blackie.'

'Oh, she's always had a little thing for him.'

'I never knew that!'

'Didn't you notice how she'd disappear every time he visited the café and then she'd come back smelling of Californian poppy? She kept it in the drawer in the kitchen.'

'I didn't know.' Rainey was wide-eyed.

'Well, I lived there, so I knew all their secrets. Her little passion was never going to go anywhere – Blackie's only got eyes, one brown and one blue, for your mum!'

'Shh! That's my stepfather you're talking about!' Both started giggling.

'Oh, I do love you,' said Bea. 'Promise me we'll always be friends?'

Rainey stopped laughing and said very seriously, 'You'll always be my best friend, I promise you that.'

'So,' Bea said, 'tomorrow this place opens its doors to the punters. What made you decide to invite us all tonight?'

'Just wanted to say thank you to everyone who's helped us along the way.'

Bea was looking down at Max sitting alone at a corner table and nursing a pint. 'Even that German helped.'

'You're right. He's worked as hard as any of Eddie's blokes on this place. I couldn't leave him out, or any of the Germans, for that matter. The rest of Eddie's men are probably propping up the bar.'

'Oh, look!' broke in Bea. 'There's Syd Kennedy dancing with his wife. She's so pregnant she looks ready to drop at any minute!'

'That's their second baby!' said Rainey. 'He could have been my stepfather at one time.'

'Not once your mum set her sights on Blackie!' Bea poked Rainey in the side with her elbow. 'Look down there,' she said. 'Isn't it wonderful that your family, my family and Ivy's lot all get on so well?'

Rainey saw tables had been moved and chairs brought over so that people were grouped together, talking, drinking and laughing. Elsie and Doris Waters were sitting with their family and friends.

'Did you ever read Bing's letter?'

Bea's blue eyes flicked back from the scene below. 'You've waited a long time to ask me that,' she said.

'Not because I've never wanted to ask you before,' she said quickly.

'Of course,' said Bea. And Rainey watched, spellbound, as Bea put her hand inside the top of her dress and wriggled it around before opening her palm and showing Rainey the folded piece of satin. 'I keep it pinned inside my bra close to my heart.' Carefully she unwrapped the small piece of material. The folded paper inside she smoothed out and turned towards Rainey so she could read the words it contained:

Bea
 Wherever I go
 Whatever I do

You are always in my heart
Now and until the end of time
Bing

Rainey put her hand across her mouth and forced her lips into a straight line to stop herself crying. After a few moments of silence, she took a deep breath and said, 'You carry it everywhere?'

'Always, except when I'm asleep. Then it's beneath my pillow.' She began refolding the small piece of paper. 'You see, Rainey, just like you and Charlie, I loved and was loved in return by a very special man.'

Rainey watched the safety pin being slipped into the satin. Bea's voice caught her off-guard as she said, 'Now you must tell me the truth. You're no doctor, so how did you know that making me sing the song that reminded me of Bing would make me cry and return me to my senses?'

Rainey said, 'I didn't, not really. I gambled on us singing songs that reminded us of good times, happy places we sang them before.' She paused. 'We only have to sing a few notes of "Where The Bluebird Goes" and we're back at St John's School, singing for Mrs Wilkes. Music does that, doesn't it? Transports us to a different dimension. I thought if I could get you remembering when you sang that song, especially to him in Dartmouth, it might help you break down the barrier you'd created against thinking about Bing. Then, hopefully, you'd cry. To get you to cry was Bert's idea.'

Bea put her arms around Rainey, who heard her sniffle. There was no need for more words between them.

A sudden guffaw broke into the ambience of soft music rising from below.

Rainey felt Bea's hands push herself away. Loud laughter filled the air and floated upwards.

'Gert and Daisy,' said Bea, signalling that their previous conversation was at an end.

'Aren't they funny?'

Rainey and Bea laughed: they'd chorused the same three words.

'I bet they're used to being invited out and then asked to do a comic sketch.' Rainey was looking over the balcony.

'Probably,' said Bea. 'They must like what they do or they wouldn't do it. They remind me of a couple of very funny aunties,' she said. Then, in a serious voice, 'They've been good to me . . .'

'Not just you, me too,' said Rainey. 'Oh! Look at them!' For some reason Elsie had stood up and was holding her skirt just high enough to allow a pair of elasticated bloomers to peep above her dimpled knees. This caused great merriment among the people sitting about her. Doris was miming pulling a piece of elastic.

Bea shook her head. 'They're like a couple of kids,' she said. 'I shudder to think what's going on down there. It's got something to do with knicker elastic, whatever it is!'

Rainey said, 'And just look how besotted your brother is with Ivy. You'd think no one else had ever been pregnant.'

Ivy's head nestled against Eddie's neck. Gracie was sprawled across her lap, fast asleep, and wearing a pretty pink dress that Maud had made.

'Think Ivy'll ever return to the stage?' Rainey asked.

Bea shook her head. 'Maybe, but I doubt it. She's been on at him about a house in Western Way in Alverstoke. Says they'll need more room when the baby comes . . .'

'She could have got to the top with that voice of hers,' mused Rainey. 'It rivals Billie Holiday's.'

'When Ivy sings "Strange Fruit" she sends shivers down my spine,' Bea added.

'But with Ivy, the heart wants what the heart wants.'

'And above all she wanted Eddie and a family.'

Rainey finished talking and gave a deep sigh. But it was a happy sigh. She could smell cigarette smoke rising in *her* club. Hear laughter floating up from below. Then she said,

'You coming down with me? They'll expect me to make a speech and, of course, for us to sing . . .'

'Sing what?' Bea frowned.

'I can only think of one song that fits everything that's happened to us during the war and during our lives . . .'

'"Where The Bluebird Goes"?'

'What d'you think?'

'Excellent choice. If it hadn't been for Alice Wilkes and her choir, we wouldn't be this contented now,' said Bea. 'Wait a minute, have you decided on a name for this place? I mean, there's no sign up outside. People can't make reservations to eat and dance in a club with no name.'

Rainey suddenly blushed. 'I sort of have, but . . .'

She got no further for Bea's attention was taken and she was busily waving to Eddie and Ivy downstairs. 'We'd better go down,' said Bea. 'Ivy has something planned. We can't disappoint her.'

'And you're not going to tell me what it is?'

'You know what Ivy's like,' Bea said, 'and you'll find out soon enough.'

'Come on then! Race you downstairs!' said Rainey.

'Don't be daft – film stars don't race anywhere!' Bea said haughtily. Then she smiled. 'We could walk quickly, though!'

*

Max finished his beer and set the glass on the table. He looked across the floor to where Eddie was sitting among his friends and family. Earlier he had shared that table with them. Gracie had been asleep, draped across Ivy like an extra piece of clothing. Clutched tightly in her podgy hand was a peg doll. It was chewed and ragged but Max didn't care about how his gift to her had worn. What mattered to him was she would not be parted from that one small toy.

Rainey and Bea were standing beside Ivy, who looked across at him and waved. Soon he would need to make the presentation. It had been Ivy's idea and Bea had gone along with it. Pregnancy certainly made Ivy easier to get along with, he thought. Max was sitting alone because he thought it was an honour to have been asked to do this and he wanted to compose himself. A scroll of paper lay beside his empty glass.

Over the past weeks working with Ivy meant he had come to understand her more. It had also shown him how passionate and fiercely protective Ivy's feelings were for Eddie, Gracie and the coming child. In a few months he would be returning to Germany. Repatriation had already begun. Now there was no need for him to try to escape he realized how sad he would be to leave these people who had welcomed him into their lives.

Max was probably Gracie's biological father. But he knew he wasn't her daddy. The man who had saved his life when the chimney pot fell through the rotted building was giving his daughter more family love than Max could ever hope to. All his life Max had lied and done wrong, and luck had allowed him to wriggle out of distasteful situations. A sudden thought struck him. Before he left Gosport he must not forget to remove the fake documents from the chimney in Alma Street. Sunshine's name deserved to remain untarnished. Max owed her that. Some things were better never coming to light.

Up on the stage the girls were being applauded for singing the folk song that had begun their careers. They'd sung in front of the red velvet curtains, a perfect backdrop for their hair colouring and looks. For once, each of them was individually dressed. These three special young women had wrung the hearts of their audience with their song's words.

At her table Alice Wilkes was emotionally dabbing at her eyes and being comforted by her blind husband. Even her little white dog, Toto, hugging her feet, looked downcast.

Max rose from his seat, picking up the scroll of paper. It was an important moment for him and he didn't want to make a mistake. After his presentation, Rainey would make her speech. He would return to the other table and rejoin the friends he would probably never see again, once he had returned home to Germany. In the years to come, he would go on mourning for the innocent people he had destroyed. Hans and Sunshine had deserved more for loving him.

His heart was beating fast as he climbed the steps to the stage and stood to the side of the three young women. He began talking not just to them but to the audience. 'I wish to make a presentation to Rainey from Bea and Ivy,' he said. He handed her the scroll.

Puzzled, Rainey began to unroll the paper. He saw her lips lift in a small smile as she saw the copperplate handwriting he had laboured over.

'There is as yet no name outside this beautiful club,' he continued, speaking to Rainey. 'On that small piece of paper is written Bea and Ivy's gift to you. I was asked to sign-write the name they hoped you'd eventually choose. The completed sign is out the back, ready to be hung, before your official opening tomorrow evening. That's assuming you agree and like it, of course.'

There was a moment of complete silence. Then the people began to clap after Rainey had read what was written on the scroll.

Rainey quietened them with a wave of her hand. 'This is a wonderful gift. I want to thank everyone who had a part in either making or deciding on this for me. It's exactly what I wanted but I hadn't got around to discussing with Bea and Ivy. They've beaten me to it. I can't wait to see it up, outside the entrance,' she said. Max could see the tears in her eyes.

'Tell us what the name of the club is, then,' came a voice from one of her friends out front.

Rainey laughed and shook the piece of paper. Then she linked arms with Ivy and Bea. 'Why, Bluebirds, of course!' she said.

Acknowledgements

Thank you, Florence Hare, for your excellent advice. Thank you, Juliet Burton for being so easy to talk to. Thank you, Jane Wood for always being there. Big thank you to Hazel Orme for righting my wrongs. I am indebted to all at Quercus who work so tirelessly for me. Finally, to my loyal readers, thank you.